Blood Will Tell...

a novel by L. Lee Shaw

Blood Will Tell...

Library of Congress Control Number: 2008902673

ISBN: 978-0-9814709-1-7

Printed in the United States of America

Boho Books paperback edition / March 2008

To Those Who Wear No Flesh But Teach Me Still

Prologue

It was told in legend the northern lights encircled the thatched roof of the great shelter the night she was born, shifting and shaping as though in expectation. They said she emerged, not with the cries of a new life forced into an uncertain world, but with a howl of triumph as though she had escaped some dark prison...this babe with the caul.

And when the wise ones were summoned from the Samhain to bless the birth, she looked on them with no unfocused blueness blinking against the firelight. They claimed she stared with crystal clarity into their faces as if reading their very souls.

They spoke of her in song, poem, and remembered history passed from the light of one fire to another. And they spoke of her seed; weaving blessings into their words if one of her blood came to be among them.

But the ashes of the fires were scattered by time and the collective memory sank beneath the greening of civilization. The remembrance of her, her deeds, even her name disappeared. There was nothing except her essence, arising generation after generation in those who carried her forgotten blood.

No longer a blessing, it left her descendants alien, walking just outside the light in the shadows of the unknown.

Chapter One

Daphne leaned against the flaking paint of the window frame and stared out. The sun was beginning its descent into the opening maw of darkness. It was the interval when the edges of day reality blurred as the night shadows crept from under trees and spilled between buildings. It was the loneliest of hours, Daphne thought, when you faced the home coming. The daily proof you were uncoupled and scrabbling to give purpose to your heart.

"But, you're going to meet a man, my dahhhling."

The words cut delicately across Daphne's thoughts.

"I meet dozens of men every day, Mom. I work in a hospital, remember. And knock off the Zsa Zsa Gabor bit, it dates you."

"Touchy tonight, aren't we? Well, maybe I need to cook up something to put you in a better mood."

"Mom, you don't cook. You've never cooked. To you pot is something to be smoked and pans happen to bad movies."

"Touchy and snippy, too. I can see when I'm not wanted or appreciated. I'm history."

"That you are, Mom. That you are," Daphne murmured.

Turning her back to the window, she looked across to her cousin sitting in the old Morris chair, feet up on a thread-bare tapestry covered stool. Katlyn was busily reordering index cards while making meticulous notations in an old notebook. The Victorian beaded lamp pooled its light with the Art Deco torchiere to illuminate her work and cast shadows across her face.

"Have you ever wondered why we are the way we are, Kat?"

Katlyn Talmek stopped her shuffling to look over the top of the half-moon glasses resting on her slender nose.

"In what way are you referring to, dear," she asked.

Daphne turned again to look out the window. "You know…the family gift…the family curse…the family weirdness." She paused and wrinkled her forehead in thought. "Like how come mother and I still talk?"

Edmund Broadhurst had glided into the room, pausing before the tarnished, gilt mirror over the fireplace to scrutinize himself. He was, as usual, impeccable from his burnished golden hair to his highly polished loafers.

"It's not particularly unusual for mothers and daughters to talk," he said to his cousin's reflected image.

"But my mother's been dead 17 years."

The tiny crystal bell on the mantelpiece tinkled indignantly.

"See what I mean?" Daphne said, gesturing toward the sound.

Edmund surveyed the bell's shimmying movements thoughtfully. "You may have a point. Well, m'dear, we must be off." He dropped a kiss on the cheek Kat inclined towards him.

The large white cross on the back of the maroon windbreaker caught the light as Daphne pulled it on. Crossing to the lawyer's bookcase, she pulled up one of the dusty glass doors and studied the hand weapons before reaching in to select a modern switchblade from among the chipped stone knives and medieval daggers.

Another thought began to slip into Daphne's mind as she led the way to the front door. She blocked it before it could be heard. Opening the front door, they heard the little crystal bell begin to ring. Daphne firmly shut the door behind her.

Edmund tilted his head slightly toward the living room windows listening to the faint sounds. "Are you and your mother squabbling again, cuz?"

"Oh, she's being Madame Althea, teller of fortunes. 'You're going to meet a man, my dahhhling'." Daphne mimicked her mother's words.

"With her, ah, different perspective, she just might know something."

"Edmund, as I told dear old mum, I meet dozens of men everyday and I wouldn't have most of them on a golden charger with Béarnaise sauce," she said as the two cousins began to descend the three tiers of stairs leading from the old house to the sidewalk.

Inside, Katlyn glanced up at the bell which continued its dance of anger. "Althea, please, I can't concentrate. Besides," she said, watching the bell begin to lean slightly over the edge of the mantel, "if you aren't careful, you'll make a smash of yourself." The bell subsided and gently tinkled itself back from the precipice.

* * *

The harvest moon loomed behind the treetops. Its baleful face bathed smoggy, blood red as it stared down the retreating sun. The air was sharply crisp and tangy with the smell of smoke and moldering leaves. At the sidewalk, the cousins turned downhill from the Heights toward the Corners.

Even a small city has its human sewer where the waste products of the community wash and collect, breeding after their own kind. In Kelton, it centered in the Corners. Once the thriving heart of a younger community, it was now just a collection of decaying structures.

In and out of its raddled facades moved the street entrepreneurs. Hiding in the darkness behind the broken strands of neon, they serviced the nightly feeding frenzy of unnatural hungers. At the Corners, sins and sinners found each other in the fractured shadows.

Dusk had already dimmed the front of the building where Edmund and Daphne stopped. Daphne tweaked the key back and forth in the lock, shaking the door simultaneously until the ancient tumblers fell into place. She reached a hand inside and flipped the switch. Sputtering, the florescent lights ignited, dribbling illumination out of the old narrow storefront, and backlighting the small, elegantly calligraphied sign announcing 'Free Clinic'.

Inside, Daphne shrugged out of her jacket and hung it on the listing coat tree.

Edmund began to straighten the six chairs forming a right angle along the front window and wall. Running his fingers over the curling duct tape patching the split vinyl, he forced it to hold one more evening.

"You've been looking for the answers your whole life, Edmund. What do you think makes us the way we are?" Daphne asked as she passed him on the way to the back of the clinic.

He shrugged as he tugged the sleeves of his grey tweed jacket back down to reveal just the right amount of pearl grey shirt cuff. "A gift of the angels. An ancient pact with the devil," he said as he crossed to the old staircase. "Most likely an errant and, I should say, rather stubborn gene."

Daphne's face was a mask of sour dissatisfaction as she sprayed disinfectant over the old examining table, the little metal cabinet beside the sink and the chipped, rust stained sink itself.

She set about replenishing medical supplies from her hidey-hole storage place under the stairs while Edmund climbed up them to satisfy himself the door at the top was still securely nailed shut.

He ambled back down, lightly flicking his handkerchief over dust that might have settled on him. "Well, m'dear...."

Ears practiced in hearing the wavelength somewhere between sound and thought felt the faint cries even while her hands were stacking crackling packages of gauze squares. Daphne stopped, cocking her head to isolate and identify the sound. She held up a hand to silence Edmund.

Edmund paused as a peculiar jolt shot through him, lighting all his nerves and making him feel as though they were standing outside his skin. He turned his head and listened carefully. Like Daphne, he sensed it more than heard it. It felt like a soul breaking.

The gauze packages slithered into disarray as Daphne ran to answer the scream for help she heard in the non-sound. It was coming from the alley beside the clinic.

The upper brick walls still caught the setting mid October sun, backlighting the shadows rising from the ground. The rapidly cooling air captured the malevolent perfume of the alley.... urine, rotting garbage…putrefying incense of the land of dying.

Daphne's nose barely registered the smells, accustomed as she was to the odors always hanging just under the strong hospital deodorizers. Edmund masked them with his handkerchief.

She stopped deep in the gloom to aurally focus in on the cries. Normal sounds were drowned out by the rumble of a tired old truck coughing its way home. Still she heard what she wanted to hear.

It was coming from a place behind the rusted dumpster. She pulled out a tiny flashlight and used it to bore holes in the deepening dusk. It caught a rat waddling out to peruse the leavings.

Daphne giggled as the creature tried to scamper off, its small feet scarcely able to carry its obese middle.

"You are a prime candidate for a heart attack, my man," she called softly after it. "Better start hanging out in a healthier alley."

The sound of her voice caused a sharp intake of breath somewhere behind the dumpster. In a moment, Daphne was crouched and playing her flashlight in the narrow space, Edmund looming over her head.

A small boy was wedged in behind the dumpster, his arms tightly hugging something hidden by his drawn up legs.

Edmund widened his eyes to capture details in the feeble light. He took in the stained, ragged sweatshirt jacket and shoes with the sole duct taped to the split uppers. The boy was huddled with his head tucked in tightly to his knees.

Edmund reached over Daphne and placed a hand on the boy's head. The hair felt greasy and sticky. He gently but firmly pushed until the boy was forced to raise his face.

One eye was swollen nearly shut. Blood was mixed in the mucus oozing from his nose. Dark redness ran from across his cheek to a swollen lower lip. He clutched a tiny, wet bundle of tabby fur.

Although the man's face sharpened into feral fury, his voice was hypnotically gentle and soothing.

"Son, does your kitten need help? This lady is a nurse. Let her have the kitten. She can help it."

The boy hugged the bit of fur closer and shook his head. Abruptly a great roar of anguish tore out of his thin little frame. "He made me do it. He made me hold her under. Just like he did Kelsey." The pain in his sobs threatened to rip his small body apart.

Edmund straightened and gave a mighty shove to the dumpster, making room for him and Daphne to reach the boy.

Gently, Daphne extracted the kitten from the boy's arms. Its icy limpness told her there was nothing left to do. She cradled it gently in her hands and stepped away as Edmund reached in to scoop up the boy. The boy stiffened, trying to push out of Edmund's grasp but the fight was only momentary. With a despairing groan, he collapsed.

Edmund laid him carefully on the examining table and reached for one of the old thin hospital blankets folded on the shelves beside the sink.

Daphne shook the remaining diapers out of a box. She arranged the kitten's body in it, tenderly wrapping it with paper towels before turning her attention to the boy.

Although covered, his shivering was almost convulsive. As she busied herself with peroxide and cotton cleaning up the face, Edmund stood lightly stroking the boy's temples, his voice resuming its hypnotic cadence.

"It's alright. You're safe now. No one can hurt you."

Gradually the boy quit shaking and began to drift into a twilight sleep. "What's your name?" Daphne asked replicating Edmund's soft steady tones.

"Justin," the boy answered sleepily. "Justin Floyd."

"Where do you live?"

"Briarwood."

Briarwood…a street where even hope did not try to grow.

"Who was Kelsey" Edmund asked. He felt the boy's body go rigid against the memory and his fingers moved in a different pattern. As the boy's body relaxed, Edmund again asked the question.

"The baby. My baby sister."

"Where is she now?"

"Under the old refrigerator. In the backyard."

"Who put her there?"

"Gary."

"Who's Gary?"

"Momma's boyfriend."

"What did he do?"

"He put her in water. He didn't want a baby. He beat Mom lots trying to make the baby die. When she was borned, he put her in the water. Then he put her in the backyard."

Edmund and Daphne communicated silently. They felt the truth of the boy's words.

"I think I best go make a phone call, Daph," Edmund murmured.

Chapter Two

The old rolling chair groaned loudly as Dennis Cobb stretched. He pressed his hands against his eyes a moment before tossing the file in front of him on the stack precariously perched on the corner of his desk. It was time to go home.

As he straightened up his desk, his brow furled in thought. He mentally cruised through his refrigerator and cupboards trying to remember if he had anything even semi-nutritious to fix for the kids. He really didn't want to have to stop at the store but he was afraid one more Happy Meal and the children's protective services would be on him.

Jerry Rickham wandered in, his utility belt squeaking as he fastened it around his waist. He glanced at Dennis as he checked his gun, clips, taser, and cuffs. He flipped open his briefcase and riffled through it.

"What's the matter, Cobb? Getting bored with the same old slime, crime and grind? Don't forget Halloween and a full moon all in the same week. Guaranteed to bring out the weirdos."

Something between pain and disgust passed over Dennis' face. "Thanks for the reminder but actually I was trying to decide if I had anything in the house to fix for dinner. Slime, crime and grind are easy in comparison."

Jerry's face sobered as he was reminded of Dennis' widower status. "Yeah. I guess a hot pastrami and six-pack from Johnny's joint isn't recommended for kids."

Dennis' face pulled up into a tired, lop-sided smile. "The six pack might be okay but they'll never go for the pastrami."

Ron, the evening dispatcher, leaned through the pass through window and hollered. "Hey, Cobb. Take the call on line one. It's some guy at the Free Clinic. Says they got a murder, maybe."

Chapter Three

The boy was sleeping quietly when two women arrived. One was holding a bloody washcloth against her face while the other firmly guided her through the door.

Daphne hurried to them. Violence was the clinic's chief supply agent.

The young woman flinched as Daphne gently pulled the cut together with steri-strips. The eye was already swollen and blackening.

Tearing open a wipe, Daphne spilled sterile water on it to wipe away the blood from the bruised face and dab at the clots in her hair.

"Has he ever hit you before?" she asked quietly.

The girl started to shake her head but her companion intervened. "Yes, he has. Every time the SOB gets drunk, he punches her out."

The girl lowered her eyes as mute shame burned across her cheeks, deepening the red marks.

As Daphne busied herself cleaning up, she covertly studied the young woman. Long untrimmed hair, faded jeans stretched over a broadening bottom, out-of-date top; it told a familiar story. Probably married before finishing school. No money. No job skills. No hope. No way out.

Tossing the paper towel she had dried her hands with into the garbage can, Daphne sat on the old examining stool and scooted forward until she could look into the face where mascara bled over the bruises. Tears were dropping onto the hands twisting a sopped tissue into a hard little ball.

"No person in the world has the right to do this to you. You're not some guy's punching bag or doormat. You need to get out of this situation and you need to do it now. It's not going to change or improve, no matter how many promises he has probably made to you."

The words bubbled thorough the tears. "But, I don't...I mean I have noth..."

"That's okay. You don't need anything. There is a place where you can go and be safe. They will help you get your stuff and give you what you don't have to get started again. They'll help you get a job and finish school. And he can't get to you there. He can't ever get to you again. Trust me. All you have to do is go."

The venerable glass door slammed open with a force that sent a near fatal shudder through the old pane. A booze-soaked block of a man swayed in the doorway. He glared at the trio of women, finally focusing on Daphne. He ran the back of his hand over his mouth, mixing spittle in beard stubble.

"She ain't going nowhere unlessen it's with me, bitch. Get your dumb ass off that chair. Only place you're going, pigface, is to fix me chow. Now move it or do I have to kick your fat ass again?"

The boy awoke with a terrified whimper.

Daphne came off the stool with a speed which sent it careening into the battered wall, her petite frame taut with fury. Her crystal blue eyes solidified until they were as hard as the three precious stones edging each small ear.

She jabbed at the man with her words as she advanced across the room. "So you're the big, bad bully who gets his rocks off beating women. I bet you're a real tough character. Bet there are lots of people afraid of you, aren't there."

She was close enough now to smell regurgitated beer on his breath.

He shifted in the doorway, simultaneously jerking his jeans up over his belly and belching in Daphne's face.

"You got about two seconds to get out of me and my old lady's way, slut," he said as he leaned aggressively into Daphne's face.

In a movement too quick for his bleary eyes to catch, Daphne's hand dipped into the pocket of her scrub jacket. The six-inch switchblade snapped upright, stopping just under his hairy nostrils.

He took a startled step back and raised one fist across his chest.

"Swing that hand and I'll make sure it's the last time you ever raise it to anyone again."

"Yeah, you and what pack of Marines?" he said with less certainty in his belligerence.

Daphne advanced forward, motioning to him with the blade. "If you think you are man enough to take it away from me, come on in."

They were out of the building now and in the path the clinic's light made across the sidewalk.

He glanced right, then left out of the corners of his eyes.

"Oh, don't worry. Nobody in this neighborhood is going to come to anyone's rescue. So how about it? Ready to try it?"

Somehow being backed across the sidewalk by a small woman stung his male ego enough that, despite the weapon, he took a swing. The knife cut smartly across his hand. He howled in painful outrage.

"Next time, it'll be your balls."

He backed up two more steps and stopped. Daphne swung the knife at him one more time, forcing him to step back again. His feet tangled with something and suddenly he was falling, landing with a bone-rattling jar flat on his back in the street. For a moment, the stars were much closer.

The tall man who had been leaning against the decapitated parking meter bent down to run a silk handkerchief over the top of his shoe and carefully brushed his pant leg before looking at the man gasping for his lost breath.

"Oh, I say, old man, I am sorry. I didn't see you coming." The British accent came coolly foreign out of the night.

Blue lights began to strobe as a car pulled out of the line of traffic. The trio was thrown into bright relief when a set of headlights swung into the curb.

"It seems the law has arrived, Daph," Edmund murmured as he shifted his position so his elbow now rested on the meter.

A second car pulled in behind the police cruiser.

"We have a problem here, people?" the broad shouldered officer said as he emerged from the car, automatically slipping his baton into the loop of his belt and loosening his gun. He stepped around the open car door.

Daphne shielded her eyes against the blue flashers. "Jerry?"

The chunky man grunted as he used the front bumper of the police car to lever himself out of the gutter. He made it unsteadily onto his feet and stood, wavering back and forth in the car's headlights.

"You a cop? I want you to arrest this bitch. She done assaulted me with a goddam switchblade and them things are illegal. Look what she done to me," he said as he held his bleeding hand out in the headlights.

"This true, Daphne?"

"I nailed him with my," she paused as she slowly dipped her hand back into her scrub jacket pocket and drew out, "bandage scissors."

The man began to spit in his anger. "That ain't true. It was a goddam switchblade." Suddenly, he lunged at Daphne. "You lousy little piece of...."

Edmund quickly stepped in front of Daphne. Officer Jerry Rickham also stepped between them, placing his baton firmly across the man's chest and backing him up. "Whoa, buster. Get a hold on. Daphne, tell me what went down." A third man, standing just out of the range of the lights, tensed but didn't move.

Gesturing to the two women huddled in the doorway. "The little gal with the battered face is this man's wife. Her friend brought her here for medical attention after this guy beat the hell out of her. I was treating her when he shows up and threatens me. I had to protect myself and my patient. You're welcome to search me." She held her arms out.

"Nah, that's not necessary." Jerry pulled out his handcuffs and dragged one of the man's arms behind his back and snapped a cuff on, followed by the second arm and cuff.

"What're you doing? I ain't done nothin' wrong."

"We're going to let this nice lady have tonight to think things over and maybe by morning she will decide not to press charges against you." He hustled the profanity spewing man into the car.

Turning back to them, he gestured to the tall man now stepping into the light. "By the way, this is Detective Dennis Cobb. He's here about your call."

The three people stood examining each other for a moment. The first thought through Dennis' head was these people were as strange as the occasional stories he had heard suggested. The woman was tiny, maybe five foot one or two, ninety eight pounds soaking wet. A mass of blonde curls was pinned on top of her head, tiny tendrils escaping here and there framing the small oval face.

He transferred his study to the man standing behind her. Expensively dressed and groomed, he had the languid and delicate movements of an effeminate personality although he had moved quickly enough in defense of the woman. Still, there was a hooded, watchful look in the eyes that put Dennis in mind of a predatory cat.

Daphne was having trouble bringing the man into focus. He seemed to be wrapped in mist. She stepped towards him and held out her hand.

"I'm Daphne DelaVeque and this is my cousin, Edmund Broadhurst." As soon as he gripped her hand, she was encompassed in wet sadness and the sound of weeping filled her ears.

"Edmund, do you mind helping Detective Cobb. I need to finish up with the others."

She preceded them into the clinic. The two women had taken refuge in the chairs by the window and the one whose husband had just been taken away was weeping inconsolably.

Inside the clinic, Dennis looked around. "This place wouldn't pass code for a dog pound," he thought to himself, "and they are treating people here?"

Daphne turned to him. "The place runs entirely on volunteer services and donations. What money we get goes into supplies and helps pay for medications. Frankly, a mother whose baby has 104 degree temperature, no money, or insurance could care less if our walls are falling down."

Dennis whirled, startled. He hadn't spoken consciously, had he? A chill climbed his spine.

The petite woman hadn't waited for his response. She was already perching on a chair next to the two women, handing out tissues and talking earnestly.

A light touch on his elbow drew his attention back to Edmund. He caught himself pulling his arm away from the fingers. Edmund immediately dropped his hand and turned away so the smile playing across his lips was not seen.

He stood back and motioned for Dennis to pass in front of him to the examining table. Justin had again pulled up into a shivering huddle under the blanket. Edmund placed a gentle hand on his shoulder and spoke. Dennis could hear the soothing tones but the words were too quiet for him to catch.

Keeping a protective arm on the boy, Edmund came around the table and hoisted a hip to balance on the edge of it. He brought the boy around and sheltered him under his arm, drawing him close.

"Justin. This is Detective Cobb from the Kelton Police Department. You need to tell him what happened to your kitten and your sister, Kelsey."

Still not lifting his head, Dennis observed the boy's shoulders begin to rise and fall rapidly as though in terror.

Edmund pulled his arm back and began to rhythmically massage the boy's neck. "It's all right, Justin. You can trust the detective. He will help us look after you."

When the boy finally raised his head, Dennis swelled with rage at whoever had perpetrated such abuse. The boy sensed his anger and huddled against Edmund.

Dennis caught sight of the rolling stool. He went to retrieve it, using the few seconds to bring himself under control.

Then with assistance from Edmund, he coaxed out the story including how Gary had apparently broken his mother's arm as she fought to try and save her baby.

As the two men stood studying the kitten's body in its makeshift morgue, Dennis said softly, "I'm making this child a ward of the state. I'll call and get a matron down here."

Daphne spoke from behind him. "I have the authority to take the child into custody."

Dennis turned, startled by her voice. She reached in her pocket and pulled out a black I.D. case, flipping it open to reveal a photo ID card and badge.

She turned back to Justin, gently stroking his hair back from his forehead as she talked. "Justin. I am going to take you to the hospital with me. That's where I work. Detective Cobb is going to the house to get your momma and bring her to the hospital, too. I want to make sure she is all right. And, Justin, Gary won't be able to get to you or your momma again. Understand. He won't ever hurt you again."

Turning back she fixed her clear blue gaze on the detective. "Could you get someone to drive us over? I don't usually bring my car to the clinic."

"You walk here?" Dennis said surprised.

Daphne shrugged. "Beats having my car stripped while I'm patching up the aftermath of a gang fight."

"Well, I believe everything here is under control. I shall leave you both to your duties."

"Ah, Mr. Broadhurst, I will need you to come down and make a formal statement."

"Would morning be soon enough? I suspect you shall be somewhat occupied for the balance of the evening."

Dennis nodded his concurrence and Edmund evaporated out the door.

Dennis turned back to Daphne, who had her arms around the boy, gently rocking him back and forth.

"If you need me to come to the station, I need to come in before I go on duty at 7 a.m. or after I get off at 3:30 p.m.," Daphne said.

"You work at Kelton Community?"

Daphne nodded. "Peds unit."

"I'll call tomorrow and arrange a time with you."

He found her clear steady gaze disconcerting. He started towards the door and then turned back.

"I'll radio for a car to pick you up. You gonna be okay here by yourself?" he said glancing out the door as a couple of the street regulars drifted by, eying the action in the clinic.

"I am quite capable of looking after myself. I've been doing it a long time."

Dennis gave a short nod. "Keep the knife handy, okay?" he said as he strode toward the door.

Watching the broad shouldered man depart, Daphne mentally threw a question after him. "Who weeps for you, Cobb?"

Chapter Four

Following the shadows, the man approached a small house sitting on its tiny overgrown lot. The naked porch light burned low as though ashamed. It revealed a screen door hanging brokenly against the peeling exterior. A couch, its mangy skin mottled with mildew, lay discarded across the end of the tiny porch. The rusted corpse of a washer stood stiffly by the dilapidated steps.

The split wood on the steps creaked painfully as Edmund climbed them.

He had just stepped on the porch when the front door flew open and a roar engulfed him.

"Where the hell have you been, you little bastard?"

A thick necked man charged out the door, expelling foul fumes with every breath. Deliberately choosing to view the man through the eyes of the child, Edmund felt as though he was being swallowed by hell itself. And for a moment there was the briefest flash of sensation as though he had himself felt this way once upon a time as he came back into himself.

From inside the house, a woman appeared and grabbed at the man.

"No, Gary. Stop. Don't hurt him anymore."

She was as pathetic in her appearance as she was in her attempts to deter the man's objective. Her hair hung in dirty hanks around the shoulders of a filthy robe. She clutched at the diaper pin holding it together at the bosom.

He flung her off with a single backward jerk of his arm.

She huddled in the open doorway, a hand crammed in her mouth. Within her eyes, Edmund saw someone screaming for help beneath a sea of utter despair.

"I don't know who you are but get your ass off my porch before I have to throw it off."

Edmund deliberately threw a hip forward and swished a hand in the man's face. "Oh, I do like the physical ones," he said sweetly.

The man reached out and grabbed Edmund by his jacket while doubling up a scarred fist. "When I get through with you, a dog wouldn't have you, you lousy fag."

The limp hand seized the man's wrist, the long, sensitive fingers ruthlessly compressing the nerves.

The man could not maintain his grip under the excruciating pressure and the pudgy fingers reluctantly relinquished their hold.

The man stared at the hand. It was as if he was being held by death itself. His blood chilled under its icy touch.

A growing darkness seemed to swallow the light on the porch.

The man struggled against the hold on him. "You sonvabitch. I'll teach you."

The woman stared fearfully at the contest before her. She knew too well the brutish violence of the one man. Although tall and well built, the other man was lighter and somewhat sissified in appearance. He was obviously overmatched.

Edmund let go of the man's wrist and stood, hands on his hips with indolent disdain.

Anger poured like hot lava through the heavy-set man. He lowered his head and charged into Edmund with fists flailing.

Before the eye could blink, Edmund had his hands about the man's throat. The thumbs pushed the chin up while the long fingers dug into the cervical spine. The man's arms sagged and dropped as he felt his strength being sucked away.

Edmund's face seemed to float above him, the brown eyes beginning to glow with an eerie fire.

"Frightfully bad form, old man. You are much too old to be the school yard bully." The tensile fingers caused every nerve in the man's body to scream out with agony at the same time preventing him from making a sound. His eyes bulged as the pressure built inside his head.

A half-smile played over the lips of his captor. Then Gary could hear the man's voice ricocheting through his brain bringing a wash of horrible images in its wake. He tried to run from the monstrous thing pursuing him through his own skull. He couldn't get away. He mentally cowered under its approach. It demanded to be faced. He couldn't do it. He wouldn't do it, but it dragged him up until he had to look at it. He screamed as he looked into his own face, bloated with hideous malevolence.

Abruptly Edmund released his grip and the man fell heavily to his knees, whimpering and struggling to crawl away from himself.

Melting back into the shadows, he directed his last words to the woman. "Courage, m'dear."

As a rich laugh echoed out of the darkness, something long quenched flickered within her.

Chapter Five

Dennis was still struggling with the facts portion of the search warrant. Right now, it was pretty thin. One small boy's statement even with the obvious abuse and the dead kitten might not move Judge Greene to let them start digging up a back yard. He wished he had more.

Ron's voice echoed through the empty room. "Cobb, it's someone else calling about the Free Clinic thing on line three." Dennis punched the call onto the line.

The voice was cool and feminine. "I checked the hospital records. Kelsey Jeanne Floyd was born February 17 to Brenda Joy Floyd and Gary no middle initial Stallman, 1427 Briarwood. Obstetrical records indicate two cracked ribs and bruising on the mother's abdomen. She claimed she fell over the dog. Kelsey was seen in the Well Baby clinic at two weeks of age. All indications she was proceeding normally. She was scheduled to be seen at two months. Mother never returned with her. There are no other records relating to the baby including morgue records. Mother was treated for broken arm in March. Said she missed a step and fell off her porch. Doctor's notes suggest abuse. I am faxing them through now. HIPAA be damned." The caller hung up the phone crisply. Almost simultaneously, Dennis heard the fax line ring and engage.

"Cobb. Judge is on four."

Dennis recited the facts he had just been given. "Send it over. Call the DA in now. If this checks out, Cobb, I want the bastard in front of me tomorrow morning."

The fatigue he had felt earlier dropped off on his way to the dispatch office. The records from the hospital were already neatly tagged and waiting in his basket. He shoved them into the copier and issued orders as fast as the machine spat out duplicates.

"Get Rickham in here and have him get the warrant to Judge Greene. I want the 'ghoul squad' and backup. Also get me a matron. Everyone meets me at the all-nighter in the Corners. We go together. I don't want this scuzz bucket jackrabbiting."

It took nearly 45 minutes for the entire team to rendezvous. The first to arrive was Dr. Hal Grissum. As soon as Dennis got out of the car to meet him, the small groups of people hanging out in front of the store began to melt away in the night.

Grissum, as usual, was complaining. "What is it with you guys? I have one lousy night off from call and who do I hear from? You people got a law against a man staying home and watching a ball game?"

He was just relighting his cigar when Dave Colby wheeled his little Miata in, nearly barking Dr. Grissum's shins.

"I'll be glad when he finally gets old enough for something with an engine," Grissum grumbled out of the corner of his mouth.

Dennis watched with fascination as Colby unwound his six foot frame from under the wheel. Although he had seen it any number of times, it still amazed him.

Dave shambled around the car and joined the other two in holding up Grissum's Bronco. A turn of the wind soon encapsulated the photographer's head in the pungent cigar smoke. Coughing and sweeping at the air with his long, freckled hand, Dave moved away. "Hey, Doc, don't you know those things will kill you."

"Not a chance. I'm gonna get run down in a sleazy parking lot by some lunatic in a kiddy car."

Both Colby and Dr. Grissum were part of what the Kelton police department referred to affectionately as the 'ghoul squad'. The department was too small to budget for professional crime lab personnel. The state police furnished both facilities and personnel upon request but its services had to be shared with every other small community throughout the state. To fill the gap, Kelton had several citizens who were willing to place their professional skills at the city's disposal for nominal fees. Dr. Grissum served as medical examiner in addition to being chief of staff at Kelton Community Hospital and overseeing the emergency department. Dave Colby had a small photography studio, earning the bulk of his income from school and wedding pictures.

A police car pulled in on the other side of Grissum's car. Jerry got out waving a sheaf of papers. "All signed, sealed and ready to be delivered, Cobb."

Dennis was so busy scanning the documents to make sure everything was properly signed; he didn't notice the other person getting out until Grissum groaned.

"Oh, god, not you, DelaVeque."

Dennis looked up in surprise at the woman smiling sweetly at their group.

"Why, Dr. Grissum, what a pleasant surprise."

"Fellows, despite her appearance, you are in the presence of a vicious she-devil. I suggest you keep your distance and your guns ready."

Daphne looked down at her hands folded demurely and then peeped up through long dark lashes. "Dr. Grissum, are you still pouting? I was merely assisting by lighting a small fire under you."

"You singed the hair off my ass," he shouted.

The other three men goggled a moment, then Dennis took charge. He began to explain the purpose of their nocturnal visit to the Floyd residence.

Dennis led the way out of the parking lot with Grissum and Dave sharing the Bronco. Jerry and Daphne brought up the rear.

As the vehicles pulled in along the curb, the occupants could see a man splayed out on the couch, an empty whiskey bottle lying on the porch. There was no reaction from him even as the car doors slammed.

"Shit," Jerry said. "Can we serve a search warrant on him when he's passed out drunk?"

Daphne cocked her head. She could hear a choking wheeze as though air was being squeezed through an ever diminishing space. She stared at the house hard.

Suddenly she sprinted for the house. "Ohmigod, she's hung herself."

She flew up the steps and tried the door handle. It was locked. She flung herself at the door, her light weight not even raising a groan from the old wood. Dennis raced after her. He pulled her up by her shoulder.

"What in god's name are you doing?"

She grabbed his arms. "Kick the door in. Kick the frickin' door in now," she ordered.

Dennis never knew why he turned and drove his size 11 shoe against the old door lock. The wood splintered and the door fell in. Daphne shoved off of Dennis' arm and shot into the house. Dennis followed the maroon windbreaker disappearing through a door.

In the back bedroom a woman was dangling from a makeshift noose, her breath gurgling from between bluish lips. Daphne grabbed her legs and tried to push the woman's weight up away from the material twisted around her neck. She was flung aside as Dennis roared for Rickham and took her place. He readily was able to lift the woman high enough to release the pressure.

Rickham jumped on the sagging bed and cut the pieces of sheet which had been woven into a hangman's noose.

The two men laid the woman on the bed and instantly Daphne removed the strangling loop. Immediately the woman's breathing eased and the blue began to diminish. Dr. Grissum arrived with his bag. With meticulous cadence, the two medical personnel worked on the woman.

As the ambulance pulled away from the curb with the woman and Daphne inside, Dave looked at Dennis and Grissum. "How the hell did she know what was happening? I didn't see anything, did you?"

"How could we, the Floyd woman was in the back of the house," Dennis answered.

Grissum turned back toward the house. "I tell you, men, when that female ain't giving orders, she's giving the willies."

Chapter Six

Dennis' eyes were red and gritty feeling when he arrived at the police station the next morning. It had been nearly midnight by the time they had been able to get Stallman sober enough to serve the search warrant and begin their work in earnest. It hadn't taken long to find the tiny mummified body wrapped in the garbage bags exactly where the boy had said it would be.

The clock was leaning on four a.m. by the time Stallman was booked, the paperwork had been completed to send the body to the state medical examiner, and Dennis had made his weary way home.

Agatha McIntosh, his babysitter cum next door neighbor, was comfortably asleep on the couch. He dragged a blanket and pillow from the linen closet in the bathroom and stretched out between Eric's youth bed and Cortlyn's crib.

He awakened three hours later to the smell of coffee and the sensation of being strangled. Eric had crawled down beside him and now had his arm wrapped tightly across his throat. Cortlyn was methodically bombarding him with crib toys.

Agatha poured him coffee as soon as he came into the kitchen with Eric clinging to his back and Cortlyn hanging on his neck. Concern etched her angular Scots face beneath its thick shock of iron grey hair as she peeled Cortlyn off her father and expertly tucked her into the high chair. Dennis reached back and lowered Eric onto a chair.

"Ach, you be lookin' like death warmed over, laddie," she said as she thrust the coffee cup into his hands.

Dennis smiled tiredly. "Mrs. Mac, what am I going to do when the Captain sails home to claim you?"

A shadow crossed his mind as he watched as Mrs. McIntosh filled small plastic bowls with cereal and sippy cups with juice. It had been his very good fortune to have 'Mrs. Mac' move in the other half of the duplex. A former school librarian who was waiting out the last year until her husband retired from the merchant marine, she had become a surrogate grandmother to his children, never minding the crazy hours a cop had to keep sometimes.

"What am I going to do when that man is underfoot all the time? The Lord will just have to provide for us both," she answered

The children had acted out and fussed during his preparations to go back to the police station. His tired mind was riddled with guilt by the time he was buzzed through the door.

The arraignment went as expected with the judge setting a million dollar bail and ordering a competency examination. The man who battered children and drowned babies stared sullenly at the floor.

When it was over the jailer prodded him towards the door. "Come on, Stallman. We got lots of people eager to meet a man who kills little bitty babies." Dennis saw the man's eyes darting around looking for the hole that would let him escape the nightmare he woke up in.

Dennis tugged the knot in his tie down and undid the neck button on his shirt as he came back into the station house.

"Hey, Vern. What's the name of that psychologist we contracted with to do the forensic psychological evaluations?"

"Ashe, sir. Lygia Ashe."

"Call the DA's office and give 'em her name and number, will you?"

It was after mid-afternoon when Dennis pulled into the parking lot of the hospital. He stopped at the front desk to ask the location of the Floyds.

The receptionist patted her well-spritzed hair, batted her stubby eyelashes and simpered at him.

"Why, Dennis, it's been a long time since you paid us a visit. Is it professional or," she lowered her eyes and looked up at him coyly, "personal?"

Inwardly, Dennis cringed. He had become extremely leery of females following Melanie's death. It had seemed he had no sooner called the ambulance than the house was swarming with women all applying to take her place. Every possible service had been hinted at and in some cases openly offered. He had felt as though he was suffocating in perfume and unwanted attention. Thank god for his sister. Susan had taken him and the children in, and then, in her forthright manner, turned off the flood.

Much later Susan had sat him down for a discussion. "My dear brother. You are a good looking man. Attraction number one. You are a cop. Cops aren't called blue knights for nothing. Attraction number two. You are now a single man. Big attraction number three. You have three choices. You can just pick one, like picking a name out of the hat, and remarry quickly. You can learn to like men. Or just think of them as gnats and brush them off." He had become a human fly swatter.

"Professional, Joanne," he said. "Could you tell me where Brenda Floyd and her son are?"

"Medical unit. C wing."

Dennis lightly slapped the counter with his hand and turned away. "Thanks."

"You'll come back to say good-bye won't you," she called after him. He waved a non-committal hand.

The years of remodeling and expansion had added wings in every direction. The only way to get anywhere in the hospital was by a circuitous route but, finally, Dennis was pointed to a small day room.

It was close to 3 p.m. when he finished with Brenda Floyd. It had been the all too familiar story of a woman's need to have a man trapping her and her son in a life that ended not in happily ever after but hell.

The pediatric unit was on the second floor of what had been the original three story hospital. Dennis stepped out of the elevator checking his watch. It was nearly shift change time. He spotted Daphne standing at the nurse's station, flipping open charts and recording information from bits of paper she shuffled periodically. She had her back to him. Without raising her eyes or turning, she spoke to him. "Be with you in a minute, Cobb."

While Dennis waited, he studied the situation. Unless the woman had eyes in the back of her head, there was no way for her to have seen him. No one had spoken to him and indeed no one else was even at the station. Another feeling of eeriness swept over him.

With a final snap of a chart, Daphne gathered up her bits of paper and stuffed them in the pocket of her teal blue scrubs. She picked up a bright yellow stethoscope and slung it around her neck, hooking the bell over an earpiece.

"I need coffee and you're buying," she said to Dennis as she passed him and punched the elevator button.

In the closed environment of the elevator, she was again aware of the misty sadness surrounding the man but she did not hear the weeping this time.

Back on the main floor, Dennis followed Daphne to the end of the cafeteria counter where the coffee pots squatted on their heating elements. She held up the pot and looked through it. It was black as death.

"This stuff would probably cure Ebola fever," she said as she poured it into two foam cups. "Hold it away from you," she instructed as she made her way to a table beside the windows. "It'll probably eat through the bottom any second."

She sat her cup down and then stopped an orderly. "Yo, Tim. You got a cigarette?"

He fumbled in his pockets before bringing out a pack and shaking one up. He handed her his matches, "Keep 'em. I got more" and scuttled off.

Daphne opened the window, sat and scrunched down in her chair until she could put her feet up on the chair beside Dennis. Then with total disregard to the numerous "No Smoking" signs, she lit up.

Dennis shifted uncomfortably.

"DelaVeque!" It was a familiar bellow echoing through the nearly empty cafeteria. Dennis looked up to see Grissum charging in their direction. Daphne calmly took another drag off the cigarette. "I wonder why all the pleasures in life are so bad for you?" she asked.

Grissum loomed over the table. "I am going to bring you up before the Board for flagrant violation of hospital rules."

Daphne coolly blew out a cloud of smoke. "Fine and I'll tell them who keeps getting ashes all over the O.R."

"That is insubordination."

Dennis suddenly became aware the cafeteria was filling up with hospital staff sidling in to watch. His discomfort grew. Despite his profession, he loathed scenes.

He looked back to see Daphne's crystal blue eyes calmly looking at him.

"I hope you don't ever let this old fossil treat you, Cobb. He thinks leeches are modern medicine."

"I'll have you know I have never had a malpractice suit in my life, woman."

"Dead people can't sue."

"That's it, you're fired," Grissum howled.

"You can't fire someone who quit ten minutes ago," she countered.

Grissum glared, his cigar working up and down, but the eye farthest from Daphne winked at Dennis. Daphne took one last drag and then flipped the butt out the window.

She skewered Grissum with her clear blue look. "Look, Cobb has had a long day. Let's let him get his business done. Go torture the helpless, chase down a cute ass to pat, malpractice. Anything. Just go away."

Muttering to himself Grissum swung away from the table, the capacity crowd parting as he went through. Grissum growled at them, "Just who the hell is taking care of the patients around here with all you yahoos standing around goofing off." As soon as Grissum cleared the doors, a cheer went up and one of the men made a careful mark on a small blackboard. Then the room emptied as rapidly as it had filled.

When Dennis turned back, he found Daphne's eyes back on him. It was a cool, clinical gaze. They seemed to take in everything and yet revealed nothing to him. The interview proceeded quickly. Daphne gave short concise responses. There was no side-tripping, no unnecessary explanations, nothing except the facts.

Dennis clicked off the small tape recorder he had set between them to record his questions and her answers. "This should be transcribed in a day or two. You can sign it then."

Daphne nodded, straightened up and then stood up. "See you around, Cobb."

She had vanished by the time Dennis had finished gathering up the tape recorder and his notebook. As he passed the little board with its neat rows of marks carefully divided into groups of five, he stopped to study it.

"I think we are going to make a new record," a man's voice said over his shoulder.

"What is it?" Dennis asked.

"That's the number of times Grissum has fired DelaVeque this year. If we beat last year's record, Grissum has to provide a big New Year's bash. We only need twenty more to beat last year's record and we still have better 'n two months."

Dennis stared at the board reviewing the whole scene in his mind including Grissum's wink. Suddenly, he understood. It was all a game between two people, who apparently had enormous respect for one another, in order to provide an ongoing diversion for people working in a high stress field. Dennis walked away with an unexpected glimpse into the odd little woman. He had known Grissum a long time. It took a hellava lot to gain the old curmudgeon's respect. She must be some kind of female despite Grissum's insistence to the contrary.

Chapter Seven

Lygia Ashe, PhD. clicked off the small dictation recorder and leaned back in her chair. She had interviewed and tested the alleged baby-killer for the past several days. She had been unsurprised by her findings, a sociopathic con man, mean and manipulative, with the probable start of organic brain syndrome from his drinking. He was totally competent to stand trial.

There was only one thing bothering her. It was his strange tale of a foreign sounding "demon" that attacked him the night the police arrived. He described it in such clear and vivid detail; Lygia was hard pressed to say it was an alcohol induced hallucination. The man was quite adamant in his denial of concomitant drug usage and just as adamant in standing by his story. Regardless of what had triggered it, it was real in his mind.

She had even gone to the hospital to talk with Ms. Floyd, the only other one present that night. Brenda Floyd had listened to the story with a stony face staring out the window at the brilliant Indian summer day.

"No," she said emphatically. "Nothing like that happened."

"Are you sure? It was a pretty bad night for you. Perhaps, you are hazy in your memory. Please think about it carefully."

Brenda looked out at the trees flaunting their final flaming glory. "'Courage, m'dear', as if he knew what was going to happen," she murmured. A demon? No, an avenging angel who saved her and Justin. And one did not betray their angels.

Lygia leaned forward to try to catch her words. "I'm sorry, I didn't catch that."

Brenda turned and looked at Lygia. "I'm sorry. I saw and heard nothing like what you described that night." Her gaze was unshakable.

Lygia sighed and glanced at her watch before picking up her little recorder again. She was due to meet Roberta at the hospital's meeting room in less than an hour. Maybe she'd ask her opinion. Regardless, she would not include it in her report. It appeared to be a single isolated incident triggered by what she couldn't say. It was not enough to alter her conclusion.

She pressed the record button. "Subject was interviewed and tested with the following findings. . ." Her words continued in a concise rapid-fire stream.

Roberta was sitting on a bench in the hall when Lygia arrived. Roberta looked at her watch as Lygia walked up. "Right to the second as always. What'd you do, wait outside until just the exact moment to walk in?"

"No," Lygia smiled. "I just have a hyperaccurate interior clock."

"Yeah, it figures your heart beats in Greenwich Mean Time. Do you know anything about the guy who's speaking tonight?" Roberta asked as she pushed up to her feet.

Lygia shook her head. "Not a thing, and if he is as dull as the last two speakers, I'm dropping my membership in the Washington County Psychological Association. I don't need to spend three hundred bucks a year to be bored out my skull."

They strolled into the meeting room with about ten minutes to spare. "Well, do we sit in the back so we can escape or towards the front so we can see and hear?" Roberta asked.

"The back row is already taken. They must have been at the last meeting. Pickings are kinda slim if we're going to sit together. Looks like in front."

The meeting opened with the usual noting of coming events for those in the psychological field, general announcements, and a brief introduction of the evening's speaker. As Edmund Broadhurst walked to the podium, Lygia heard Roberta's audible gasp.

"Girlfriend," Roberta leaned over, "I am having an orgasm."

The talk was provocative. It struck one uncomfortable note after another in those present as it challenged the professionals to move beyond the narrow straits of the mind in diagnosing mental dysfunction. He spoke of the soul and the interrelation of it with the mind and emotions.

When his talk was over, the applause was politely scattered. Lygia caught an odd little smile playing over his lips. As she gathered up her purse and stood up, Roberta grabbed onto her arm and dragged her towards the speaker.

"What are you doing?"

"I have got to touch him. He is the most beautiful thing I have ever seen," Roberta said hauling Lygia after her.

As they waited their turn to speak to him, Lygia noticed Edmund was looking deeply into each person as though he was reading them. When they finally approached, Roberta thrust her hand out. "Hi, I'm Roberta Nickles, clinical psychologist here at Kelton Community."

Edmund bowed politely over her hand, holding it firmly for a moment. "Then, p'rhaps you are familiar with my cousin? Daphne DelaVeque in pediatrics?"

"You're related to Daphne?" Roberta used the comment to drink in the man's face. "Yes, I can see the resemblance. This is Dr. Lygia Ashe. She's in private practice."

Edmund turned to Lygia. "Ah, Dr. Ashe, what a pleasure." He took her hand.

At his touch, she had the double sensation of actual event overlaid with 'memory'. The dèjá vu was momentarily overwhelming. It caused her to embarrass herself by stammering. "Do we, er, have we met?"

"I am familiar with your forensic work from trial transcripts I have reviewed in my research."

He was looking deep into her eyes and she had the strangest feeling of something lightly touching her mind, a very delicate probing jostling her thought processes. She pulled her hand away and the connection was broken. It unsettled her. "I enjoyed your talk very much," she said with polite formality and turned away.

Roberta hurried to catch up with her. "What was that all about?"

"I don't know. Did you feel something when he looked in your eyes?"

Roberta nodded. "I sure did."

"What?"

"Lust."

Even after she was home, curled up on her couch and sipping a cup of tea, Lygia could not quite shake the peculiar feeling clinging to her. Although he was startlingly attractive, it wasn't a physical response to him. In truth, his presence frightened her a little. She sensed darkness within him.

It was a sensation similar to one she had experienced in high school on the day she was supposed to go out with Jimmy Tonelli. When they met between classes to confirm their date, she had felt something emanating from Jimmy. It, too, had frightened her. The feeling had grown until by the time she got home from school, she felt a physical terror of going out with Jimmy that night. She wrestled with herself because she had been trying to get a date with him for months and months. But, her fear finally won out and she had called it off with an excuse.

His car had sailed off a back country road that night and all four occupants had been killed.

Her friends had been so shocked to see her at school the next morning. They had assumed she was one of the four. It had been difficult to explain why she was not sitting beside Jimmy when the Camaro shot into the night. She felt almost guilty as though she had somehow contributed to the accident. It was a secret guilt she carried for years even after it was determined Jimmy had been acid tripping at the time of the accident.

It was certainly one of the occurrences which pointed her in the direction of psychology. She had entered the field to learn to answer and control the knowings she shouldn't know. It had taken years but she was, at last, master of her mind. No more hocus-pocus…until tonight.

She sat behind her desk the next day, her head buried in her hands. She couldn't believe she had done it. Whatever possessed her?

Her secretary peeked in the door. "Dr. Ashe, Mrs. Tallman left without paying. She ordered me to cancel all her other appointments."

Lygia lifted her head and nodded dully. "I am not surprised, Rebecca. Don't bill her for today and cancel her out."

Rebecca withdrew. Lygia looked down at the open file in front of her. Neatly chronologized was Mrs. Tallman's steady complaint of emotional abuse and deprivation by her husband. They had been working on her ability to be more assertive in her dealings with him. Today, when Pearl Tallman sat down and pulled tissue out of her purse signaling the beginning of her session and tears, Lygia had looked at her and knew. She knew Pearl was using the story of an emotionally abusive husband to justify her relationship with her tennis coach, her female tennis coach.

"Pearl, perhaps, we should move away from your husband for a while and explore some of your other relationships."

Pearl just looked at her. "What other relationships are there to explore," she asked with a hint of wariness in her tone.

"Well, for instance, some of your friends. Say, your tennis coach, Connie. You and she are, ah, very close, am I correct?"

Pearl's face lost some of its usual high color. "Who have you been talking to? I don't care what they are saying but it's not true. They're just jealous. They're just trying to cause trouble. To get Connie fired from the club. Because she chooses me over them."

"Perhaps, we should work on your fear of that aspect of yourself, Pearl."

"Dr. Ashe, I think you are the one who needs some work." She had hurled herself to her feet, giving an automatic yank to her short tennis skirt. "Anyone who would accept such filthy rumors and sick gossip as fact is obviously not the person I want to expose my deepest self to. Not one word of this conversation better ever leave this office or you won't believe the lawsuit I'll slap on you." She stormed out, slamming the door for good measure.

Lygia wrote in her conclusion. "Patient terminated treatment."

"Doctor needs head examined," she added between gritted teeth.

Chapter Eight

Dennis was reviewing files two mornings later when the chief appeared in front of his desk. He tossed a manila folder down.

"There was an attempted date rape last night. Fourteen year old girl was beaten up pretty good. She's in Kelton Community. Parents have signed consent for her to be interviewed. Father wants this guy busted and castrated. Not necessarily in that order. I need someone who can handle this without screwing it up. Take Overman with you to handle transcription."

Dennis read over the sketchy report taken at the hospital the night before. The girl, Paula Lovett, had been too hysterical to supply much information. He dialed up the hospital and asked to speak to the charge nurse on duty on Lovett's floor.

"Pediatrics, DelaVeque speaking."

"Ms. DelaVeque, Cobb over at KPD. I understand Paula Lovett is a patient on your floor."

"That's correct."

"The parents have signed a consent form allowing us to interview her. Could you tell me if she can talk now? She was pretty incoherent last night. I need to try to get a full statement from her."

Daphne's soft breathing accompanied the sounds of a chart being pulled. "She is sleeping right now. There are no more sedatives ordered for her at this time. I would suggest she will be clear of medication by 2 p.m. You should be able to talk to her then without worry of a tainted statement."

Dennis noted the time on the inside of the file folder.

At five minutes of two, Dennis and Louise Overman stepped off the elevator in the pediatric unit. "Dennis," one of the nurses bleated as they approached the desk. Almost immediately several more staff women appeared and the air became heavy with competition flirting.

Louise turned and spoke so only Dennis could hear. "Bees to honey, Cobb. What is it you have?"

Dennis glared at her.

Daphne came out of a room down the hall holding her stethoscope and scribbling on a sheet of paper. She glanced up at the commotion at the nurse's station. Dennis looked distinctly uncomfortable. She recognized his companion as the sister of one of the women she had worked with in emergency until they had both made their escape to saner parts of the hospital.

Dennis saw her check her watch and jot the time down before she stuffed the paper in her pocket and walk briskly towards them, flipping her pink stethoscope around her neck.

Tall, heavy set Louise bent over and hugged Daphne when she reached them. Daphne exchanged small talk with Louise while she quickly moved them down the hall. At a door with Lovett written on tape and stuck to the name plate, she paused before quietly opening it and admitting them.

Dennis closed the door as Daphne went to the bed and took the hand of the teenage girl. Paula's face was badly bruised and there was tape across the bridge of her nose.

"Paula, this is Detective Cobb and Louise Overman from the police department. They need to ask you about last night." The girl clutched fearfully at Daphne's hands.

Cobb's voice came gently from his position just inside the door. He had pushed his hands down in his pockets and made no move to approach the bed. "Paula, would you feel better if Ms. DelaVeque stayed with us?"

Paula nodded and shifted closer to Daphne. Dennis hoped he was doing the right thing. This was going to take some delicate footwork to get what they needed and he didn't want it screwed up by the wrong thing being said at the wrong moment.

Louise slipped into a chair on the opposite side of the ward's empty bed. She knew Dennis liked to run his own show and was surprised he had offered to have Daphne stay.

Not moving any closer to the bed, Dennis explained to the girl what he was going to do, what her rights were as the victim, and her freedom to end the interview whenever she couldn't handle it.

The interview took nearly 45 minutes. Throughout, Dennis kept his voice soft and gentle. Little by little he had edged up from the door to the bedside. He had carefully placed one hand on the bed while keeping the other in his pocket. In precise orchestration, Daphne had gradually released her hand from the girl's and pulled back slowly. When the interview ended, Daphne was the one by the door and Dennis was holding the girl's hand.

The girl had looked into Dennis' face, relief lighting her own. "Wow, I just realized I didn't do anything wrong. He's the one who got out of line. Even when I told him to back off, he kept forcing the issue. Yeah, he needs to learn females aren't just things he can use as he wants to. Nobody gets to tell us what to do with our bodies but ourselves." She pondered the thought a moment. "You know what. I'm starved. I could sure do with a double cheeseburger, fries and a strawberry shake from Big Bill's."

Dennis tugged the end of her hair. "Thanks, Paula. You did great. You're going to be okay." He turned towards Louise. "Ready?"

Daphne opened the door. "Give me a few minutes, Paula, and I'll see if I can get you something to eat."

"Onion rings sound good, too."

Daphne didn't wait for them. She was heading back down the hall when a screech erupted from one of the wards ahead. Dennis started and stepped quickly into the hall.

"We have an escapee from Ward C," the same voice yelled. At that moment, a small Hispanic boy looking to be about five years old scooted into the hall. He had one arm in a surgical soft cast. The edge of his hospital gown was caught in the waistband of a pair of Superman underpants.

Daphne broke into a trot. "Enrique."

He came at her, swinging. "She ain't gonna give me no poke in my butt." Daphne put her hand on his head and stayed back letting him take swings at her.

While Enrique grunted in his efforts, Karen came out of the infant room. 'Daphne, Berman wants a blood draw on the York baby. You know me, I can't draw blood from an elephant. Could you. . ."

"Just let me get this desperado corralled and I'll be right there."

The swings were slowing considerably. Daphne looked down. "I think you have about whipped me, hombre. I'm ready to surrender, if you are."

He stopped and she took her hand off his head. He looked up and burst into tears. "Don't want no poke." Daphne bent down and picked him up; he was half as big as she was. She just stood in the hall and gently swung him back and forth in her arms for a minute while she whispered to him. He giggled reluctantly. Then he giggled again. They disappeared into the ward.

"You two make a good team," Louise said as she and Dennis walked down the hall. "You danced perfectly through that, like you were reading each other's minds."

Dennis glanced at her. "No matchmaking, Overman, okay?"

Louise grinned in amusement. "Cobb, I can tell you don't know a thing about our Daphne. Your ego will take quite a beating if you think she is going to join your fan club of panting females with heaving bosoms. She's not the swooning type."

"I coulda guessed that. First time I saw her, she was backing a nasty tempered drunk about three times her size across the sidewalk at the point of a knife."

Louise laughed. "That's Daphne."

"Her cousin was there, though. I doubt she would have done something like that if she was alone."

"Oh, yes she would have," Louise nodded. "Carol worked with Daphne for years in ER. We may have the mean streets but they have the mean cubicles. It was Daphne they ran at the nastiest drunks, most hysterical parents, most confused, combative oldsters."

Dennis punched the elevator. As they waited for it, Louise noticed a couple of the women find reasons to drift in their direction. Dennis was avoiding eye contact with them. Daphne crossed the hall, never glancing in their direction as she went into the baby ward. Louise noted Dennis' eyes followed her the whole way.

"That tough, heh," he said as they stepped into the elevator.

Louise leaned back on the rail. "Yeah, you could say so. Carol tells of a night when all hell was breaking loose in ER. KPD dumped a fighting drunk on them, fresh from an auto accident. Daphne was assigned to do the preliminary assessment. The guy didn't take to it kindly and backhanded her a good one, slammed her into one of the cabinets, breaking her collarbone. She didn't say a word about it for better than two hours, kept right on working. Finally, she bumped into something." Louise screwed up her face remembering. "An IV pole, I think. Anyway, she went down. Grissum about had a stroke when he found out. Stood over her gurney and yelled at her. Know what she said to him?"

They were stepping out into the lobby. Dennis shook his head.

"She told him she was waiting until a real doctor came on duty."

Dennis stopped to look at Louise's grinning face. "You're putting me on."

She raised her hand and crossed her heart. "Gospel, Cobb."

Dennis glanced back at the hall leading to the main part of the hospital. "She does have guts."

They pushed out the door into the crisp fall day. Louise drew in a deep breath of fresh air. "Yup, fierce, feisty Daphne. Afraid of absolutely nothing…except trusting another human being."

Chapter Nine

Although the paper trail of evidence he was forming was still in its preliminary stages, Dennis was pleased when he left his meeting with the district attorney several days later. The DA had listened carefully to his work product and determined he would not be offering Gary Stallman any deal other than life without parole if he pled or the death penalty if he chose to go to trial. It wasn't a replacement for a whole lifetime lost but it was all Dennis could offer up to tiny Kelsey now.

It was already dusk as he turned his car towards home. Darkness now dominated each twenty-four hours.

The radio near his knee crackled. "E-24, E-24, we have a 10-56 at 2389 S. Donnymeade Road." Although the prowler call was being dispatched to the patrol officer, Dennis realized he was only a few blocks from Donnymeade. He picked up his microphone. "E-16, E-16, this is E-8. I am in the vicinity and ETA is 2 minutes. Request E-24 as back-up."

"That's an affirmative, E-8. E-24 will back-up."

Two houses from the address he had been provided with, Dennis cut the lights and engine, drifting into the curb quietly. He picked up his big flashlight, and quietly exited the car. He approached the house laterally, edging his way around to the back.

As he cleared the corner of the house, he could see the dim outline of someone pulled up on a windowsill.

He moved quietly. His intention was to come within a few feet and turn on his light, using the element of surprise and blinding light to control and contain the situation. As he stepped up onto the patio, his foot struck something that skittered away with a metallic sound. The figure froze and then dropped, creating an even bigger metallic crash.

As the figure sprinted into the gathering gloom, Dennis turn on his flashlight and illuminated the red and white back of a letterman jacket. He was so busy keeping the perpetrator in the light, he missed seeing the humpy side of a toppled Weber bar-be-que. His feet tangled with it and he went down heavily on the exposed end of a leg that had broken free. A fiery pain tore into his side, taking his wind and his voice. He lay gasping shallowly. The flashlight had spun away and now lay with its beam trained on him.

The patio flooded with light and voices came at him from all directions. "Did they get him?" "Jeremy, where are you? Are you alright?" "Geez, Mr. Cobb, you scared me to death."

Dennis found himself looking up into three young faces, one of which belonged to Police Explorer Jeremy Jamison. "Are you alright, sir?" Dennis was too busy trying to breathe to be able to talk.

Officer Burns came around the corner in time to see three youths trying to assist Detective Cobb to his feet. Ultimately, he and the Jamison boy achieved it.

Dennis was finally able to speak only by carefully saying one word followed by a shallow breath. "Would" "someone" "like" "to" "tell" "me" "what" "is" "going" "on?" He had his hand inside his jacket and could feel the warmth of his own blood trickling down his side. He kept it there, not letting the kids see it.

Jeremy started, "Well, you see Amy and I are going together and she got grounded..."

"Cuz of a D in chemistry," Amy interjected.

"Anyway, I just came by to see her and since she can't have anyone in to visit until her folks are home, we were just talking through the window."

Burns picked up the questioning. "So neither one of you called to report a possible prowler?" They shook their heads mystified. Then with a pregnant look at each other, they turned sharp eyes on the younger boy. "Mickey?"

"Well, I thought I was doing what I should. The cat wanted in and when I opened the patio door, I could see someone out there. I couldn't tell it was you, Jeremy."

"You did the right thing, Mickey," Dennis said although the words came out thin and forced. He squeezed the boy's shoulder. "Jeremy, could you get..." He pointed towards his flashlight.

"Yes, sir."

Dennis started towards his car feeling light headed from being unable to draw a deep breath. He heard Burns instructing the young people back into the house and sending Jeremy home with orders to phone next time.

Dennis was leaning against the hood of his car when the officer returned. Burns turned his flashlight on and carefully lifted Dennis' coat away from his side. The torn shirt was soaked in blood. He could see the edges of a bad gash through the tear.

"I think I best drive you to the Emergency room, sir."

***

Dennis winced and drew in his breath painfully as Grissum mopped away at the wound. "This is the first time I have had to patch one of you guys up for being attacked by a bar-be-que. Tell me, Cobb, was it high on charcoal fluid or had it been smoking something?" His assistant rolled her eyes toward heaven.

As the nurse helped Dennis to a sitting position and adjusted the rib belt over the thick layer of gauze protecting the wound, Grissum came back stuffing items in a small plastic bag.

"Okay, you got two cracked ribs in addition to that nasty gash. Here's some pain killers to help for a couple of days. Also here's a tube of antibiotic salve. I want that dressing changed once a day. Keep it dry for 48 hours. No lifting, and avoid bending as much as possible. In fact, I'd like it if you would keep your ass down for the next 24 hours. Got that?"

Dennis rewarded Grissum with a dubious nod and gently worked his way off the table. As the nurse began to help him into his shirt, Grissum gave him a hard look. "I know that attitude. You aren't going to do a damn thing I instructed, are you?" His bushy eyebrows beetled and he turned his glare on the nurse. "Next time, we're gonna use the leeches. They respected doctors in those days. Be back here tomorrow." He stomped out of the room.

The nurse flashed Dennis a grin. "He studied with Hippocrates, you know." Dennis smiled wanly back.

The children raced towards their father as soon as the door opened. Officer Burns headed off a frontal assault just in time. "Whoa, big guy," he said to Eric, "your Dad's been hurt."

"You mean somebody shooted him? Wow!" Eric said and raced to the kitchen shouting. "Miz Mac, Miz Mac, Daddy's been shot. Isn't that great. I bet it's gonna be on TV tonight."

Cortlyn toddled towards her daddy holding her arms out. Dennis watched her. "Oh, baby, I don't think Daddy can pick you up." When Burns reached for her, Cortlyn turned diaper to run howling all the way to the kitchen.

Mrs. McIntosh hurried into the front room. She had an old fashioned baker's apron over a long lavender lace evening dress.

After Burns had helped Dennis ease onto the couch and departed, Mrs. Mac managed to quiet the children and hear the story of the run in with the very real bar-be-que while chasing a phantom prowler.

"Ahh, Denny, my lad, I need to be finding someone to come stay with you. Tonight's the Eastern Star dinner and I am the mistress of ceremonies. There be no way I canna go."

"I think Eric and I can handle it for a while. You just go and have a good time. If things get too bad, I'll call and round up some help."

She untied her apron uncertainly. "Well, if you be promising me."

"You have my word." Dennis winced as he lifted his hand.

Chapter Ten

The nurse was just carrying the small plastic bag to Grissum when the doors of the cafeteria burst open and a flood of people poured out, indicating the in-service was over.

"Dr. Grissum? Your patient, the policeman, forgot his medications."

Grissum grabbed the bag just as he became a sole male island in a sea of women dragging him opposite of his prior destination.

In the swirling tide, he spotted a mop of pale golden curls washing over a bright pink warm-up suit.

He reached out and managed to snag the backpack draped over the pink shoulder.

"DelaVeque."

She pulled up short and turned with stormy blue eyes on her captor. Before she could speak, Grissum held up his hand, waving the bag under her nose. "A mission of mercy, DelaVeque. A mission of mercy."

Daphne rolled her faded Geo Metro into the left hand driveway of the duplex. A plastic baby swing hung from the one lone tree planted squarely in the middle of the duplex yard. A child's bike lay where it had been dropped near the walk. There was a scattering of trucks, plastic sand pails and balls. An all too familiar spasm squeezed her heart as she made her way to the front door. She wondered if she would ever get over this reaction when catching a glimpse of family life.

She rang the door bell and heard small feet racing towards her. She could hear Cobb's voice calling weakly "Don't open that door until..." She lost the rest of what he was saying when the door flew open and a small boy of six or seven looked up at her with bright inquisitiveness. Behind him she could see Dennis staggering off the couch to his stocking feet. His well-muscled chest was bare except for the white band of the rib belt.

"Hi," the little boy announced. "My daddy got beated up in a fight with a bad guy."

"Yeah, I heard," Daphne answered and drew the bag out of her pocket. "You forgot your meds at the hospital. Grissum asked me to drop them by."

Just then a bare bottomed toddler made a dash from behind a worn brown recliner toward the open door. Daphne deftly caught her and swung her up in her arms. Dennis lurched forward. "No, she's afraid of strangers."

The baby put her fingers in her mouth as she and Daphne gravely surveyed each other. The little girl plucked gently at one of the blonde curls floating around Daphne's shoulders then laid her head against the curve of Daphne's neck and looked at her father.

"That's Cortlyn and Eric," he informed her. Suddenly he went putty colored and sagged abruptly to the couch, unable to hold back a gagging moan.

Daphne kicked the door shut and swung Cortlyn and her backpack to the floor.

"Eric, get me a big bath towel now," she ordered and the little boy sprinted for the back of the duplex.

Dennis swallowed back the wave of nausea engulfing him. Daphne's small hands were warm against his clammy skin as she felt his forehead, checked his pulse and respiration.

Eric was back with the towel dragging behind him. Daphne took it and draped it across Dennis' knees.

"I think we better put Dad to bed," Daphne said. Dennis clutched her arm and shook his head.

"Daddy doesn't sleep in there anymore. Not since momma went away. He sleeps here," Eric explained.

Daphne nodded, her heart making an unexpected leap at the news of the apparent lack of a female in the family unit. She set about plumping and turning the pillow. "Now, Eric, I want you to take your Daddy's feet like this," she demonstrated how to put his hands under Dennis heels, "and when I give you the word, you lift and bring them around to the couch like this. Can you do that?"

He nodded and carefully positioned himself in an excellent imitation of Daphne's demonstration.

It was fortunate the couch stood apart from the wall, the back forming a narrow passage toward a closed door on the left. Daphne was able to get a good grip on Dennis' shoulders. "Okay, together now."

Dennis felt a little foolish as the tiny woman and his even smaller son efficiently helped to lay him back again but it was a lot less painful than the first time.

Daphne came around and got down on her knees beside him. She unbuckled his belt and slipped it out, shaking off his hand when he tried to stop her.

"Eric, could you show me where the bathroom is?"

Eric importantly led her through an entry leading straight into the kitchen. To the immediate left was a short hall with first the children's bedroom and then the bathroom.

Having secured a washcloth and a pan of cool water, Daphne returned and sponge bathed Dennis's face, arms, and chest. An old crocheted afghan was piled under the coffee table. Daphne pulled it out and carefully covered Dennis, tucking it across his shoulders. As she lightly brushed the hair back from his forehead she was struck with the most absurd desire to kiss the place between his eyebrows where the pain plowed little furrows.

Astonished by her turn of mind, she slapped it down by jumping to her feet and surveying the room.

Dennis felt the nausea and pain ebbing. A light, warm drowsiness took its place. He had nothing left to fight with and he surrendered.

Eric stood importantly next to Daphne awaiting further instructions. Cortlyn was methodically smashing dried cereal flakes with her hand on the coffee table. Next to the overturned box of cereal was a jar of peanut butter with a baby spoon stuck in it.

"That's nutritious," Daphne commented.

"We was fixing supper for Daddy," Eric explained.

She went around the table and scooped up Cortlyn. When she was safely tucked under one arm, Daphne picked up the cereal and peanut butter with the other. "Let's see what else we can find after we get some bottoms on this young lady."

With a freshly diapered Cortlyn riding on her slim hip, Daphne searched through the nearly bare cupboards and refrigerator.

"Your dad ever hear of a grocery store?" Daphne asked Eric.

It was the silence which woke Dennis up. He listened and then called, "Eric, Cortlyn?" Unable to put any depth of breath behind his words, he felt they only drifted as far as the end of the couch before disappearing. Panic jumped up in him. He forced himself to be calm and think. The DelaVeque woman had been here. She was a pediatric nurse. She knew kids. But what did he know about her? Not a damned thing except that Grissum trusted and respected her. Okay, that was probably enough. And Eric would be okay but Cortlyn was terrified of strangers. He was picturing his tiny daughter struggling, fighting, screaming when he heard the gravel crunch in the driveway and headlights flashed across the picture window.

A car door opened and he could hear Eric's voice chattering a mile a minute. The front door opened and Eric came into the living room carrying a grocery sack nearly as big as he was. Behind him was Daphne with a large bag of groceries in one arm and Cortlyn in the other. His daughter was hanging onto the front of Daphne's jacket totally at ease.

The trio disappeared into the kitchen. In a moment, Daphne was back. She laid her hand on his forehead before picking up his wrist and checking his pulse. Then she slipped her fingers inside the rib belt and slid them around to his sides gauging its fit.

Eric's voice came in a stage whisper from the doorway of the kitchen. "How is he?" It was louder than his normal voice.

"I think he's going to make it," Daphne whispered back.

"That's good to know," Dennis said opening his eyes.

"Well, 'Dances with Hibachi', how do you feel," Daphne asked as she fluffed his pillow. Her hand struck something shoved down in the couch cushions. She leaned over him and her hair fell, tickling his shoulder as she felt around and finally pulled his gun and back holster out.

'What are you going to do, shoot the Puffalump?"

"I forgot to take it off and I didn't want the kids to get it."

'Where do you keep it?"

"Closet...bedroom," he said gesturing over the arm of the couch.

"I'll put it away."

Dennis started to sit up. "No, that's okay. I think I can take over now."

"No way, Cobb," Daphne said. She placed her free hand on his chest and put her weight into it, forcing him to lay back.

Suddenly he was very aware of the feel of her hand on his bare skin, the smell of new mown flowers that emanated from her and the place where her hip contacted his thigh. His belly caught fire and he flushed with embarrassment.

Daphne opened the door and switched on the light. The room was at least ten degrees cooler than any other part of the house. When she moved into the room she was surrounded by the misty sadness she had felt the first time she had met Dennis. The plaintive weeping was clearly audible as she crossed to the closet. Whatever happened had happened here, she thought.

She slid open the closet door and was engulfed in the fusty smell of clothes long unworn. She placed the gun on the shelf and then touched several of the garments. All the colors were dark; the styles stark and severe as though the wearer had been in perpetual mourning.

Closing the closet, she studied the room. It, too, had that peculiar smell and feel of someplace no longer used by the living. A thin layer of dust lay over every surface. But more than the obvious lack of use, Daphne was struck by the complete lack of personality in the room. There was nothing here except a kind of bland genericism. The whole room looked as though it had been moved in toto from a cheap furniture showroom. The bed was covered with a comforter printed in a Texas Star quilt pattern. The nondescript, brownish print was repeated in the pillow shams and the short curtains hanging limply in the long narrow window above the bed. The furniture was phony cherry veneer over particle board. Where were the little mementos, the quirks, the bangs and bruises of daily living that gave furniture, regardless of cost, its place in a family?

The only personal touch were pictures on one wall. Daphne went to study them. Several were shots of Eric at different ages and one was of Cortlyn as a baby. But it was the family portrait that interested Daphne.

It was a standard shot from one of the photo mills. Daphne could see Eric got his coloring from his mother. Seated beside Dennis, she was tall, dark and lovely despite being slightly overweight. The weight was probably post-partum since Cortlyn was a tiny pink face buried in white blankets. But what caught Daphne's attention were the extreme contrasts in the two adults. Dennis eyes were a hard, glacial grey and his smile forced. The coldness surrounding him had been captured visibly. In contrast, the woman's eyes were swollen with a hint of redness as though she had been weeping just prior to the picture. Her smile was tremulous, almost non-existent. There was lostness within the woman Daphne could sense even from the picture.

The pervading sadness of the room combined with the feelings elicited by the woman's image suddenly swamped Daphne. She felt as though she were being sucked towards a dark, cold, empty place.

She ran from the pain in the room.

She observed Dennis as she passed behind the couch. He was dozing again. There was a sensual softness in his mouth; a boyish vulnerability in his face. Gazing at him, she felt something akin to a flutter in the vicinity of her heart. But what of his heart? Was it cold enough, hard enough, dark enough to create a hole in which a woman could fall and be lost forever?

Watching, a sigh rose unbidden from her most hidden parts. Looking up, she could see the dual reflections of herself and the sleeping man in the night-blackened picture window. "Of what matter is his heart, past, present or future, to you, DelaVeque? Of what matter is anyone's heart to you?"

She turned toward the kitchen without another glance.

Daphne and the children fixed dinner. Then she sluiced them through the tub. When freshly scrubbed and outfitted in pajamas, they set about baking up a batch of chocolate chip cookies. She popped a chocolate chip into Cortlyn's mouth while Eric snitched a bit of dough.

For Daphne it was like having a role in one of the TV shows she had watched so avidly growing up. The ones she had pulled bits and pieces out of to concoct a dream place she was going to go live with her mother. Her mother had helped build it, too, telling endless stories on nights when she had no one or no place more impressive to go than their latest room.

Someday, they were going to live in a little house with real rooms like a sunny kitchen and a pretty pink bedroom. Someday, they were going to have trees to climb, a yard full of flowers, and maybe a pony. Someday they would quit moving from motel to motel and then Daphne would have friends, birthday parties, and a Christmas tree.

Her mother had kept up the stories long after Daphne's hopes had ossified into painful pebbles to stumble over now and again in her mind.

Someday never came.

The warm aroma of cookies woke Dennis. He carefully sat up. The room was neat as a pin. The marvelous odor was mixed with the delighted giggles of his children. He guessed Mrs. Mac was back in command of the family unit.

Gingerly, he got to his feet and moved quietly to the entryway. It wasn't the burr of Mrs. Mac at all. It was the throaty voice of Daphne telling a fantastical story about a little bear who was trying to steal cookies. The children were so involved they never noticed him.

It was only on his return trip from the bathroom that he came face to face with the trio making their way to the bedroom.

"Hi, Daddy," Eric said cheerfully. Cortlyn leaned out of Daphne's arms all puckered up with a kiss.

Dennis lowered his head. "Goodnight, angels. Have you had fun?"

"Yeah, Daffy's super."

"Daffy?"

"As in loony tunes," Daphne said as she finished herding them into the bedroom. She tucked Cortlyn in and then Eric. She kissed them and turned on the nightlight. She lingered a minute, gently stroking Cortlyn's hair and then carefully pulling up the blanket and tucking it around Eric.

Dennis had remained and watched the tenderness emanating from her face. When she turned and caught him watching, she looked guilty as though he had witnessed something shameful.

He smiled in his slow way that lifted one side of his mouth first. "Got a cookie for a hungry bear?" he asked.

"I could probably give him a roast beef sandwich first."

Dennis followed her little figure back to the kitchen and sitting gingerly in a chair, he watched her pull out bread, lettuce, tomato, a package of roast beef from the deli, mayo and mustard.

"Where did all that come from?" he asked.

"There are these marvelous places called grocery stores, Cobb," she answered. "You ought to visit them. You'd be amazed at what you can find."

He looked down at his folded hands. "I haven't quite pulled everything together yet," he said quietly.

Daphne sat the plate in front of him. "I'm sorry. I wasn't being critical. You're doing a fine job. They're great kids." Her voice had a soft misty sound to it and he looked up to see her gazing toward the bedroom with something between pain and longing.

The back door opened and Mrs. Mac bustled in. "Ach, laddie. You're up and looking better." Daphne immediately grabbed her jacket off the back of a chair. Her moment in the show was over.

Mrs. Mac looked at her in surprise. "Daphne? Whatever are you doing here, lass?"

"Heading home, Mrs. Mac. I am returning custody of the Cobb family to their rightful keeper, although, I did enjoy the loan. Catch you around, Cobb," she said as she headed towards the living room.

Dennis noticed her face was once again set in its cool, non-expressiveness. He listened to the sounds of her departure. There was nothing but silence by the time Mrs. Mac returned from checking the children.

"So how do you know DelaVeque?" Dennis asked while Mrs. Mac put two cups of water in the microwave and reached for the instant coffee.

"I be knowing her grandmother, God rest her sainted soul, and her cousin Kat. Kat and Elmore finished raising the poor wee thing."

"What happened to her real parents?" Dennis asked through chocolate chips.

"Oh, I don't think the family ever knew who or what her father was. Her momma claimed he was some foreign correspondent she had married, got himself killed overseas. Shows up one day here in Kelton with this wee babe and story. Hands the little thing over to Rosalind Wyckham, that be Daphne's maternal grandmother, and waltzes out. See Althea was a journalist herself, wrote under her maiden name of Wyckham. Always chasing all over the country. Bylined some big stories in her time, even got herself nominated for a Pulitzer."

"So Daphne grew up here in Kelton? I don't remember her from school."

"You be rememberin' right. She weren't more than three when her momma swoops in and takes off with her. Liked to kill Rosalind it did, knowing what kind of life the babe would have."

Mrs. Mac sat the coffee in front of Dennis and took a seat opposite him. "Did it turn out to be as bad her grandmother feared?"

Mrs. Mac nodded grimly. "Aye, laddie. Rosalind be knowing." She took a sip of her coffee. "T'was a pathetic little bag of bones Kat and Elmore found lying at her mother's grave in the cemetery. Near death herself with pneumonia."

"They found her in the cemetery? Didn't they know where she was when he mother died?"

"Not with the likes of Althea's haphazard ways. Daphne dinna even know she had family until she be waking up in bed at the old house. Hitchhiked here from Sacramento looking for her mum, carrying everything she owned in a duffle bag. It took them near a whole year before she would unpack that bag for good."

"How old was she?"

"She was fifteen going on fifty. A week after they be finding her, Kat comes home and Daphne was gone. Scared her to death, them still not knowing about the child and all. T'was a couple of hours later, the lass staggers in, so weak she could hardly stand. Seems she had gone and found herself a job, her still coughing till it like to tear her in two. She was worrying about the rent she was owing Kat and Elmore. Kat and Elmore had a time trying to make her understand she didn't have to pay to live with them. They wanted her to just rest, get well, start school, and enjoy being a kid. She had no idea what they were about. She thought they were thinking she hadn't done the best she could to take care of her mother and help out with the money and all."

Dennis shook his head, "At fifteen, it was all my parents could do to get me to take the garbage out. I never even wondered where the money came from."

"And that's the way it should be, but best Kat and Elmore could figure out, Daphne was taking care of herself by the time she was seven or eight. She was lying about her age and working every place they went by the time she was twelve. It was a matter of survival. Althea would get herself so wrapped in a story or a man, she would forget the child. She would be gone sometimes three and four days from wherever they were camping out."

"The little thing even signed herself into school. Lord, what a nightmare for Kat and Elmore when they registered her at Kelton High and had to start tracking her records. They had records from twenty six schools by the time they went back to the third grade. Even the school district was willing to give up by then."

Mrs. Mac paused to drink her coffee while Dennis contemplated his grimly. "She had a pretty rough way to go," he said softly.

Mrs. Mac nodded. "That first Christmas about broke Kat's heart. She cried and cried for the lass. Here she was nearing sixteen and had never decorated a Christmas tree. When they finished, Daphne would sit for hours and stare at that tree as though it was the most magical thing on this earth. When they asked her to make a list of what she might want for Christmas, she couldna understand putting down more than one thing. That's all Althea had let her chose. Know what she was asking for? A book of fairy tales from the used book store. Then she worried it was asking too much, it being about two dollars."

"Kat told me about the child's Christmas before coming to Kelton. Althea gone off to a ski trip with some man and leaving Daphne alone. Her mother had even forgotten a present. The lass stayed by herself and ate out of the vending machines. She celebrated by walking around town looking at the lights till the wee hours of the morning."

Dennis shook his head as he looked down the hall to where the children were sleeping. "How can people not appreciate the miracle they have in a child."

"Well, you'll not be hearing Daphne crying about it. She wonna be anyone's victim," Mrs. Mac said as she put her cup in the sink. "And Althea being paying for it in her way. Now Denny me lad, you need to be laying back down and get some rest. I'll see to you in the morning."

* * *

Daphne let herself in the old manse. The living room was murky with only the wall sconces above the fireplace gilding the shadows in the room. To her left, the double pocket doors were closed to the old parlor that served as Elmore's office/study when he was alighting between travels to primitive societies. Down the hall, Daphne could see light under the swinging door to the kitchen. She did not have to enter it to be able to picture Kat sitting at the table, a heavy earthenware tea pot at her elbow, going through sheets of data spit out by the computer, extrapolating information and clues for Elmore to chase in his travels.

She bore to the right and climbed the graceful stairs. In the upper hall, she could see the light was on in Anne's room. Just as she was about to go and check on her aunt, she heard Edmund's voice drifting out. The strip of light extinguished and he opened the door simultaneously with her opening her bedroom door. He did not see her stepping just inside her room as he closed his mother's door. He stood for a moment, his forehead resting against the old wood. Daphne's heart spasmed for him. Death was not always the worst ending.

Daphne slipped out of her clothes and into an oversized shirt striped in neon pink, yellow, green and purple. She ran a brush through her hair before beginning her nightly ritual of checking on her wards in what she called the queendom of misfits. Dolls, stuffed animals, china and porcelain figurines, even dough and papier-mâché representations sat on shelves, chairs, old chests and the floor. Each and every one was damaged.

She touched the harlequin marionette that was missing an arm. A porcelain headed doll sat in a wheelless buggy, her empty eye sockets carefully protected by a child's pair of sunglasses. A china dog who had lost its upraised paw leaned cozily against a cat without ears. The armless teddy bear was hugged by the legless doll.

Daphne could not pass up anything being disposed of because of damage. She loathed the idea the world could only belong to the whole and beautiful. She did not repair the damage for the same reason. They were as they were and she would give them her love because they were damaged.

Her last stop was before the one object in the room which was perfect in its appearance. A large doll house sat in a place of honor on the window seat. Kat and Elmore had made it for her the first Christmas she had been with them. Here, finally, was the sunny kitchen with tiny, ruffled curtains in the window. A miniature hutch held wooden bowls and pottery dishes to set the little farm table. Minuscule herbs and flowers bloomed in the window. The pink bedroom had a canopy bed with lacy coverlet. The living room was cozy with overstuffed furniture, a big fireplace and bookcases full of books. Elmore had even placed it on an artificial turf covered board to simulate a yard. Shrubs and flowers neatly edged the house while the little tree held a tire swing, and a pony waited patiently inside a split rail corral.

But, even this lovely little house was flawed, she thought as she straightened a pillow, smoothed the coverlet and stroked the wooden pony's real horse hair mane. It was empty; devoid of the laughter, tears, love and pain which made a house a home. It was waiting for the family that never came. Waiting to be filled up with life. Waiting...just like her.

She knelt down on the floor in front of the house. For some reason tonight, old emotions and long deceased dreams were stirring within her. They rattled their skeletal bones in the closets of her heart.

She stared at the house while trying to block the noise emanating from within. Then she saw movement.

A blonde woman with hair piled on her head was setting the table while pans simmered on the stove. A toddler with light brown curls was busy arranging magnetic letters on the front of the refrigerator. A boy with silky dark hair was swinging in the tire swing, trying to touch the first evening star. And a man was coming through the door. A man with a slow smile pulling up one side of his mouth first.

Daphne jerked herself to her feet and snapped the threads of reverie.

"You know, DelaVeque, you have got to get a life," she scolded herself as she crossed her arms fiercely over her chest.

And there was the problem. That was the life she wanted. Hot tears gathered just under the surface. She quelled them with icy splashes of water in the bathroom. Then making her way back to her room, she clicked off the light and slid into the empty bed. Pummeling a pillow into shape, she struggled to fix her mind on the actuality of her days.

"I have to get gas in the morning. And it's my turn to take out the garbage. And I need stamps. And...."

"Shush, baby, shush." She felt the weight of Althea on the side of the bed and a cool touch on her forehead as the words glided into her mind. "Don't fight so hard. It's okay to dream."

"No it's not, Momma. Dreams only grow till they tear you in two and then they die, leaving behind nothing but their rotten, stinking corpses."

"The death of some dreams is a way of having fertilizer to grow better dreams, sweetheart."

"I can't dream anymore. I have nothing left to hope with."

"We'll see." Then an old lullaby began to croon softly in her head rocking her gently into sleep.

Chapter Eleven

Edmund strolled through the dark chill toward the five story building housing his office. Built in the 1950's, it appeared now as then, a graceless, charmless, cement block of a structure housing a variety of professional offices. Even at this late hour, lights shone and the parking lot across the delivery alley still had a scattering of cars.

In the stillness of the street, he heard the light click of a woman's heels. Edmund saw the CPA whose office was down the hall from his own step out of the shadows of the building and begin to cross the alley purposefully, her long legs beating out an efficient little tattoo.

* * *

She was at the parking lot when she realized other feet had fallen in behind her and were quickly gaining on her. She hurried to get to the sole pool of light in the center of the lot. Once there she stopped and whirled around hoping to see another weary worker trudging to their car. Not tonight.

They approached with their limbs moving loosely and confidently inside their black leather jackets…mutated sons of Hell's Angels.

Keeping her eyes on them, she began to step backward carefully.

The taller was obviously the leader. He eyed her up and down and licked his lips in an obscene manner. The other kept his small, piggy eyes on the leader and mimicked his actions.

"Will you look at what we got here, Jaimie. Now, baby, didn't your mother tell you about being out alone after dark. Course, could be you're one of them liberated women. How about it? You liberated?" He shoved himself up against her offensively.

The woman had been adjusting her keys so they were protruding through her fingers. She used them now, raking across his face and eyes. He spun away with a yelp of pain and immediately swung back, his hand catching her hard across the side of the head.

She stumbled, desperate to keep her balance. She almost succeeded when her high heel caught against the speed bump. With a cry she fell, striking her head on, of all things, her dropped briefcase. The world faded away in a rush of darkness.

The two punks dropped down beside the woman. One began to rummage through her handbag. The aggressive one looked at the slender leg revealed by the hiked skirt. He began licking his lips with sexually aroused savagery. His hand reached out and began to slide up the leg, pushing the skirt ahead of it.

"Well, how refreshing. Good Samaritans still abound in this day and age."

The deep voiced British accent caused the two attackers to freeze. The slower of the two dropped the purse and began to slowly slide backwards as though to make an escape.

The leader quickly sized up the man leaning so casually against a car, arms nonchalantly crossed over his chest.

He rocked back on his heels, slipping his hand into his pocket where it closed around the cool reassurance of a pistol grip. Slowly he straightened to a standing position, assuming his loose jointed stance while he challenged the man with his eyes.

With deliberate casualness, he pulled a pack of cigarettes out of his other pocket. Shaking one up, he dragged it out with his lips, letting it dangle as he dug around in the same pocket for his lighter.

In a movement so smooth and quick, he didn't see it coming, a lighter flared in his face, startling him into stepping back.

"Please allow me," the man said as he held the fire to the end of the cigarette. To cover the moment of fear that had passed through him, the punk drew deeply on the cigarette and then blew a stream of smoke out into the man's face.

"Thanks, queenie," he said as he simultaneously flipped the cigarette into the man's face and pulled the gun, holding it under the man's aristocratic nose. With a motion of his hand, he signaled his partner to move around behind the man.

The man under the gun neither began to snivel nor to try to make a run for it. Instead, unnervingly, he threw his head back and laughed. It was a macabre sound bouncing around in the circle of the street light.

The laughter stopped abruptly and the man was staring deep in the punk's eyes. "I have always preferred the taste of wild game," he said. Slowly he smiled, drawing his lips back and revealing what looked like a pair of fangs.

Lunging, Edmund sent the gun skittering into the night with a swipe of his hand. He grabbed the man, dragging the head back until the throat gleamed against the black leather.

It was difficult to tell if the scream was torn out of a human or an animal throat.

A moan as soft as the air ruffling her hair slipped from between the woman's lips. She tried to open her eyes but they seemed curiously weighted and uncooperative.

She was aware of gentle fingers probing about her face and slipping lightly down her neck. She must have had an accident although she couldn't quite remember it. Somewhere someone was moaning as though in great pain.

Where was she?

Fear forced words out to catch the exploring fingers. "I'm not dead?"

"No, indeed you're not. Though a bit shaken, I suspect." The voice glided through her darkness tender as a caress.

By concentrating only on one function, she finally managed to get her eyes open. A beautiful masculine face drifted above her.

The light glinted in the soft waves of his hair. It illuminated the brow and high cheek bones and the faintly smiling lips. "Hush, now. The police will be here any moment."

As the fog faded from her mind, she realized this was the man whom she passed occasionally in the hall. "You're....you're 313."

Sirens could be heard faintly in the distance now. Edmund's voice took on a soft, hypnotic cadence. "Hush, hush, now. You are quite safe. Just rest till they arrive."

She felt herself drifting away to a place that was soft and warm despite the swelling sound of sirens.

* * *

"Vampire? What the hell do you mean vampire? It ain't friggin' Halloween yet." The police chief stood in the doorway of his glassed-in office shaking a fistful of papers under the noses of two patrolmen as Dennis pushed his way gingerly into the squad room. "You guys go back and rewrite this thing, and I don't want any vampires in it, you understand?" He shoved the papers back at them. As he swung around to his office, he caught sight of

Dennis working his way slowly to his desk. "Cobb? I thought you were taking a couple of days medical."

"Truth is, chief, with my two kids, I'll heal quicker on the job."

"Well, whatever. As long as you're here, help these two try to write a decent report, and, remember," he shook a warning finger in their direction. "No vampires."

Dennis carefully sat and edged his chair up to the desk. The two patrol officers handed their report over to him.

"We know it sounds crazy but this is just the way it went down. I mean, the guys must have been whacked on something. But, damn it, this is the way it went down."

Dennis quickly scanned through the incident report. It described the response to a call of a woman being attacked in the parking lot over in the old Glenover side of town, an area comprised mostly of furniture stores and scattered older professional buildings.

Upon arrival the two officers found the woman lying in the parking lot, stunned by a blow to the head though not seriously injured. Nearby they had found her two assailants, writhing, moaning, and fighting something invisible. When the police officers appeared, they had crawled to them and begged for assistance; protection from the vampire who attacked them.

Dennis looked up from the report. "Any marks on them?"

"No, sir. Not a one that we could see. We even put them in front of a mirror but that just made them worse. They kept grabbing at their throats and trying to make us see the 'fang' marks."

The other officer picked up the story. "The only way we got them to settle down was to find a couple of crosses for them to hold. When we left them at the jail, they were clutching them as though their very lives depended on it."

"What about the woman? She see anything?"

Both men shook their head. "No. Apparently one of the punks smacked her pretty hard and she hit her head when she went down. The only thing she vaguely remembered, after being hit, was 313 somehow came to her assistance. At least she thinks so. She said she might have dreamed it, too."

Dennis raised his shoulders in puzzlement. "What's 313?"

"That's a man who has offices on the same floor as hers. She has a CPA practice on the third floor of the old Hansen Building."

"So what does he have to say?"

"Well, actually, we never got to talk to him. When we got in the building to check, there was no name, business or otherwise listed beside 313 on the directory. When we went to the office, there was nothing on the door except some kind a symbol and no one was there."

Dennis picked up the phone and punched in the number to the jail. "Wayne? Tell me what's going on with the two Benton and Hardeman brought in last night. They crash yet?"

The two patrolmen watched the phone intently, trying to make out the deep buzz of the jailer's voice rattling into Dennis' ear. When he cradled the phone, Dennis continued to stare at it for one long moment before looking up.

"Wayne says they are still clutching their crosses and jumping like two scalded cats at every shadow and sound. They haven't budged from their story and Wayne is willing to bet a week's salary neither one of them is loaded on anything now."

"So how do we get rid of the vampire for the chief?"

Dennis glanced at his watch. It was pushing nine o'clock. "You two go on home and get to bed. I'll do some checking around. When I find a logical explanation, we'll put it in the report."

"And if you don't, Cobb?"

Dennis grinned. "Better buy him some garlic, boys."

As soon as the two patrolmen vacated, still muttering to each other, Dennis buzzed the dispatcher. "Vern, give me the name and phone number of that psychologist again, please."

Dennis scribbled the information on his desk blotter and then punching up an outside line, keyed the number in.

The voice answering was young and breathy. "Dr. Ashe's office."

Dennis identified himself and waited for the doctor to come on the line.

The next voice was a deeper, cooler voice. "This is Dr. Ashe."

"Dr. Ashe, this it Detective Cobb, KPD. How familiar are you with vampires?"

"Are you asking personally or professionally, Detective?"

"I'm not really sure, Dr. Ashe."

"Personally, I've had the usual brushes with Anne Rice and Bela Lugosi. Professionally, I had case studies of people who believed they were vampires."

"What about people who are convinced they have been attacked by a vampire?"

"Sounds like a hysteria-induced case. Too many movies or books, I suppose."

"I don't know about the movies, but I would bet these two haven't read a book between them since the third grade. They aren't your usual candidates for self-induced hysteria. They happen to be a couple members of one of the street's rougher gangs. A gang we suspect to be behind some drug related slayings."

"Last night, they attacked a woman in a parking lot. This morning they are claiming they, in turn, were attacked by a vampire. They practically begged to be arrested and last I knew were huddled on their jail bunks clutching crosses. Would it be possible for you to go by the jail and see them? I don't need anything in depth, just a handle on what may have set them off?"

Lygia was instantly reminded of the baby killer's story of his battle with a demon. "Fascinating. If you will clear the red tape, I'll head over now and phone you a report this afternoon."

* * *

Dennis pushed his car seat all the way back, then very carefully swung his legs out and levered himself into a standing position. He took a breath of accomplishment. That wasn't too bad at all, he thought as he walked carefully to the door of the Hansen Building.

The guard nodded his head. "Yessir. 313, that would be Edmund Broadhurst. He does some kind of research. Something about crime, I think. No sir. He's not in now, hasn't been all morning. Yessir. I always go round and check all the doors when I first get here at 6 a.m. His door was locked up tight and the place was quiet as a tomb. Well, sir, Broadhurst kinda comes and goes on his own schedule. Comes in often during the evening or night. Tells the other guards he talks with people all over the world and he has to accommodate their time zones. No, sir. I have no idea where he lives or how to get in touch with him, main office keeps those records. I'll be glad to give you a call when he comes in. No, sir. I won't say nothin' to him."

The Broadhurst name was familiar but Dennis couldn't place it until he reached the car. It was his cracked ribs that reminded him as he swung unthinkingly into the car. The pain wiping out his breath cross connected with last night's nursing care and the baby killer. DelaVeque would certainly know where to find her cousin.

Chapter Twelve

Like most of her patients, the child was dwarfed by the sturdy hospital crib. Great, dark eyes filled the tiny, pinched face. A small brown hand and arm were firmly taped to a padded board, protecting the IV tubing snaking to the bag hanging at the head of the bed. One leg curved towards the other, the little foot ceaselessly rubbing and pushing against the fiberglass cast trapping her from waist to toes.

The mother rose from her chair and came to stand with Daphne. A grayness gathered from many wakeful hours dulled the golden brown skin. Traces of a softer, sibilant language colored her words.

"My baby's hurtin' so much. She ain't slept a minute since she woke up from surgery," she said as she watched the little curly head turn restlessly on the bunny sheets. "I wish I could take away her pain," she said softly. "I wish I had the 'touch'."

She looked up to Daphne. The fine eyes were blurred with fatigue. "Granny wanted to teach me but I was too smart to be wastin' my time on that fool stuff." Tears brimmed. "And now my baby's hurtin'."

Daphne patted the hand clenching the crib railing. "Well, I didn't have a granny but I have a cousin," she said. Leaving the odd comment hanging in the air, she turned her attention to the small child.

"Keesha, honey, I'm going to turn you over now." Pulling the crib out from the wall, she expertly changed the IV pole to the opposite hole and deftly turned the child on her stomach. Exhaustion reduced the child's protest to a small whimper of pain. Daphne adjusted the little girl's gown while she focused her mind as Elmore had instructed her. Then closing her eyes, she rubbed her hands together a moment. Gratifyingly, she felt the heat rise in them.

Following a prescribed pattern, she massaged the child's shoulders, neck and back. Then resting her hands over the fiberglass covering the incision, she concentrated more energy into her hands. The fiberglass grew warm and the little girl closed her eyes. She slept.

Her mother looked up, eyes rounded by surprise and welling over with gratitude. "You got the 'touch'," she whispered.

Daphne gently eased the crib back into place and covered the sleeping child with a blanket.

Turning her attention to the woman, she smiled. "She'll sleep for a while. I suggest you get something to eat and then get some rest yourself. I'll fix the chair for you to nap in when you get back."

Firmly, she guided the woman towards the door. "Come along. I'll direct you to the cafeteria."

* * *

Preparing to get out of the car again at the hospital, Dennis remembered Broadhurst's address would have been on the statement he signed in the baby killer case. So why was he levering himself out of the car once more?

Of course, Grissum had told him to come by today to get his ribs checked. And it would impolite not to thank DelaVeque for her kind assistance last night, And...

Dennis had thought of a half dozen reasons for taking the long route around to finding Broadhurst by the time he reached the front entry of the hospital. None of them included being intrigued by a petite blonde nurse.

Dr. Grissum was standing at the admissions desk signing papers, his unlit cigar working up and down in time with his pen.

At Dennis' approach, he glanced up. His mouth fell open with the cigar drooping dangerously toward the floor where it stuck to his lower lip.

"My god, the patient is returned per orders."

"That'll be a first." A voice came from behind Dennis.

He turned in time to see Daphne place a medical chart on the counter. She pulled a pen out of her hair and made a couple of cryptic scribbles before pushing the chart across the counter.

"I also came to thank Ms. DelaVeque for all her help last night."

Grissum had the cigar firmly clenched in his teeth again where it now it jutted dangerously toward the ceiling. "You were just dropping off meds. What help?" he demanded.

Daphne stuck the pen back in her hair and turned her blue eyes on him. "That is none of your damn business," she said sweetly. She turned her gaze on Dennis. "You are welcome. I enjoyed it very much."

"Enjoyed what?" Grissum demanded.

He was ignored. For a brief moment, something wavered in the air between the two.

Then Daphne turned and walked briskly away. She was acutely aware of the renewed rattling in her chest, pressing on her heart.

Dennis' eyes never left the retreating figure until she disappeared around a corner. He felt a peculiar emptiness gnawing somewhere in his middle.

Grissum's wiry eyebrows beetled together. He seized Dennis by the arm and began to steer him briskly across the hospital's foyer. "Has anyone ever told you about the birds and the bees, Cobb? Well, you're a big boy now and it's time you heard about the facts of life."

Grissum hunched over to lean one elbow on the counter while Dennis was buttoning up his shirt. "Tell me, Cobb, you developing a hard on for my nurse?"

"What?" Dennis looked up startled. "What nurse?"

Grissum came over and hoisted a hip up on the exam table beside Dennis. "DelaVeque, that's what nurse."

"We barely know each other, Doc. She was just teasing you about last night."

Grissum's tone dropped to gravelly seriousness. "I like you, Cobb. But Daphne is the closest thing to a daughter I've ever had. She's one spunky little girl who's made something of herself despite a rough, miserable life. When I first got to know her, she was working three jobs, practically around the clock, so she could go to college. Now, she's one of the best nurses this or any hospital could have. I'm real proud of her."

Dennis nodded but his expression was puzzled.

"Now, I think you're a fine man and I know that you've had some rough spots yourself. But, Daphne's more than just a good nurse. She's got some...er, some special gifts. The whole family does in one way or another. You saw an example the night we went out to find the baby."

Dennis' mind flashed back to the memory of Daphne knowing the woman had hung herself without seeing it. He nodded more slowly.

"What I'm saying is, I won't have my girl hurt. God knows, she's had enough to last two lifetimes. You know what's cooking now. Be sure you can stand the heat before you go into the kitchen. You understand?"

Dennis gave a vague nod. His mind was no longer focused on Grissum. It had caught and held on the words he had used "...she has some special gifts." She heard or saw someone choking to death when there was nothing to be seen; to be heard. A family of similar talents. The cousin who had an office in the same building as Benton and Hardeman's victim...

There was a sharp report as a metal gurney slammed through a swinging door. Dennis jumped and found himself alone in the cubicle.

Chapter Thirteen

Dennis had just dropped the baby killer's file on his desk when the intercom on his phone buzzed. Then Ron, in his quirky manner, stuck his head through the pass-through window and hollered back at Dennis. "That lady psychologist is here. Dr. Ashe." Dennis waved his hand to indicate for her to be sent on back.

A tall woman pushed through the security door. The general rumble of conversation in the squad room diminished as the officers watched her progress. She had a full, womanly figure she skillfully downplayed in an expensive, grey suit. Her dark hair was cut short and winged back from a face betraying an exotic heritage. Her large dark eyes tilted slightly above strong cheekbones and a firm chin. The generous mouth softened and balanced the distinctive face.

She seated herself, hooking her shoulder bag over the back of the chair after withdrawing a pair of glasses. She perched these on her nose and flipped open the grey suede portfolio she carried. "Absolutely fascinating, Detective. I appreciate you calling me on this."

Dennis leaned forward. "So what's the verdict? Were they high or are they nuts?"

Lygia pulled off her glasses. "The truth is I don't know. What I do know is that they truly believe they were attacked by a vampire. I spoke with each of them separately. They both gave me a similar story. Now, I am aware they could have cooked it up between themselves but one of the two defendants will probably test borderline retarded. He does not have the capacity to remember anything complicated that is not real in his mind. And this 'vampire' attack is very real to him."

"I don't know what triggered this event in their minds but it is similar to another case I worked on recently. Remember the Floyd murder case. The baby killer?"

Dennis gave a quick glance at the file folder resting under his elbow. "Of course."

Looking off into space, Lygia began to absently twirl her glasses by the earpiece. "I did the competency workup on Stallman. During the course of my examination, he told me a story about being attacked by a demon. 'A foreign demon'."

"A vampire?" Dennis asked sharply.

"No. It was something else. It was something that made Stallman think he was being dragged into hell."

"Not a bad place for him," Dennis said. "How?"

"I'm not exactly sure. He says it appeared on his doorstep and he engaged it in physical battle. He claimed it was incredibly strong. That it bested him and dragged him down to hell."

"None of that was in your report."

"No. I spoke with Mrs. Floyd about it. She was quite adamant that nothing had occurred. It seemed to be an isolated incident perhaps dreamed by an alcoholic."

"And now?"

"Now I find an interesting coincidence, but no explanation."

Dennis picked up the patrolmen's' report. "Looks like the chief is stuck with a vampire."

"Sorry, I wasn't any help in explaining this away." Lygia began to collect her things.

"Send your bill to my attention and I'll get it through ASAP."

"This one's on the house on one condition."

Dennis looked up.

"You call me if you get anymore strange attacks." She held out her hand. "Deal?"

Dennis shook it. "Deal. And thank you, Doctor."

Lygia turned to leave, then glanced back.

"Oh, by the way. Both men said their vampire spoke like 'he weren't no real American.' Interesting, huh."

Dennis rubbed the back of his hand thoughtfully along his chin. "Very interesting," he murmured.

* * *

The hall in the office building was a microcosm of working America. Doors opened and closed as people came and went. Dennis could hear ringing phones, the whir of computer printers, the squeal of fax machines. Through the louvers of mini-blinded door windows, he could see desks stacked with files, bodies hunched over key boards and people in a variety of poses talking into phones. Wood-grained plastic signs identified accountants, lawyers, investment firms.

Half-way down the hall, the monotony of the metal and glass doors was broken by an expensive wood door. Baroque styled numbers spelled out 313 and beneath it was the symbol the patrolmen had spoken of. Like them, Dennis had no idea what it was but he felt it was very old…something from another age.

When he opened the door and stepped into the office, he was stunned by the elegance filling the waiting area and the spacious office beyond. A brush of the wall showed they were covered in rich and probably genuine ivory brocade. The two small loveseats were upholstered with kid-glove leather glowing like burgundy wine. The satin sheen of the display cases reflected costly woods.

Through the open door into the office, Dennis could see Edmund talking on the phone. After listening just long enough to discover the conversation was in French, Dennis began to discreetly study the several glassed in cases. Unusual collections were carefully displayed. They ranged from bits of twisted wood and roughly carved figures to pre-Columbian stone carvings and opulent medieval crosses and amulets.

African masks, shields and spears were arranged on the walls between the expensive cases. Dennis wondered what connected these items other than their ownership by a single man.

It struck him there was a tremendous amount of money invested in this room and the office beyond…odd for a man whose home address was in an area decaying in genteel poverty.

"How may I help you, Detective Cobb?"

Dennis jumped, startled by the nearness of the man's voice, and whipped around only to be surprised further to find the man was leaning casually in the doorway between the two rooms. He had sounded much closer. Dennis glanced surreptitiously around. It must be a trick of the acoustics.

"I wanted to talk to you about an incident that occurred in the parking lot last night."

"Ah, yes. The violent assault on our attractive CPA."

Dennis focused in on the man. "You have knowledge of the incident then?"

"Only second hand, Detective. Only second hand. The building was absolutely throbbing with the news when I arrived today."

"Then you weren't on the scene last night? You didn't assist her in any manner?"

Edmund spread his hands in a helpless gesture. "Alas, no. I was denied any moment of chivalry. But do come in, I will provide whatever meager assistance I might."

Dennis surveyed the inner office. Floor to ceiling bookcases filled one wall. The partially opened door of an antique armoire revealed an elaborate computer setup. Two tall narrow bookcases flanked a glass case. In them were numerous books, all identical. The word 'Journal' was stamped in gold on the spine. Beneath were dates written in copperplate. One such book lay open in the desk. The same writing partially filled a page.

"What is it you do, Mr. Broadhurst," Dennis asked as he brought his study back to Edmund.

A half-smile played over Edmund's face. "I am student and a seeker of answers."

Dennis glanced slowly around the room again. "What exactly is it that you study, Mr. Broadhurst?"

"Evil, Detective Cobb. Evil."

Dennis' eyes narrowed and his face became a cool mask. "Would you mind telling me what a 'student of evil' does exactly?"

Edmund wandered to look out the window. "Every day, in your profession, you are in a war with evil. It is the root from which all crimes grow. We have given it many names and disguises throughout history. Hate, greed, mental illness. But still curled within whatever name we wish to attach, we find the most basic element. Evil. As constant as the sun and air we breathe, it is the base rock of man's history. And while we all recognize its effects, we have yet to reduce it to its empirical state. A state in which we can name the elements, map their configuration, and armed with that information, intervene to alter its course."

Edmund moved from the window to the small glass case standing between the two narrow bookcases. He looked deeply into it for a moment then lightly, almost reverently, brushed his long slender fingers along the edge.

Dennis examined the contents. Pillowed on glowing, golden silk were a rough hewn carving out of some wood he did not recognize, a small leather bound book open to a curious language, and a stole, richly embroidered with religious symbols on the tails. Rusty stains marked both the book and the stole.

"How do you fund your, ah, studies, Mr. Broadhurst?"

Amusement tugged at Edmund's face as he turned back toward Dennis. "I am independently wealthy. An uncle, who made a bit of a fortune in bricks, was quite generous in his will."

"I would think, under those circumstances, you would be living in New York, Los Angeles, or London, even. Kelton seems to be an odd choice for a man with your particular interests."

The careless air fell away from Edmund as he turned back to stare once more into the small display case. "Kelton is my mother's birthplace. She has not been, er, well for some time. I brought her here hoping the familiar, familial surroundings of her childhood and youth would assist in restoring her."

An almost palpable pain emanated from the man. Dennis' question came gently. "Have they?"

There was a bitter twist to Edmund's mouth for a moment. "Not as I had hoped." He looked down and seemed to pull himself back from some unseen place.

Dennis started as the phone on Edmund's desk rang. Edmund glanced at it and then at Dennis. "Is there anything else, Detective?"

'Curioser and curioser.' The old lines from *Alice in Wonderland* came unbidden into Dennis head as he closed the office door behind him. He wondered what Dr. Ashe would make of this man.

Chapter Fourteen

Lygia sat down on her couch, leaning forward to place a glass of wine on the coffee table. Every since the night she met the disturbing Mr. Broadhurst, barely perceptible ripples flowed in and around her. She felt her hard won homeostasis had been shifted slightly. A faint distortion altered the perception of her world and it made her edgy.

Roberta's gift stared at her from the coffee table. Apparently Broadhurst was also a published textbook author. A slip of paper protruded from the book, Roberta's voluble writing visible from the couch. "If they had texts like this when I was in college, I might actually have read one."

Lygia stared at it and knew she was avoiding it. She reached for her television remote. But her hand brushed the book and, then it was in her hand. Oh, well, if she didn't, at least, do a quick scan of it, Roberta would ask questions she didn't want to answer. She opened it.

It was hours later when Lygia stopped reading because her eyes would no longer focus. Roberta was right; the book was a far cry from the dust dry tomes of her college years. This one ensnared the reader, pulling them into a primeval world. She could see the fire flicker on the cave walls, its dance of light and shadows bringing animation to the paintings and carvings; smell the fear of man huddled close to the burning light; feel the night pressing against the mouth of the cave; and hear the screams of survival and death as a world yet unnamed, untamed stretched to the edge of the stars. It was dark and evocative. Like the man.

She stretched mightily. Bed was going to feel so good.

Someone was calling her name. She got up from her bed and pushed back the curtain hanging over her door. Crossing the small living room, she stood just outside her mother's 'reading room'. She could see the crystal ball sitting in its small wooden bowl on the table at the center of the room. She stepped through the beads in the door and listened. The call seemed to be coming from the table. As she drew close, she could see a form in the crystal. She cupped her hands around the ball, drawing it to her. She saw Edmund Broadhurst standing in the center. A black fog roiled behind him, slowly filling the crystal. It began to swell about him, pulling him into its black mist. His face was so empty, so bereft. As he disappeared, he held a hand out toward her, upturned, plaintive. She snatched her hands away and his hand became bleached skeletal bones before dropping into the black.

Her eyes flew open, seeking the familiar shapes of her bedroom. She rolled on her back and stared at shadows swaying in the moon's reflection on her ceiling. There was a low thrumming in her. It had the same resonance of a call too distant or poorly connected to be understood. She was aware she could clarify the reception, but it required a part of her she had immured. Under no circumstances would she disturb the seal she had set. She turned resolutely on her side.

Across town, in an attic room, another set of eyes watched and listened. He, too, had been called forth by her dream. He felt now her repulsion at the cry emanating from the dream. The strength of her will deflected it back into the void of night.

Wearily, he reached out and turned on the light in his monastically stark room. He pushed back the rough woven bedding and reached for a vicuna robe. It was not a luxury, but a necessity in the unheated space Edmund had chosen to occupy in the old house.

He went to sit on the worn settee, stretching his legs over the denuded velvet. Bracing his elbow on the back, he let his fingers support his head. There was only a little left now. The old monk had spoken the truth all those years ago.

Edmund closed his eyes and once again he was lying on the pallet in the monk's cell. He was fever gaunt, his body burned up in the fire of his illness. The old monk had propped him against his arm as he forced him to swallow the bitter broth of herbs. As he had sponged the soaking sweat from Edmund's body, he had spoken with the deep, quiet of a mystic who walks upon the eternal.

"My son, your resources will not go on forever. You are feeding on yourself to sustain your quest, your work. And the work you do requires you must pay with great pieces of yourself if you are to remain out of the grasp of the dark places. The scales lean heavily on the life side now. But the day will come when they will fall the other way. On that day, the darkness cannot be satisfied and it will claim you. To survive, you will need an infusion of life from one who overflows with it. When it is offered, drink deeply for it is in the receiving you will give the blessing."

"Who has this life? How do I find them?"

"You cannot find. You must be found."

"Will I know?"

"Yes. But the gift must given willingly. You may ask but not take. You may watch but not influence. It will be a time when you must wait upon the judgment of the heavens."

"And if the choice is to withhold?"

"Then you shall surrender to abyss. To fight will increase your pain many fold."

Some weeks later, the old monk had come again to him as he sat in the monastery's garden listening to Compline in the gathering dusk. He had foretold the meeting with Kat and Elmore and their leading him to the place of his waiting for the life giver. He had followed the holy man's instructions explicitly.

He had waited through the years, continuing to spend himself in the work to which he had been called. Now, he had been rewarded with the knowledge he had seen, touched, knew who carried his life. But Dr. Lygia Ashe was not a likely giver.

He lifted his head and stared across the dark end of his room. It was there, yawning before him. The abyss.

In the cool night, his life source slept.

Chapter Fifteen

Daphne was transferring vitals from her notes onto charts when the elevator door slid open. Three Candy Stripers emerged, heads together, as they hurried past her. She heard only a fragment of their conversation. "...I got the coolest costume...." Halloween flowed and bubbled around her like a cauldron coming to full boil.

She rammed the chart home in its slot with more force than was necessary. Holidays were the worst, always the worst.

Susanne entered the nurse's station and collapsed on a stool as she dug a couple of folded over hospital menus used as notepads out of her pocket. "Lord, I can't believe it is Friday afternoon already. I am never going to get it all done. I still have half a Power Ranger costume to sew. A lion's mane to put together and six dozen cookies to bake up for the PTA Fall Festival tomorrow afternoon. The Sunday school is having a hayride after church on Sunday to pick out pumpkins. Monday, I need a dozen cupcakes for the Brownie Halloween party. Tuesday, I am in charge of goodie bags for Ricky's school Halloween party and then it's trick or treating. I tell you, Daphne, I am not going to make it."

Daphne was silent as she drove the last chart home, stuffed her notes into her pocket, and flipped her teal blue stethoscope around her neck. When she finally looked at Susanne, her words came soft as a prayer. "You have no idea how very lucky you are." Susanne was about to give a smart reply but Daphne had already hurried away from the station and was fiercely stabbing the elevator button.

Arriving in the basement, she gave a vicious shove to the slow opening elevator door, stamped across the hall, yanked her name tag off and slapped it through the time clock.

The series of brief, explosive actions punched a hole in her frustrated anger and she sagged against the wall, burying her face in her hands as she fought to equalize her emotional state.

"DelaVeque, you sick? Genuine concern was buried in the brusque, gravelly tones.

Daphne lifted her head but did not turn to look at her interrogator. "Nope. Just a bad case of the blue means."

"Blue means....blue meanies. That would be a great costume for you to wear for x-raying the candy this year. I could come as the yellow submarine."

The blaze in her eyes caused even the formidable Dr. Grissum to take a step back. "I don't want to x-ray candy for other people's children this year. I don't want to work a second shift so someone else can hold wonderful, sticky little hands while they trick or treat. I don't want to hear about another costume or party or....." The flash fire of anger burned out and washed away in a flood of tears. She went into Grissum's arms, her fists pounding out her pain on his chest as the tears threatened to choke her. Wrapping his arms protectively around her, he whispered comfort into curls atop her head. "Go ahead baby. Get it out. It's okay. I'm here for you. I'll always be here for you."

In a few moments, Daphne's strong will gathered up her shredded emotions and she pulled back. Searching her pockets, she found a crumpled tissue and blew her nose loudly. As she wiped her eyes, she saw smears of mascara and make-up on the front of Dr. Grissum's white lab coat. "Oh-oh," she said. Pulling a well-chewed cigar out of his pocket, he stuck it in his mouth at a jaunty angle. "Now that'll give 'em something to talk about for the rest of year."

Gripping her elbow, he began to steer her in the direction of the doctor's lounge. "Now, young lady, I prescribe a cup of coffee and a heart-to-heart."

"And when did you acquire a heart," Daphne asked, her voice still tear smeared.

Behind the door marked 'Physicians Only' was standard issue. Pale green tile walls, tan asphalt flooring, vinyl couches in aqua and beige colored the room institutional. A couple of cots were pushed up against the walls. Pillows, sheets and hospital blankets neatly folded on them. Styrofoam cups with various amounts of unfinished coffee were scattered among a spray of tattered *Golfer's Digest, Field & Stream* and the occasional medical journal.

Grissum gave Daphne a shove towards one of the couches. After securing two cups of coffee, he paused to rummage through several white coats hanging in the minuscule closet. Triumphant he delivered not only the coffee, but a pack of cigarettes to Daphne.

When smoke was wafting towards the ceiling vent, he turned a clinical eye on Daphne.

"So you're finally getting tired of being Kelton's Mother Teresa, heh? Wanna a piece of the action now? Wanna get right down there in the gutter and wallow around with those dirty diapers, and, what did you say? Sticky little hands?"

Daphne hung her head as though ashamed of her very feminine longings.

Grissum shot another cloud of smoke toward the ceiling. "I suppose we better find you a man. Useful device for making babies. Not entirely necessary, of course, but still the accepted norm. So whom should it be?"

"Yeah, right. How about a Ghostbuster?" Daphne twitched off the couch and stalked to the back wall to stare at the bulletin board buried under in-service schedules and notes scribbled on prescription pads.

Grissum studied the person he loved as though she were the spawn of his loins. "You know, you're not a bad looking specimen as females go. I suspect that you could get most anyone you decided would be appropriate material."

"Just a couple of problems, Doc." She held up two fingers as she turned back. "One, there is a great white shark cruising in my wake who has left the impression around most all this place that to approach Nurse DelaVeque is certainly hazardous to your career, let alone your life span."

Grissum's wiry, grey brows knitted together defensively. "I'm just heading off the small fry and bottom feeders," he muttered.

"And every other species known to woman," she countered.

"Yeah, okay. Reason number two?"

"The familial affliction carried on with great vigor even by the modern generation. How do you explain to a man about people who hear things no one else can hear? See things that aren't visible? Can carry on conversations with people who have been dead for seventeen years, for god's sake."

"It isn't as though your family is born with two heads or transform into fanged creatures during the full moon. You have unique talents, that's all."

Daphne shot him a bitter glance.

Their conversation was interrupted by the entrance of two of the hospital's young interns. Seeing Daphne, one of them huffed up. "Excuse me, this is the doctor's lounge," he said pompously. His companion's elbow jabbed him sharply in the ribs. He caught sight of Dr. Grissum. Gulping, he turned a whiter shade of pale. "Oh, boy," he whispered.

Grissum pulled himself up from the couch. Clasping his hands behind his back, he stopped inches from the intern's face. "You know the last wannabe doctor that interrupted one of my assignations found a fine future as a cook on a shrimp boat in Alaska."

"I'm sorry, sir. I didn't mean...I shouldn't have....I...."

Daphne took pity. She headed towards the door, calling back over her shoulder. "Yo, Jaws. Time to blow this dump anyhow."

At the elevator, Daphne punched a button and then drooped against the wall. She forced a smile for Grissum even as tears once again gathered in the corners of her eyes. "Well, I guess, I better go back up and sign up for the second shift. Yellow Submarine, huh?"

Grissum looked at the stubbed out cigar before ditching it in the wastebasket and pulling a new one out of his pocket.

"The only thing you're going to sign right now is the check for dinner. Come on, you're buying," Grissum said as he shoved her through the still opening elevator doors.

The blue neon of the beer sign behind the bar provided most of the light by which Daphne and Grissum glanced at the menus. Grissum reached in his pocket and pulled out a tiny examination flashlight and shone it on his. "As much money as Gus rakes in here, you would think he could afford to pay the electric bill."

The waitress standing with pencil poised over her little notebook stifled a giggle.

Daphne tossed hers aside. "Since the menu hasn't changed from the time Gus bought the place in nineteen ought six, it should be etched on your genes by now. I'll have the steak sandwich with fries and he'll have the broiled chicken salad with whatever fat free dressing you have. And two coffees."

Grissum threw his menu down petulantly. "Listen, young lady, I have been managing to order my own meals since...."

"My mother was in diapers, I know, but I saw your last cholesterol count."

"It wasn't since your mother was in diapers and what the hell are you doing snooping in personal records."

"Extending the life of your wizened, old heart despite the rumor Grissum is the one human born without any vestige of the organ."

"At least they acknowledge I am human."

"There is some serious debate on that and, I understand there is an extensive list of volunteers waiting to perform an autopsy on you.... death is not a requirement."

The waitress set their food in front of them and Grissum immediately reached across the table to skewer a french fry. "What, no catsup," he said as he chewed happily on the grease laden potato.

Daphne took a small bite of her sandwich. The food tasted as flat as her life.

Grissum was poking among the greens piled in the plate before him. "The only way this could be called a chicken salad was because Gus walked the chicken by it. On a short leash." He glanced up at Daphne's lack of response. In a brief instance of her unawareness, he saw the deep pit of loneliness she was hiding in her heart.

"You know, DelaVeque. Hospitals aren't the only places open on the holidays. Instead of working a second shift at the hospital, you might volunteer to take somebody's kids trick or treating."

"Yeah? Whose?"

"Oh, I dunno. There are lots of people that have to work on Halloween. Waitresses, bus drivers, cops." He caught the brief flash in her eyes.

The nonchalance with which she turned her attention back to her food fooled Grissum not a moment.

"Speaking of cops. What's the story behind Cobb? I keep picking up the strangest vibes around him."

"Want to explain?"

"I keep hearing, er, feeling a wet sort of sadness. Like there are tears being cried for or about him." She mentally walked into his bedroom once again. "When I helped out the other night, I saw a family picture. They didn't look like a happy family. Eric mentioned his mother went away yet all her clothes were still in the bedroom. And Cobb keeps the room all closed up, unused. It was a bit weird."

Grissum took his time pulling out a cigar, flagging the waitress for more coffee and then settling back.

"Cobb's wife died in that room better 'n a year ago. It was never decided if it was deliberate or accidental."

Daphne's eyes opened wide. "You mean nobody knows how she died? Or why?"

"I didn't say that. She died of an overdose of CNS depressants combined with alcohol. It just wasn't determined if she meant to go all the way or if she just used bad judgment this time."

"This time? You mean she had tried suicide before?"

Grissum nodded gravely as he tapped the ash off his cigar.

"Well, did she leave a note, a letter, something to show her intent?"

Grissum studied the end of his cigar before putting it back in his mouth. "She left a letter, lots of letters as a matter of fact."

"So what did they say?"

Grissum shrugged. "The usual, I guess. How much she loved him, needed him, missed him, yada, yada."

"I'm confused. Were they separated, getting a divorce? Did he have someone else on the side?"

"Nope, nope and nope. The letters were all to a dead man."

Daphne drew a deep breath and placed her hands flat on the table as though to stabilize herself. "Okay, let's take this from the top one more time. And please do your best to remain coherent and cognitive. Now, what is the story behind Cobb?"

"I guess it starts a long time ago. Dennis has pretty much always been like he is now, kinda on the quiet and sober side. Just one of those real steady people, keeps his head and his own counsel. Oddly, his best friend was Frank O'Conner, a real wild man. Totally opposite."

"Frank was always a pistol, literally as well as figuratively. Raised on stories about his grandfather, a Chicago police officer who once worked with Elliott Ness on a case, and being the nephew of Kelton's then police chief, Frank had no doubt in his mind he was going to be a police officer."

"After graduation, Dennis headed over to Emerson U. Frank applied for the police academy, sponsored by his uncle. He surprised everyone by graduating first in his class. At the ceremonies, he and Dennis took turns polishing his shiny new badge with their shirt sleeves." Grissum was looking in the mirror of memory, and a sad, nostalgic smile played around his cigar.

"Sometime after Frank was on the force, he started dating Melanie Garber. Melanie was one very pretty young woman who looked like your perfect little parochial girl. You know, all sweetness and Peter Pan collar on the outside. But underneath that prim little school uniform was a real hell cat. She and Frank fought, broke up, made up daily."

"They got engaged as soon as she graduated from St. Mary's. Dennis, of course, was all set to be the best man."

"At Thanksgiving that year, Melanie was out of town with her family. An ice storm moved through the area and with the holiday, it was a regular three-ring circus here. Frank was at Dennis' house when they called him to help out. Frank was killed a couple of hours later."

"He was thrown to the pavement and struck his head, breaking his neck and crushing his skull pulling a child out of the path of a sliding car." Grissum paused. "I'm the one who pronounced him dead," he said quietly.

"Dennis was a pall bearer at the funeral. Frank's badge was pinned to a navy blue ribbon stretched across the wreath. At the end of the grave side services, Mr. and Mrs. O'Conner gave it to Dennis."

"Dennis went home and sat in his room alone for hours with that badge. The next morning, he left without saying a word to anyone. He had correctly surmised Frank's uncle would be at the station. A man who ate, breathed and slept his job was sure to turn to it for comfort."

"Dennis marched to the desk, the chief told me later, drawing up all 6'1" of himself. 'Sir, I would like to ask a favor. Yesterday Mr. and Mrs. O'Conner gave me Frank's badge.' He pulled the badge from his pocket and held it out. 'It's a great honor but I am not worthy of it yet. Would you please keep it for me and give it back to me on the day when I have qualified to wear it?'

"Six months later, he made good his word. The entire O'Conner family together with the Cobb family stood as Chief O'Conner pinned Frank's badge to Dennis' uniform."

"Now, Melanie had taken Frank's death hard and time only seemed to worsen the situation. She wouldn't eat or sleep. She spent all her time in her room writing letters to Frank. It finally reached the point, while Dennis was at the academy, Melanie attempted suicide. 'To be with the man I love,' she said in the letter she left for her parents. It was pretty clear that Melanie needed some serious help. Donaldson signed the papers for her parents to get her committed."

"Dennis was on the force when she was released. Although functioning better, Melanie was still very fragile. The Garbers were very particular whom she was exposed to, but they couldn't keep her sheltered entirely either. Dennis seemed like a good choice to see Melanie now and again, maybe help ease her back into the world a little bit. And Dennis was a good choice. He seemed to know just how far Melanie could go before she got wobbly. Just his naturally calm and steady nature seemed to help keep Melanie on firm ground."

"It might have gone on for a while like that. Just a couple of people with a shared past who would have eventually drifted on to other things if Dennis hadn't become a hero."

"Hero? When? Where?"

"Yep. Genuine, bona fide, Governor's award winning hero. Right here in beautiful downtown Kelton." Grissum slowly chewed his cigar from one side of his mouth to the other and back as he thought. "Must have been about the time you were in nursing school."

"Seems he was coming back from forget where. Anyway, he's on his way back and taking a short-cut on a back country road. He catches a whiff of smoke drifting over the road. Told me later, it wasn't wood smoke. It had a chemical smell. That's what made him look for the source. He found an old trailer house on fire. He went in. Rescued a woman, her two children and the family dog. Burned the shirt right off his back doing it. Spent a while recovering from the smoke inhalation. There was a lot of hoopla in the media at the time."

"It was at that point, I think, Melanie began to mix up Dennis and Frank in her head. Regardless, she set her cap for Dennis and he was like a lamb to the sacrifice. Before he knew what hit him, he was married to Melanie."

"The marriage was in trouble from the honeymoon. Melanie thought she had her Frank all over and, of course, she didn't. She started a slow downward spin within the first year of their marriage. Dennis couldn't save her, though, Lord knows, the man tried."

"You mean when she died?"

"No. He wasn't there. He had taken the kids and gone to his sister's for a couple of days. Melanie was over the edge by then. I don't think Dennis could take it anymore. He was half out of his mind worrying about whether or not Melanie was taking care of the kids while he pulled shift. The endless fighting, her self-destructiveness, the alcohol. The man was about to come undone himself."

Grissum looked deep into his almost empty coffee cup. "Melanie had been dead for over twenty four hours before Dennis found her," he said quietly. "There were a lot of rotten questions and nasty insinuations at the time. Even the O'Conners and Garbers blamed him, as though Dennis had somehow failed Melanie by not being Frank. Neither set of people have spoken to him since the funeral. He puts on a good solid front, but the man took a serious hit. There's a lot of damage there."

Daphne sat quietly absorbing the information; then she stood and grabbed her knapsack off the empty chair between them. She bent down and planted a quick kiss on Grissum's grizzled cheek. "Catch you around."

She was almost to the door when she called back over her shoulder. "Thanks for the dinner."

Grissum half rose out of his chair. "Come back here, you cheap hussy." But she was gone.

He sat down, a broad smile framing his cigar.

Chapter Sixteen

Dennis was wishing he had taken Mrs. Mac up on her offer to stay and help out one more evening. He was losing ground rapidly as he tried to cope with a six year old wired on the upcoming Halloween and an eighteen month old who had declared herself liberated.

"But, Dad, you promissssed," Eric wailed when his father had tried to explain he just wasn't up to carrying Cortlyn through Wal-Mart to find a Halloween costume.

Cortlyn was perfecting her autonomy and a loud, decisive "no" answered her father's every request.

The ringing of the doorbell was almost drowned out by the duelling vocalists.

Dennis staggered to answer the door, trying to hush the children.

"Well, Cobb, I am truly impressed with your control of the situation."

Eric let out a delighted whoop and raced to tell his tale of woe about the Halloween costume to Daphne. Cortlyn trotted up on her stubby legs and held up her arms. Daphne reached down and swooped her up before stepping past Dennis as she entered the house.

"Okay, first things first." She looked at Dennis. "How are you feeling?"

His smile lifted one side of his mouth first, "Better, but I'll probably have to scratch the triathlon this week."

"Pity, you would have been a shoo-in at the chaos event."

Daphne went to sit on the couch. She patted the spot beside her and directed her steady look at Eric. "Okay, you next. What seems to be the problem?"

Dennis noticed she listened with her full attention on Eric as he related once again the story of the lacking Halloween costume with no diminishment in drama.

Daphne nodded her head slowly and thoughtfully. "I think that is something that we can handle." She got up off the couch. "Let's get cleaned up and we'll go find you a costume. Maybe your father can get a little rest."

She went into the kitchen and deliberately raised her voice when she saw no signs of dinner preparations. "And maybe we can round up some chow while we are out."

"McDonald's," Eric's voice answered.

Dennis was just settling his jacket over his broad shoulders when the trio came back ready for their outing.

"And where do you think you are going?" Daphne asked.

"I never miss a Happy Meal."

* * *

A black ninja costume complete with plastic katana and throwing stars hung in the closet beside a small plush bumblebee outfit. On the shelf above were two treat gathering bags. Dennis smiled at the costumes as he checked on his two children. Last night's adventures kept them sleeping later than usual.

He ran water to start the coffee and wiped up a bit of pulp from the counter. A huge pumpkin sat on the kitchen table grinning at him. A large plastic cauldron was on top of the refrigerator filled and ready for the invasion of the candy snatchers Tuesday night.

With a cup of the fresh brew in his hands, he went back into the living room. The transformation was amazing. Black and orange crepe paper ran from the corners of the room to a large spider hanging from the light. Cardboard cut-outs created a miniature graveyard of the picture window. Soft foam rubber pumpkins and candles leaned crookedly on the coffee table. It looked like a home where a family was celebrating the holiday.

And it had been fun. The whole evening had gone without any stress or mishap. Although, he kept his guard up out of habit, there had been no need for defensive tactics. Daphne had behaved in a straight forward manner. He hadn't had to run the gamut of subtle hints, veiled looks, or 'accidental' touches.

He sipped his coffee and slowly studied the room again. It had never been like this. Every holiday had been a disaster. Melanie always dove headfirst into depression dragging Frank in her wake. The day would deteriorate into tears, fighting, some grand dramatic scene, the children upset and crying. It had torn him apart as he struggled to make the holidays special for his children so they could have a trunk full of pleasant memories like his parents had created for his brother, sister and himself. But there was always the need for keeping everything low-key to try to head off one of Melanie's miserable fits.

People accused him of being cold about her death. He hadn't been cold. He had nothing left. Part of him had died long before her. Beaten to death by the constant emotional and occasional physical battering he had taken at her hands. Whatever feelings he originally possessed had been pulverized to an unrecognizable state. And none knew the depth of her madness when saturated with her booze and pills.

Not one of his accusers had known what drove him from the house the last days of Melanie's life. Only his sister and brother-in-law knew the truth. Melanie had tried to kill Cortlyn. He carried the scars on his arm where he had stopped Melanie from plunging a knife into his daughter's little chest. The lividity of death hid the bruise on her face where his hand had come crashing down as he struggled with her.

When he had stood by the bed and looked at her cold body spread across her own vomit and urine, relief was his first emotion. Guilt soon scalded his soul but he would never forget that first moment of being overwhelmingly grateful she had finally chosen Frank over him.

* * *

Daphne was in the supply closet pulling out gowns, sheets, and blankets to begin the morning bathes and bed changes when Susanne stuck her head in the door. "Kristi tried to call you last night. She wanted to ask if you would work second shift for her on Halloween."

"I can't. I'm not working a second shift this year."

"But you *always* help Grissum with the x-raying and do the treats up here. Kristi just figured....."

"Not this year. I have other plans. Sorry." Daphne's crisp tones shut off any further queries. Those tones concealed the part of her rolling and bouncing like a puppy.

Last night had been a sweet fantasy come true. The children had been delightful. They seemed so hungry for a woman's presence. And not just the children. She could feel Dennis' warm hand on her back as he guided her out of the path of a shopping cart; the strength in his arm he had offered as she got up and down off a chair while hanging the crepe paper; and the briefest contact of his body when he had taken the filled cauldron and reached over her head to place it on the top of the refrigerator.

And in three days time, she would go trick or treating for the first time in her life...holding wonderful, sticky little hands.

Chapter Seventeen

The arriving morning found her head turned towards the Heights.

Huge black silhouettes leaned against the paling sky. The durable old dowager manses clustered along the brow of the hill. The fronts, cobwebbed with gingerbread, stared out at the tract houses burgeoning beneath them. Their ample rears sat blind to the cracker box apartments and duplexes sprung behind them.

Relics of a gentler age, they stood...metachronisms amid the cheap housing, quick food joints, and disposable humans.

The morning breeze blew a bit of paper across what remained of her face, catching and holding it in her gore drenched hair.

* * *

The phone was ringing and Dennis searched his dreamscape looking for it. It was so odd. Here he was fishing in Grandpa's creek and a phone was ringing somewhere in the trees. The persistent sound finally punched through. He lurched up onto one elbow and reached over the arm of the couch to find his cell phone on the end table.

"Cobb?" It was a short yelp rather than a question. "We got a body. The Corners. White female in the alley between the all-nighter and the free clinic. The ghoul squad has been called. The mobile unit is cordoning the area. Looks nasty."

Dennis swung his legs around, still entangled in the afghan. "Female? Who is it? Any identification? Description?" His breath was painfully sharp and not just because of his ribs.

"Blonde in those pajama things they wear at the hospital is what the prelim said. Beyond that all I know is Chief says it's your baby."

A chunk of ice formed in Dennis' midsection, chilling him as he punched the speed dial.

"Dennis?" the sleepy burr of Mrs. McIntosh's accent rolled through the line with steadying familiarity.

"I have a call."

"I'm on my way, laddie."

He pulled on some clothes and, ran his fingers through his light brown hair before settling his Glock 9mm into the holster at his back, and shoving his badge and wallet into his inside jacket pocket.

By the time he hurried from the bedroom, he could hear Mrs. Mac already moving around in the kitchen. He avoided her in case his face should betray him. Mrs. Mac had known Daphne for years. He didn't want to be the one to tell her if his fears were realized.

Dennis swung into his car, the ribs unnoticed. He backed out of his drive in a screech of tires as he floored the gas pedal. They would have called Grissum. It would be too late to head him off. The best he could do was to get there to provide support for Grissum. "Dear God, don't let it be Daphne," he found himself saying over and over as he raced to the Corners.

The street was so full of vehicles Dennis was forced to park a block away. He made his way through the knots of spectators and clumps of officers all watching the alley with fascination.

Dr. Grissum was just coming out of the shadows, pulling off a pair of bloody latex gloves, folding them inside each other. The ambulance crew started forward with the body basket, red blanket neatly strapped inside.

Spotting Dennis trotting towards him, Grissum motioned the crew off.

"Doc." The word was a prayer of thanks. Grissum's expression, although coldly grim, told him it couldn't be Daphne lying in the alley.

"Hell of a way to start the morning, Cobb." He turned and started back into the alley, Dennis hard on his heels.

She lay on her back midway up the alley. Dennis drew in a breath to counteract the rise of nausea in his stomach. He looked away a moment as he steadied himself. Looking back, he asked, "What the hell did you do, lady, to earn this?"

Dennis squatted by the body, careful not to disturb the blood patterns. He pulled a pen from his pocket and carefully hitched it under a name tag clipped to the edge of her scrub shirt. Through the spatters of blood, he was able to make out the name Olivia Sawyer, Housekeeping. Kelton Community Hospital. He glanced up at Grissum. "You know her?"

Grissum shrugged. "There's two, three hundred people who work at that place. I couldn't tell you. The name doesn't ring any bells. Somebody sure wanted to make sure she was dead though."

Dennis straightened up and continued to stare. Grissum spoke. "Double barrel shotgun is my guess. Won't be able to give you a gauge until I get some of the shot out of her. She took the first shot to the gut, the second to the face." He gestured with the latex gloves. "The mess at her head is from the pellets tearing everything away. There is no signs of frank bleeding. She was dead before the second round was fired."

Dennis looked around at the man who had been busy snapping pictures. "Got it, Dave?" he asked.

A sickly grin flashed amid the freckles as Dave slung a camera over his shoulder. "From every which way but loose." He ambled off down the alley, popping a lemon drop into his mouth.

Dennis motioned to the men waiting to pick up their grisly load.

Chapter Eighteen

Under the dormer eaves of his attic room, Edmund Broadhurst's golden head turned back and forth on his pillow as he tried to escape the smell of blood permeating his nostrils. Its sweet, salty tang mingled in the heat of fever, calling to him with primal rhythm. It trickled through the unguarded gate of his subconscious urging him to taste, to drink deeply of the body's wine. As the blood pooled and rose he tried to climb away into sheltering arms, crying out to God while God lay dying below him.

He fought against the hell summoning sleep until he was able to break into consciousness. He didn't know if the cry bringing him to uprightness came from his throat or mind. It didn't really matter as long as it had propelled him out of the black memory he could not remember.

He pushed off his narrow bed and staggered towards the window. Gripping its dry rot, he rested his burning forehead against the ancient glass. It was there, just below the surface of his consciousness, pulsing with palpable malevolence. Urging him to come, to surrender to the beast crouched in the center of his soul. He balanced on the edge now, feeling the strong pull to let go and free fall into the abyss. But life clung with the lightest of grips. He backed away into wakefulness, letting the first light expunge the tormented sleep.

He began to shiver as his sweat soaked clothes cooled in the unheated dawn. He became aware he hadn't undressed. The wrinkled, stained sourness from his nocturnal prowling offended him. He must rid himself of them and with them, the night.

His morning ablutions had melted the foul nightmare in hot water and rising sun. He came down the stairs carefully centering the Windsor knot in his collar as Daphne stalked out of her bedroom, flower strewn scrub jacket and purple stethoscope hanging over one arm.

"Cuz. Don't we look, ah, sour this fine morning."

"Would you believe that miserable old fossil had the hospital call at 5 a.m. on my day off just to stick me in emergency again. They claim just for today and I'll tell you this, Edmund, it better be for just today or I'm telling that jerk joint where to get off and you can support me."

Edmund stepped back in mock aghast. "On my pitiful pittance."

"Pittance, my eye. Your damn shirt cost more than my whole month's salary."

"Exactly, m'dear, I might be forced to trade down from Savile Row to Brooks Brothers."

Daphne just turned on her heel and sputtered off down the stairs to the main floor, Edmund's soft chuckle dancing behind her.

He raised a hand and gently knocked at the door across from Daphne's. There was no response. There never was a response but he continued with the little courtesy because of his love for the woman inside. Carefully, he opened the door.

It was a room filled with the softest colors and materials he had been able to acquire. Light and delicate, it could have been home to an angel. Instead, it housed the remains of a woman already seated in the rose colored slipper chair before the window.

He dropped his jacket on the eiderdown comforter and went to kneel on the white carpet before her. Tenderly he took her hands and held them until she found her way back and turned mild eyes on him. She smiled a small acknowledgement for the kindness of a stranger.

"Good morning, Mum. How are you today?"

It was not a good day for already her eyes were sliding away from his face and drifting to the window. He kissed both hands before relinquishing them back to lay motionless in her lap.

He stood and got the silver backed brush from the dresser and began to slowly brush the waist length hair. Once it was the pale gold of a spring morning but now the silver frost of fall was traced throughout. When he had finished brushing, Edmund expertly plaited it and tied it with one of the many velvet ribbons he kept for her. He arranged it over her shoulder just as the door opened and Katlyn's cheery "Hallo" scattered the silence.

Edmund bent and kissed his mother on the forehead, holding his face level with hers for the beat of several breaths. Never in the decades had he been able to relinquish the dream he would see recognition in her eyes and she would reach for him. But always she remained in a land hidden from him. A land he had never been able to find; a land he never quit searching for.

He picked up his coat and left the room as Kat began to spoon egg into her mouth and she ate with the automatic response of a child.

Chapter Nineteen

Daphne arrived at the emergency room simultaneously with the ambulance. She followed the men bearing the red blanketed basket in through the airlock doors. This was why she hated emergency after years of working it. It was the detonation center where lives were blown apart. She had covered too many young faces with sheets after they had been scraped out of cars. She had watched too many go to surgery only to awaken in a foreign body, the old one irrevocably gone.

She arrived at the desk as the doors on the morgue elevator were sliding shut. Several nurses huddled around the desk, watching with fascination and talking softly among themselves.

"Daphne, you're back."

"Not by choice and not for more than today."

One short heavy set nurse nodded. "I figured Grissum would call someone in since he is going to be tied up most all the day."

"With what?"

All three nurses pounced on her eagerly. "Haven't you heard?" "It was on the radio coming to work." "That was the body of the woman they found in the alley." "Right next to the Free Clinic." "Grissum will be doing the autopsy." "They said she was murdered." The soft hiss of the automatic airlock doors abruptly silenced them. All eyes glared at the other end of the emergency room, not wanting their conversation interrupted.

"Oh, god, here comes Dennis Cobb, why didn't I do my hair this morning." "If only I was twenty years younger and 100 pounds lighter." "If only I wasn't married to what's his name."

Daphne turned to see Dennis striding through the entry area. He wasn't conventionally handsome but he had that irresistible combination of strength touched with a boyish vulnerability.

In an era when women had developed a healthy wariness of the male animal as they moved through the perils of everything from date rape to battering to abandonment of both themselves and their young, Dennis gave off an aura of strength and gallantry. It was the most elusive quality of the early twenty-first century. The sense one would be truly safe sheltered in his arms.

He didn't stop as he passed them but he sought Daphne's eyes and held them for a long moment. A warm flush of pleasure rose in her, tinting her with a delicate pink.

"He is to die for," someone sighed behind her.

"Someone already did." The venom in the words splattered as a clipboard hit the counter, its sharp clap causing them all to jump. "We need a blood draw in cubicle A and C is ready to be moved to maternity. And what the hell are you doing here, DelaVeque?"

The three nurses scattered leaving Daphne alone with ER's mother dragon, Eydie Nettles. "I was just asking myself that same question, but, the fact is I am here on the orders of the Grand Poobah himself, Lord Darth Grissum."

"And drooling over the killer detective, too, I suppose."

Daphne could match Nettles attitude for attitude. "I gave up drooling right after I finished cutting my first teeth. And what do you care who the girls take home in their fantasies?"

"Well , I wouldn't take that cold hearted bastard home in a body bag. Drove his first wife to suicide, you know. Son of a bitch wasn't even there. Ran out on her. Took the kids, dumped them at his sister's, and was off screwing some hot-pants broad when she died."

"Is that a fact?" She stared at Eydie with palpable chilliness. "Where do people come up with such shit."

"It isn't 'shit', kiddo. It's the truth. I've known the Garber family a long time so I oughta know." She pushed her shaggy grey head into Daphne's face. "And what's it to you anyway, sugarcakes? Don't tell me the high and mighty detective has another convert to worship at his pedestal." She chucked Daphne on the chin.

Her touch illuminated a bit of hoary history in Daphne's mind. "You're absolutely right, Eydie. You have known the Garber family a long time and you, of all people, ought to know."

Eydie reared back as though she had been slapped. She opened her mouth but nothing was coming out as Daphne turned on her heel and left.

Daphne was just fetching an elastic bandage to wrap a strained wrist when one of the regular ER nurse's slipped into the supply room with her. "Lord, the mother dragon is positively bellowing fire and brimstone today. If it's because you're here instead of her adored Grissum, do us a favor in the future. Tell his high and mightiness to get stuffed when he asks you to fill in."

On her lunch break, Daphne spotted Grissum and Cobb sitting on the far side of the cafeteria huddled over coffee as she entered. She was surprised how strongly she felt Cobb's presence. She could almost smell the clean, astringent scent of his aftershave. She went through the line, picking up a sandwich and coffee. She covertly looked over the men a moment while waiting for change at the cash register before turning and walking to the opposite corner to sit at an empty table.

She spotted Eydie sitting in the middle of the cafeteria. From her partially hidden place behind a large post, she was able to observe Eydie's eyes locked on Grissum as she mechanically ate what was on the tray. There was sickness in the woman's obsessiveness.

Movement at the table where the men had been sitting recaptured her attention. They were getting up and leaving. Grimness was etched in both their faces as they moved through the cafeteria. Dennis' hazel eyes were two polished agates set above the hard line of his mouth.

Daphne gave an involuntary shiver. She saw something else as Dennis passed through the room. There was core of polished steel in the man, unyielding and unforgiving. Had it always been there or had it been forged in the fiery years of hell he had lived through?

As the men passed out of her line of view, she swung her attention back and felt someone's eyes on her. Eydie was getting up from her table as well. And she was staring right at Daphne with hard, angry eyes.

Daphne was just swinging her tatty backpack over her shoulder, preparatory of going home when Grissum cruised up behind her, ensnared her arm in an iron grip and wordlessly dragged her to an empty cubicle. Neither observed the heavy shadow following and slipping in behind the curtain separating the cubicles.

There was severity even to Grissum's granite carved features as he faced Daphne. "I want you to close the free clinic for a few days."

"For heaven's sake, why? Oh. Sawyer from housekeeping."

Grissum jammed his hands into the pockets of his lab coat and began to pace the short length of the area. "She died from two shotgun blasts pointblank. It isn't the how that bothers me. It's the why and who."

"Are you saying she was killed randomly, for no reason?"

"Hell, I don't know. That's Cobb's job. But about all they have right now is questions and I don't want you anywhere near that place till KPD starts getting some answers. You understand?"

"Why, Doc, if you aren't careful, somebody might get the idea you cared."

He swung back on her and clutched her shoulders, giving her a little shake. "Kid, do you have any idea what went through my mind when I got that call this morning saying they had a dead blonde in scrubs next to the free clinic?" His gravelly voice was thick with emotion. "The hardest thing I have ever done in my whole life was walk down that alley. God, if it had been you, I don't...." His words choked off and his face was suddenly old and very tired with recalled fear.

Daphne flung her arms around his neck. He answered with a hug lifting her off the floor and threatening to crush her. "Oh, baby. If I ever lost you . . .there would be no reason...I couldn't ..." He drew in a long, shaky breath as he put her down and tenderly cupped her face with his hand. "You're all I got, kid. You understand?"

Daphne looked at him through the tears standing in her eyes. She continued to clutch the lapels of his lab coat. The exposed bond of love flowing between them tore through Eydie's heart like a burning stake.

Then Daphne patted the lapels into place and pulled a well-chewed cigar out of the pocket and stuck it in his mouth. "Come on, you old reprobate. I'll buy tonight."

There was a faint rattle from the chains suspending the adjacent cubicle's curtain. Daphne heard someone rushing away.

Chapter Twenty

Eydie didn't bother to turn on a light when darkness overtook the room. She sat in a cloud of smoke as she sucked one after another of the cigarettes she had given up years ago. And she remembered.

She remembered coming to work for the hospital as a fresh, pretty young woman. Eliott said she was pretty. No, Elliott said she was beautiful. He had kissed her so sweetly, held her so lovingly as they talked of their future together. He was starting Garber's Insurance Agency. Soon, soon they would get married. Kind, gentle Elliott. Where would they be today if Hal Grissum hadn't cut across her life?

But he had with a force that exploded her world. So arrogant, so powerful, so virile, they had all run after him like bitches in heat. And he had taken them when and as it suited him.

She had scarcely believed her good fortune when he had asked her out. Hal had style all right. He always wined and dined them at the best places before taking them to bed. And there was no denying the man knew exactly what to teach a woman. One night with Hal and she had given Elliott back his ring. Elliott had taken it hard, very hard. She couldn't explain. She just walked away.

Several weeks later, Elliott died drunkenly in a car crash; Elliott who never drank.

Maybe she should have seen then. Hal had been neither caring or supportive of her. His answer had been to just hit the bed. It was too late anyway. She had become obsessed with being the one he chose permanently. But time kept rolling on and Hal remained unattached. His flings were legendary but momentary.

If she couldn't get a ring out of him, then she would stay with him by becoming his right hand, the keeper of his ego, the chief vestal in his service. She would have him by making him so dependent on her he couldn't function without her. And she dreamed daily of a time he would turn to her and say, "Oh, baby, if I ever lost you."

And, at last, he had said it.

But not to her.

Tonight she had witnessed Hal Grissum giving away everything that should have been hers...was rightfully hers.

Thirty five years of dedicating herself to the love and service of one man had been thrown on the refuse pile. He hadn't even noticed her sacrifice. Nobody existed for him except that blonde tramp.

Well, it was gonna cost. She couldn't touch Grissum; wouldn't touch Grissum. But she would hurt him just the same.

"Payback's a bitch, DelaVeque, and when I cut you, Hal Grissum will bleed."

Chapter Twenty One

He bounced lightly on his toes just inside the yellow crime scene tape stretched across the alley's entrance. It was going to be a righteous night. He could feel it in his purple haze. When you got a fine, fine product, you're just going to make some serious money. And his little sampling told him his product was gonna set people aglow tonight.

"Yo, Candy Man."

He stepped forward as a young man and his girlfriend, leaned over the tape peering into the darkness. "I is here, boys and girls. Your Santa is loaded with goodies tonight."

"Any good?"

"My man, my man. I can tell you, it will get you up and you will get it up. You are about to make some memories."

The girl giggled and hung on the arm of the young man while he pulled some bills out of his team jacket. In a moment, the exchange was made and Candy Man faded back into the alley while the couple hurried away.

He executed a couple of moves when a low-slung pick-up cruised by, its bass rattling windows in its wake.

As quiet returned to the alley, he heard the sound of someone clapping their hands. He froze in the shadows. The clapping stopped and a man stepped forward, the light from the street illuminating only a fragment of him. The dealer recognized him. He was a regular in the Corners.

"Whoa, man, you about got a nasty hole in your sweet jacket. What you doing hiding in dark alleys, anyway."

Edmund casually leaned back against the wall, his face once more obscured by the shadows. "I do my best work in dark alleys," he said.

"Well, that may be but this here is my alley for tonight and I am not open for the kind of business you're in."

"And what is my business?"

"I know you. You like candy asses. I may be the Candy Man but I ain't no candy ass so you best go find yourself somewhere else. This place is occupied for tonight."

Edmund's voice took on a soft, hypnotic cadence. "Yes, it is. But not just by us. Many creatures share the night. Have you ever looked into the shadows and seen them looking back at you. Felt their touch, smelled their breath?"

Candy Man jumped as something brushed his neck. He whipped around to look down the alley. This was stupid. It was probably a moth or beetle flying by. When he turned back, he found Edmund's face scant inches from his own. "We call them up. Summon them from the dark bowels where they hide. And when they have been called forth, they must be fed."

The man felt heat and smoke encircling his head. He heard heavy breathing growing larger and deeper with every inhalation. It was behind him. He smelled the fecund scent of rotting flesh flowing in the chilly air. He felt each breath pushing hotter and damper against the back of his jacket. Edmund gradually faded before the man's fear-bulged eyes.

"You have called them. You must feed them."

* * *

The few men who remained in the squad room were all standing around, nervously sipping coffee, and staring at the chief's door as Dennis came in. The uniformed officers were mysteriously absent.

"Where is everyone," Dennis asked as he checked his watch against the clock over the pass-through window.

"On the streets....hiding."

One of the other men mumbled, "Oh, boy. I think he just got to it."

"Who got to what?" Dennis asked.

"Oh, yeah, I think you're right. He's turning purple."

Dennis turned towards the chief's glass enclosed cubicle just as an enormous roar escaped.

The chief stalked to the center of the room and motioned the few men into position in front of him with the report he had in his hand. Reluctantly, they lined up.

"Okay, would any of you like to hazard a guess as to what is in this report?" The men looked down and shuffled their shoes on the tile.

The chief's voice expanded with each word. "It's a goddam monster who tried to devour a meth dealer in the Corners."

Dennis reached for the papers. "May I see that, sir?"

The chief swung on him. "Why? I gave you a vampire. Did you get rid of it? Hell, no. I get a necklace of garlic instead. My office smells like Luigi's Pasta Palace."

"True, but we haven't had any more vampire attacks," Dennis grinned at him. The men snickered.

"Okay, Detective Smartass, you got a dead woman yesterday. You better be ready with some answers for me today. The press is going be wanting a statement in about," he glanced at his watch, "fifteen minutes. And the rest of you get busy, I don't want a bunch of editorials about waste of taxpayer money." He turned towards his office and then swung back. "Put the word out, if I see another monster, vampire, or even Casper the Friendly Ghost in anybody's report, the writer is going to be working the sanitation department. Do I make myself clear?"

Dennis pulled his file on Sawyer and followed the chief to his office.

The chief picked up the reports Dennis had left on his desk the night before. "So the victim is a twenty nine year old white female. Olivia Alice Sawyer. Housekeeper, second shift at Kelton Community. Cause of death double blast from shotgun at point blank range. Messy. That's pretty thin so far, Cobb. I hope you got more for me this morning."

Dennis looked over his notes. "She was separated from her husband according to her mother and sister. We haven't been able to locate him to talk to yet. He's supposedly out on a week's hunting trip with some buddies from work. We're getting two different stories on her. Her family claims she was the perfect wife, hard working and devoted. Coworkers at the hospital say she was a party girl type. Bleached blonde with a boob job who always had a guy on the side and finally got caught."

"Seems the husband came home early one night and she didn't show till five in the morning after getting off work at 11:30 p.m. He didn't buy the staying with a sick friend routine."

"So whose story you buying?"

"My odds are on the coworkers. According to them her latest kick was banging her at the old Sleep Inn on Travers. That's just a couple of blocks from where she was found. They also say she used to park her car at the all-night convenience store. It was there."

"What's the reading in your gut?"

"This is a personal kill. The shooter made sure she was not just dead, but physically destroyed. That tells me we are dealing with heavy emotions."

"So who you looking at?"

Dennis rubbed the back of his neck. "The ex tops the list. But we got to take a look at the former boyfriends, jealous wives, dumped girlfriends. It's a pretty wide field at this time."

"Anything else?"

"Not much. Right now we got the game wardens looking for the hunting party. We also are trying to get a lead on the current boyfriend. Motel rents rooms by the hour. No record keeping."

The chief's intercom buzzed. "Tell Cobb he's got a call on line four."

"May be the missing husband. You better catch that."

Dennis picked up his papers off the chief's desk, managing to also get the report with the monster.

The voice on the telephone was raspy and whispery as though someone was trying to disguise their voice.

"You know the woman who was killed in the alley?"

"May I have your name?"

"They got the wrong one."

"I need you name, please."

"There's a nurse practitioner that works in the ped unit of the hospital. She the one who was supposed to buy it. Olivia was a mistake."

Dennis voice took on an authoritative harshness. "Who is this?"

"Her turn will come again." Just before the phone clicked in his ear, he faintly heard a page for respiratory. He hung up slowly. Was that call about DelaVeque?

He punched in the hospital's number. He made notations in his file while he waited for Grissum to be summoned to the phone. "Doc? Cobb. How many nurse practitioners do you have working in pediatrics?"

"What is this, inventory time?"

"No. I just had a call which I bet came from the hospital. The caller said a nurse practitioner in pediatrics was supposed to be the real victim in yesterday's shooting."

Dennis heard Grissum's sharp intake of air. "DelaVeque's the only one we have," he answered softly

"Easy, Doc. It was just a crank call. My reading on the killing and what I have learned tells me the Sawyer woman was the intended victim. There's no connection between the two. If I find out anything to make me think otherwise, I'll call you at once. Okay?"

The answering grunt was somewhat skeptical.

After hanging up from Grissum, Dennis read over the report submitted by the night shift. He placed his next call to Dr. Ashe.

Chapter Twenty Two

Lygia was staring out the window when his call came. She had come in
early to finish dictating a couple of reports but found she was unable to keep
her mind focused long enough to string together two coherent sentences.
She kept drifting back to the dreams haunting her nights.

The most recent had happened night before last. It had the strange feel
as though she had somehow shared someone else's dream. She had been
drawn into thick darkness, hot and sweaty with the smell of terror singeing
the air. Inhuman roars rode the waves of the heat. She felt scalded by hot
spray as though someone had flung blood on her. A supplication for her to
intervene, to stretch out healing arms, slipped up against her, nuzzling
piteously against her heart. She answered with stony silence, arms locked at
her sides. She stifled the soft entreaty by turning away.

She had awakened when a cry came. A cry coming from the outside of
her dream. She lay on her sweat soaked sheets feeling her heart thunder, its
echo ringing in her ears. She had the most overwhelming feeling she had just
condemned someone. Even now, sitting in her office with all its visual
reminders of her professional accomplishments, she felt diminished as
though the dream revealed she was less than she had believed she was. There
was a cold, empty place within her.

Her office was exactly what Dennis would have expected to find. Cool
tones of ecru and grey; furniture saved from being clinical by being
upholstered in genuine leather; post-modern paintings on the wall.
Everything carefully neutral and asexual.

Lygia looked up from the photocopied report Dennis had smuggled out
of the office. "No mention of an accent this time."

"No. But the dealer does say it's a guy who is in the Corners regularly. 'Faggoty' looking. That matches up with a man named Edmund Broadhurst. Broadhurst's cousin runs the free clinic next to the alley."

At the mention of his name, Lygia mentally shied away. Her interest in the strange cases abruptly cooled. She made the pretense of writing notes on the pale grey tablet in front of her to hide her disquiet. "You seem convinced already this Edmund Broadhurst is behind these incidents."

Dennis ticked off his reasons on his fingers. "He's speaks with a British accent. His actions and appearance are somewhat effeminate. He apparently wanders around all hours of the day and night according to security at his office building. He himself claims to be a 'student of evil'. He has a connection to every incident we have been able to uncover. I'd say he's our most likely candidate."

Lygia suddenly wanted out of her deal with the detective. "If you're already so sure it's him, I don't see what service I can provide at this point."

"I guess all I'm looking for now is a reading on the guy, what might make him tick, maybe an idea of how he does what he does. He is walking a fine line using tactics I don't understand. If he decides to cross it, even in the name of justice, how do we stop him?"

"Why don't you just bring him in and confront him about it? Warn him off?"

"First, he has not actually broken any law. Bringing him in would be a violation of the man's rights. I would have everyone from the ACLU to the chief howling for my head. Second, there would not be much sympathy for his victims. Indeed, if the press got a hold of this, they are apt to make the man a hero. Third, well ...the first two are enough." Dennis stopped before he admitted to the psychologist that he did not want to alienate a certain relation of his suspect.

Unable to convince him of another route to reach Edmund Broadhurst, Lygia Ashe sat in her car in the Hanson Building parking lot and struggled to compose herself. She was loathe to meet with the man again but she had backed herself into a corner in her deal with Cobb.

She earned a good deal of money each year through her contract with the Kelton Police Department in addition to the excellent publicity that followed her involvement in high profile cases. It was too much to risk by wimping out on Cobb. She compromised with herself by planning a quick and dirty job. Get in, get out, and never let her guard down. Maybe if she was really lucky, he wouldn't even be in.

Outside his door, she studied the ornate symbol. There was something familiar about it but she couldn't place it. She tried the handle. Unfortunately, it turned.

Even with Dennis' description, Lygia was still astonished by the beautiful and luxurious room. She was pivoting her head to take in everything when the man spoke her name.

"Dr. Ashe. What a pleasure." His deep, accented voice was reserved as though seeing her was anything but a pleasure.

Lygia's head came around with a snap. She found herself looking up into the face of the man she had come to study. She was startled by the change she saw in him. He was still physically beautiful but there was a somber remoteness in his face, an emptiness as though the inhabitant of his body was moving out. Gone was the warm glow in the raw honey brown eyes, the playing smile on the firm lips.

He did not hold out his hand in greeting, merely stepped back to indicate for her to proceed into his office. She wondered if she was relieved or insulted.

Lygia paused inside the door. It was a beautifully done but still functional office. She caught sight of the case. Her curiosity drew her to it. She studied the three simple objects within.

"This looks like a shrine," she said.

Edmund spoke from where he had remained by the door. "Perhaps it is. My father was a medical missionary in Africa. Those relics are all that remain."

"I don't understand what I am looking at," Lygia said.

Joining her at the case, Edmund's hand gently moved over the glass. "The Book of Common Prayer written in Swahili. A crucifix carved by one of the tribesmen in the image as he saw God. His ordination stole." His next words were barely audible. "His blood."

Lygia looked up quickly. A darkness passed over Edmund's face and there was danger in the darkness. For one inexplicable moment, she recognized it as the place she had gone in her dream. She shifted nervously away from the case. Edmund remained staring down and when she glanced back at him she saw a bereftness that was an almost audible cry in the room. Once again something pressed against her heart.

Her response was hostile. "What is it you want from me, Mr. Broadhurst?" she asked harshly.

He looked up at her without surprise. "I've asked nothing of you, Dr. Ashe."

"Ever since we met at the WPA meeting, I have had strange experiences. I have lost two patients because I started seeing parts of them I shouldn't be able to see. I keep having horrible nightmares. I don't understand how or why but you are at the bottom of it. I know it."

"Within you is a deep pool, Dr. Ashe. It is part of your birthright. It has been there all your life. I merely brushed it. You are feeling the ripples. If they have made you uncomfortable, I do apologize." He was looking someplace beyond her. His voice was fainter as though it was coming from an increasing distance. "I can assure you, you shan't be afflicted much longer. There will be nothing more to call you."

Although he had not moved, Lygia felt as though he had left the room.

The air seemed chillier. It seemed to feed the cold, empty place within her, adding to its weight and breadth. She wrapped her arms around herself as she caught a sense of death drifting in the corners of the room. She looked at Edmund and saw him looking at it as though he were expecting it.

"Thank you, Dr. Ashe, for stopping by. But if you will excuse me, I have an appointment I must prepare for."

Edmund guided her to the door. As he held the door open, Lygia noticed again the symbol. She pointed to it as she stepped into the hall. "I recognize that but I don't know why. Is it part of what's been happening to me?"

He shook his head. "No. But you are familiar with it, Dr. Ashe. It's Romany. Gypsy."

He closed the door.

* * *

Lygia got off the couch again to walk back and forth across her living room, drawing in deep breaths. She kept feeling as though she couldn't catch her breath. It was as though a solid object was sitting on her chest and it was gaining weight. It had begun after she left his office. She first blamed Edmund when she got back to the safety of her own office. But as the afternoon wore on and it continued to increase, she had finally given into a few minutes of meditation to see if she could feel him probing into her mind. She was startled to find him gone completely. It was as he had promised, the ripples were stilling. It would soon be as it was before the fateful meeting.

But something had taken his place. Something that was literally weighing on her, pressing the life out of her. She stopped. No, it was pressing the life back into her, compacting it and fitting it into a very small space. The space she allowed for emotions, thoughts, actions which were not proscribed by her concept of self and the life she had created. Pausing in front of her patio door, she stared out but could see nothing beyond the night reflected image of her condo.

She looked at her world. She was now gorgio. She was no longer gypsy. More than being not gypsy, she was the carefully constructed modern woman. Each hour of her day was delineated, and weighed against the touchstone of being importantly busy; each meticulous notation defining the landscape of her life.

And the landscape was carefully cultivated. Every activity was measured, planned, executed, and checked off. There was no room for serendipity, spontaneity, craziness or even accident. No valleys, no peaks, just a smooth level flow to her days like a never changing river. No, not a river. There was flow and life to a river. No, she was a pool. Contained, unchanging, still. She saw it clear, sweet, and serene in a verdant wood.

Edmund had named her exactly. As she studied the image she had created in her mind, it began to change unvolitionally. It transformed into dark, fetid water locked inside a stone quarry, thick and lifeless. Her chest heaved against the weight. Had she judged Edmund and turned away from him because he chose to live what she chose to wall off? Was she so locked into her narrowly defined world she would not answer the cries of another human because they did not appear in her calendar or on her short list of acceptable requests? She had been stung by the cruelty of prejudice. Was she now the prejudiced? As she stared into the reflection of her own eyes, she knew the answers. And she didn't like them.

Chapter Twenty Three

The hospital was awash in ghosts, goblins, witches and black cats Tuesday morning. Staff sported pins, earrings, sweatshirts, and vests in keeping with the calendar's date. Grissum spotted Daphne in a set of bright orange scrubs with a jacket covered with witches, skeletons and ghosts. Tinkling little pumpkins hung from her ears and two black cats perched on the combs corralling her curls to the top of her head. Even her yellow stethoscope was decorated with a jack o'lantern.

As he approached her at the elevator, he was hailed by someone. They both turned to look. It was Ryan Thetford of the Kelton Daily Tribune.

"Dr. Grissum, Dr. Grissum."

Ryan's rotund body arrived as he always did, out of breath and red faced, camera swinging under an arm and the ubiquitous notebook in one hand and well-chewed pencil in the other.

"Dr. Grissum," he panted, "you're not dressed up."

Daphne maintained a solemn face. "No, he came as something truly frightening this year."

Ryan looked Dr. Grissum up and down. He looked in puzzlement at Daphne as she stepped into the elevator.

She answered his question. "He came as himself."

The howl was most satisfactory as the doors slid shut.

Grissum turned away and started down the hall towards ER. "Save yourself a lot of trouble, Thetford, just run the same article about the candy x-rays, etc., as you've run the last umpteen years. No point in breaking with tradition. And once again, let me confirm that the inmates have indeed taken over the asylum today. God help the patients."

Ryan trotted to keep up with Grissum's long legged strides. "Huh, thanks, Dr. Grissum. But there's something else I want to ask you. About a call we got this morning. It's probably nothing, you know, one of those anonymous calls without all the heavy breathing. But Dylan said we better check it out."

Grissum stopped dead in the flow of people. "Let me guess. It was a tip we have a drug ring operating out of the pharmacy."

Ryan shook his head.

"That we are harvesting body parts and selling them on the black market."

Again a negative.

"That we are billing Medicare and insurance companies for hysterectomies on 80 year old men."

"No, sir. It was none of the regular stuff."

Grissum crossed his arms over his chest and looked down thoughtfully on Ryan's eager face. "Okay, I'll bite."

Ryan leaned close, motioning for Grissum to do the same. "It was about one of your staff members having magic powers because they belong to a devil worshiping group and they are the ones who killed the Sawyer woman."

Grissum reared back. Without saying a word, he grabbed Ryan's arm and dragged the man down the hall towards his office. He thrust him inside and shut the door with a bang.

Leaning against the door, his face was severe as he looked at Ryan. "Okay, tell me exactly what was said and intimated."

"Well, the person was calling from the hospital. I know because I could hear you being paged in the background." Grissum nodded, his steel grey eyes never leaving Ryan's sweating face. "They said you have a staff member with peculiar powers. This person does things that everyone in the hospital knows about but that they are under orders from you never to reveal on the penalty of losing their licenses. And that this person was part of a coffin..., no, what was that...coven and that the Sawyer woman had been sacrificed so this person could keep their powers. It's a pact with the Devil, you see."

Grissum drew in a long, slow, deep breath before he spoke. "Yes. We have someone like that on the staff."

Ryan's eyes bugged as he fumbled for his notebook, pencil poised.

"You'll know them because of the tail hanging out the back of their uniform and the teeny, tiny shoes they wear over their cloven hooves." His voice became a roar. "What the hell is Dylan doing following up on an asinine phone call like that? You tell that bald-headed, addlepated boss, that if he so much even thinks about printing that kind of garbage in the Daily

Trial, I'll have committal papers served on him so fast he won't see the straitjacket coming. You understand?" Ryan's sweating had become profuse.

"So your denying the story, sir?"

Grissum ripped his door open. "Get your fat ass out of my office. Now." Ryan ran, the slamming door just missing his heels.

* * *

Grissum set a cup of coffee in front of Dennis. Dennis took a sip and grimaced. "I thought I'd stop by and let you know they found Sawyer's husband. Or they found his body. He committed suicide up in the Molalla hills. Left a note over the visor. He probably did it shortly after he killed his wife. Shotgun. State ballistics will match up the shot with those you took out of her body. State examiner will set the time of death." Dennis took another sip of the coffee. It didn't taste any better. "Seems Sawyer was a diabetic, juvenile onset. His treatment affected his ability to perform sexually at times. His wife's screwing around just emphasized his failures. He lost it when he caught her with still another man."

Grissum nodded distractedly. He stopped and frowned at Dennis. "There's been another call. This time to the Daily Tribune. That idiot Thetford was in here asking his usual puerile questions about it."

"Did they name Daphne specifically?"

Grissum shook his head. "No, but they indicated there were strange instances around here that were being covered up."

"Are there?" Dennis's eyes were cool and watchful.

Grissum picked up the question within the question. His own eyes hardened as he looked at Cobb. A slight challenge entered his voice. "You tell me. During her years of working in the emergency room, DelaVeque had several instances when she prepped a patient for surgery without specific orders or apparent medical justification found in the original examination. She was correct. The minutes she saved were the difference between life and death in each case."

"There were also some instances when she overstocked supplies and set out packs of instruments on an apparently quiet shift only to have a triage event take place. Her actions meant we had what we needed where we needed it."

"She has shown a remarkable ability to tell when a child's injuries are an accident or abuse. I don't have to tell you how plausible some parent's stories can be. "

"And that, Cobb, is the sum total. DelaVeque doesn't have a familiar, rarely dances naked around bubbling cauldrons and let her broom license lapse some years ago." His smile did not reach his eyes.

Dennis' grin was genuine. "The kids will be disappointed about the broom since she's going trick or treating with us. And, personally, I kinda had my heart set on the cauldron bit."

"You know, Cobb, given another couple of decades, I may learn to like you," Grissum said as he stuck a cigar in his mouth.

* * *

Daphne arrived at Dennis' duplex a few minutes before the appointed time to dress the children and set out for the evening's adventures. Already, strange and alien creatures were swooping through the streets.

She rang the bell and the door flew open. Eric was standing there with the candy cauldron in his hand while Mrs. Mac stood behind holding Cortlyn.

Upon seeing, Daphne Eric turned and thrust the bucket at Mrs. Mac before running for his bedroom. "Come on, come on, we're gonna miss all the treats if we don't hurry."

"Ah, lassie," Mrs. Mac said as Daphne reached out for Cortlyn. "I dinna think I was going to be able to hold him down much longer. He's been counting the minutes since he got home from school. Denny called a wee bit ago and he is being held up with some clean up on that sad business in the alley. He said to go ahead and start without him if he's not made it home by the time the bairns are ready to go."

The twinge of disappointment she felt was swallowed in the shout from the back bedroom, "Daffffffy, hurrrry."

In record time, they were heading out the door, Eric skipping backwards as he urged her to run. Cortlyn's wings and little antennae bounced as Daphne hurried to keep up.

Eric's sack was bulging when they staggered up the walk to the door nearly two hours later. Daphne's arms were leaden from Cortlyn's sleeping weight. But her happiness was evident in the glow of her smile as she and Eric chattered. The door to the duplex opened and Dennis' tall silhouette filled it.

Eric leaped into the living room and spun around his father. "Wow, Dad, you won't believe how much great stuff I got. Look at this." He thrust his open bag up at his father.

Daphne beamed at Dennis. "Fortunately, we live in a small city." Dennis reached for his daughter and then noticed she was asleep. "The bumblebee fell asleep about eight blocks ago. I'll get her into bed."

Dennis followed Daphne into the kitchen. The pumpkin was the only glowing light, turning the kitchen into an eerie looking cave. "That's great," Eric stood entranced in the doorway.

"Mrs. Mac left some cold cider and warm pumpkin bread."

"You pour while I put the little honey in her hive."

Daphne's hospital experience let her slip Cortlyn out of her costume, change her diaper, and slip her into pajamas without waking her. Daphne leaned over her and gently brushed the little curls back as Cortlyn sought her thumb in her sleep. She kissed her and breathed in the baby's sweetness.

Pulling up the side rail, Daphne stepped back into something solid. Dennis caught her by the shoulders and steadied her. For a moment, they stood there looking at the sleeping child. Daphne, who had always stood at the outside of tender family scenes, held her breath in the sheer joy of the moment.

Dennis' voice was soft above her head. "You're pretty good at that."

"Lots of practice. You're pretty good at sneaking up on people, too."

Dennis dropped his hands and stepped back, "Lots of practice," he smiled at her.

Back in the kitchen, Eric was busy drinking cider. "Hey, guys, this stuff tastes just like apples." Daphne and Dennis laughed as they sat down at the table.

Daphne pulled Eric's bag to her and began to quickly check over the candy. There were several things she discreetly set aside.

Eric knelt on the chair and watched her. "Did you go trick and treating when you were little, Dad?"

Dennis nodded. "Sure did. Your Aunt Susan, Uncle Chris and I went every year."

"Did you get lots of candy?"

"One year we put all our candy together and it filled a whole pillow case."

"Wow." Eric's eyes were round as he contemplated that much candy.

"Bet Daffy got lots of candy, too, huh, Daffy," Eric said.

Daphne just smiled at him as she finished up and scooped the candy back into his bag. "Here you go, most honorable ninja." She slipped the few questionable pieces into her hand. She felt a light touch on her leg and looked down. Dennis had his hand out. She dropped them in it. He got up from the table with a wink in her direction and casually discarded them under the pretext of bringing the pumpkin bread to the table.

Dennis tapped his son on the head as he came back. "Two pieces and then bed."

"Ahhh, geez."

"Tomorrow you go to most honorable school."

Eric screwed up his face in disgust as he began to carefully make his selection from the riches in his bag. "What's the most candy you ever got, Daffy," he asked as he picked through.

Daphne was glad they were sitting in the semi-dark. It hid her embarrassment. "Well, Eric, to tell the truth. Tonight is the first time I ever went trick or treating."

Eric's eyes were enormous and his mouth was hanging open. "In your whole life?" he asked in an awed whisper.

"In my whole life," Daphne nodded solemnly.

Dennis was looking at her with much the same surprise on his face. "Was it against your religion or something?"

Daphne laughed. "Hardly. No, my mother was a journalist. Her idea of Halloween was to spend it in some graveyard or some ancient house waiting to get an interview with some dearly departed."

"A ghost?" Dennis was incredulous.

"Wow," Eric exhaled. "That sounds like fun."

Daphne gave a faint shudder. "Fun it was not. Graveyards are cold and wet. Ancient houses are cold and boring. You have to sit still for hours and hours and not move or make a sound because you might interfere with the spectral appearance."

"Your mother kept you out doing that?" Dennis' eyes goggled.

Daphne shrugged. "Only until the first light of dawn or cock's first crow. Believe me, as soon as I was old enough to stay in our room by myself, I never went out with her on that stupid assignment again."

Dennis took a sip from his glass. "How old were you when you finally quit ghost chasing."

Daphne thought for a moment. "I dunno, seven, eight, somewhere in there."

Eric tried to stifle a yawn. Daphne pushed up from the table. "Come on, you. Kiss your dad good night and let's hit the hay."

"But my candy."

"You ate four pieces already," Daphne said as she held up the wrappers. "Let's go."

Almost immediately, she was back. "He was asleep before his head hit the pillow, still in costume although I did manage to get the shoes, throwing stars and katana."

She stood looking at the pumpkin and knew the magic was about spent. "Well, I guess," she started to say as she reached for her backpack.

Dennis pulled her chair back. "You haven't had any pumpkin bread yet. Mrs. Mac will be crushed."

Daphne laughed, pleased with the brief reprieve.

Dennis studied her as she sat down and rested her chin in her hands, staring at the pumpkin. The candlelight turned her curls a faint strawberry blonde. Her eyes were luminous and her soft mouth was parted in enchantment the way a child would be seeing their first jack o'lantern. He had to ride strong herd on his hands to keep them from reaching over and pulling the combs out of her hair.

It was eerie when Daphne sat up and reached up to pulled out the combs. She lightly scrubbed the top of her head, fluffing her curls before dropping the combs into the pocket of her jacket. She caught his stare. "Those things begin to chew their way into the skull after a long day," she said.

Daphne had just taken a piece of pumpkin bread when Dennis spoke. "Tell me about your family. Grissum says you are all gifted with special 'talents' I think was his word."

She froze mid-action. Then carefully setting the bread down beside her glass, she dropped her hands in her lap and sat ramrod straight. Her face took on the cool, detached expression and her voice was distant.

"Yes. Grissum would say talents. The rest of the world would say aberration, mental defect, if you are religious, satanic manifestation."

Dennis touched her arm. "I'm sorry. Forget I asked that question."

She didn't relax or look at him. "No. You've were kind enough to share your children with me. You have a right to know what kind of person you have exposed them to." She paused and drew in a deep breath. She kept her eyes fixed on the pumpkin.

"The family 'talents' extend as far back as anyone has been able to trace. They show in every generation, whether they are wanted or not." There was a bitter edge to her voice now. "My grandmother was a medium who supported my two aunts and my mother with séances after my grandfather was killed in World War II. My Aunt Agatha has the ability to read people's lives. To know what they have done. My Aunt Anne, before she became ill, had the gift of intuitive diagnosis. She could locate and identify health problems, even in some cases, I am told, heal it. My mother had precognition. She knew in advance when events, usually catastrophic, were going to take place. My cousin Katlyn is an automatic writer. The dead are able to use her hand to write to people still living. Edmund has the ability to touch thoughts and influence minds." She stopped and when she began her voice was lower and slower. "I am able to hear things no one else can hear."

Dennis was puzzled. "Grissum told me about some things that occurred at the hospital. I don't understand how you 'heard' them. Like knowing when someone would need surgery."

"I could hear the blood pumping from a place it shouldn't be."

"Preparing for triage?"

"I heard the accidents taking place."

His voice became softer. "The children?"

"I can hear the fear and betrayal screaming in them."

She turned her head and caught herself starting to say, "And I can hear the crying in your bedroom," but bit it back. He had on his detective face, expressionless and searching. It spoke volumes to her.

She stood up and pulled her backpack off the chair. She was silent as she walked to the doorway. She paused for a moment and carefully looked the kitchen over. Then she went through the living room and she studied it before she opened the door.

"Daphne." He stopped her at the door. She looked up him with the bruised look of a child who is being banished. "I'm sorry. I shouldn't have pried."

Her voice was brittle. "You might as well get it from the horse's mouth as to hear some of the more colorful tales floating about."

As he looked at her, she dropped her eyes away from his. He reached out and caught her chin in his hand. He gently lifted her face toward him and bent over her, brushing his lips lightly over hers.

She raised her hand as though she wanted to reach for him, instead jammed it in her pocket. "See you around, Cobb." She never looked at him again as she backed her car out and drove away.

Dennis watched until the taillights disappeared, the warm, softness of her mouth echoing on his lips. He slowly closed the door and turned back. He looked around the room and wondered what Daphne was seeing. He went back to the kitchen and flipped on the overhead. As he leaned over to blow out the candle in the pumpkin, he knew. He dropped heavily into the chair. She had said good-bye. She wasn't coming back.

He stared at her glass and the uneaten pumpkin bread. A plea came from the empty place within him. "No. Don't leave me alone."

Chapter Twenty Four

In the car, Daphne kept touching the place where Dennis' lips had brushed hers.

The tender gesture had nearly undone her. She had almost thrown herself into his arms, begging him not to spurn her for abilities she couldn't help having, for the family she hadn't chosen. But she had learned, while still a school girl, not to seek acceptance. She knew to turn and walk away first, to never look back. It allowed no one else to be given the satisfaction of totting up the cost. Only she knew the price she paid.

"Good-bye, sweet babies. Good-bye, Detective Dennis Cobb," she whispered to the darkness.

The emotions of the evening all bundled together to press heavily in her chest. They made breathing difficult as she climbed the tiers of steps to the house.

Inside, she saw Edmund propped up on the old couch, his laptop computer resting on his outstretched legs. She came into the room and Edmund swung his legs off the couch just as she collapsed on it. Her face was washed out and devoid of emotion. A sure sign, Edmund knew, his cousin was in acute pain.

"So how'd you get stuck with the trick or treaters?" she asked as she gestured towards the bowl of candy sitting on the old wooden trunk that served as the coffee table.

"Kat got one of her nasty sinus headaches. I dosed her up with some valerian tea, made her a eucalyptus compress and sent her to bed. We had about the usual number. How about your evening?"

"Cobb started asking questions about the family X-files. Our talent for the strange, bizarre, and unusual." There were tears just under the words.

"And you gave him a concise and frank answer. Then picked up your disreputable rucksack and brought yourself home without a backward glance."

"Don't you start trotting around in my mind. It's bad enough mother drops in unannounced all the time."

"I have not invaded your cerebral sanctum, cuz. Just a guess based on years of living around you. "

Daphne put her head back and closed her eyes. A tear glistened in her lashes.

"Kitten," Edmund used his old pet name for her. "You must quit fighting the world so hard. We may have some rare talents, but we are not the only people to have these abilities. We do not use them for ill. We do not exploit them for gain. It will not cause some irreparable harm to the world if you fall in love, marry, have children. Admittedly, it will take a special sort of blighter to appreciate all he is getting, but you shan't find him if you put up your back and scuttle up the nearest tree whenever someone approaches you."

"You're a fine one to lecture. I may run, but you hide behind your sweet, dandy image. Oh, Edmund don't you ever want to love someone? To be a husband? A father?"

Edmund got up from the couch and went to poke the dying fire. He stood watching the sparks fly up. "I must finish the journey I have begun, Daph. Alone." The glow from the stirred fire etched his face with shadows, reflecting his inner world.

Daphne got up from the couch and went to give his neck a quick squeeze. As she stepped back she glanced in the mirror and saw them reflected back. There was family resemblance in the defined and delicate bone structure, the mobile mouths, the haunted eyes.

"Look at us, Edmund. The Prince of Darkness and the Queen of Misfits."

At that, he snapped his fingers and went to his herringbone jacket tossed over the back of the old Morris chair. He searched through the pockets and brought something out something which he presented to her with a flourish. It was a tiny ceramic bat perched on a tombstone, one wing broken off.

She gasped in delight and immediately cradled it.

After kissing his cheek, she picked up her backpack off the couch and started for the stairs. She stopped in the doorway and looked back.

"Edmund, how come with all our abilities, we never seem to know what's the thing to do ourselves?"

"Part of the rules, old girl. We have to reach out to see in. We can't reach in to see out."

"It figures we'd get stuck with stupid rules as well." She shook her head slightly and went upstairs. After preparing for bed, she placed the little bat next to the doll house. She had decorated it with scraps of crepe paper, tiny pumpkins and a gauzy ghost or two. As she sat looking at it, the whole of the evening washed over her and she finally let loose the tears she had held back since Dennis asked his question. She felt her mother's cool touch on her neck and heard her question in her mind.

"No, Mom. There's nothing you can do. I just hurt. Because I've done something stupid. Really stupid. I've fallen for him, Mom. Oh, lord, I've fallen in love. No, he doesn't love me. After tonight, he doesn't even like me."

Mercifully, there was silence in her mind although the cool touch continued at the back of her neck until she at last tumbled into bed.

* * *

Edmund sat on the couch, his hands shoved in his pants pockets, legs extended towards the dying fire. Yes, there are rules. There are always rules to govern the form and usage of all gifts. Without the rules, the gift is inarticulate. He had spent years traveling the globe, sitting at the feet of the wisest learning the rules. He had begun his quest trying to collect enough bits of the precious knowledge to fashion a key to unlock the darkness within himself. Within that darkness, he felt sure lay the map to the land where his mother had strayed.

He had crossed deserts, climbed frozen mountains, tossed in delirium fevers, spilled his blood as he dug for the precious bits of wisdom and his quest had finally come to fruition. He had compiled the rules. He had interlocked the knowledge scattered across the face of the world and he had a key. But he had also learned the key was not his to use. Someone else was guardian to his key; someone for whom the rules were written in their blood; someone who could look into hell and call the demons by name and in doing so, strip their power; someone who knew the Name.

At the direction of the old monk, he had come home to write, study, practice the arts he had learned, share the wisdom he had found with others like his cousin Elmore who were locating and preserving the knowledge first given by the stars to man...and to wait.

The burning wood broke apart and collapsed into a glow of red embers. The fire was nearly consumed. Time was almost out. Edmund knew this. Each time he had the hell spawned dream, it fed on another bit of his survival instinct. He danced longer and longer on the tenebrous edge, growing weaker and weaker in his will to pull back into the light. This last dream, he had found the scales were nearly balanced. Today he had seen death circling the corners of his office, staring at him, salivating after him. And the one entrusted with his life had spurned him. The heavens had passed judgment.

He dropped his head back and closed his eyes. He was lost.

Chapter Twenty Five

The newspaper laid splayed out over the stacks of magazines, books, empty food containers and now, overflowing ashtrays in Eydie's living room.

Sawyer's murder was solved. Nothing mysterious in it after all. A dysfunctional husband married to a horny wife. She wondered if Grissum had slept with DelaVeque. She screwed up her face as she pursued the thought. She finally shook her head. She doubted it. She had never seen him look at her "that way". Funny, how she always thought of it in quotations. "That way." A kind of slow, smoldering study of a woman. It asked a question few women were able to resist. Can you light my fire until it blows us both over the top?

No, Grissum always looked at DelaVeque like a father doting on his princess daughter. She was the precious little doll he was playing with in his senior years. Nah, it went back farther than that. It went back to when DelaVeque first started working as a ward clerk fresh out of high school. He went ga-ga then and it never stopped.

Her cheeks flamed as she remembered an incident from one of the first years the princess was out of nursing school and on staff in the emergency room. DelaVeque had run around and set out a bunch of supplies and instrument packs without checking with her as head nurse. She had been crawling DelaVeque's frame when Grissum intervened. Eydie had started to complain to Grissum. Even now she could see the cold grey steel of his eyes as he looked at her and said, "Don't push it, Eydie." and she had known if it came down to a choice between her and DelaVeque who would walk. She had been hurt and angry but she had still believed it would run its course. It had and she had been washed right out of the picture.

She lit another cigarette and watched the smoke curl up. The voice in her head grew icy hot. She had to get rid of DelaVeque. Only then would Grissum pay where it was dearest. And then Grissum would have no choice but to turn to someone else. She would be the soul of understanding and comfort. She would hold him and let him cry for his little lost toy.

But how to do it? She wasn't sure. She would have to think about that. Her eyes fell on the newspaper again. Yeah, there was time for the finale. First, she wanted to see them suffer. She would spew back some of the acid they had poured on her heart. Watch it carve runnels of fear in their faces, sear their minds, devour their lives. She would make sure when she was done there was nothing of the old Grissum left. She would own him then.

Chapter Twenty Six

Somehow the shift from October to November seemed to advance night more quickly. By the time Edmund and Daphne reached the clinic, she had to use her examination flashlight to find the keyhole. Edmund spotted the envelope lying on the floor as they stepped into the building. He picked it up. "A fan letter, no doubt."

"Sure with a large donation."

He handed it over. "It's rude to open other people's mail. I'll just read it over your shoulder."

Daphne pulled out her bandage scissors and slit the inexpensive white envelope. The paper inside had dark blotches on it. Daphne knew by the smell it was blood. She unfolded the sheet from the corners careful to avoid the blackened areas. It was composed of words cut out of the newspaper.

Ms. Free Clinic

Your end is almost upon you. Will it be tonight? Tomorrow? Next week? And how? A drive-by bullet tearing through your body? A knife quivering in your chest? A blunt object shattering your skull? The possibilities are so many. It pleasures the mind just to think on them. Now you think and wonder how and why.

"Somebody's got a sick sense of humor, Edmund. Watch the blood." She passed him the note.

"Daphne, this isn't particularly funny. P'haps, we should turn this over to your detective."

Daphne's voice was sharp. "No. It means nothing. It's probably been laying here since last night. A bad Halloween joke. Just throw it in the garbage."

"Are you sure, m'dear? After all he's just across the street." Edmund nodded towards out the window.

Daphne looked. All she could see was a light colored car; she couldn't see who was in it. She lacked Edmund's catlike night vision.

She deliberately turned her back and stripped off her windbreaker, failing to see Edmund slip the envelope into his coat pocket. "Well, I must be about, m'dear. I'll see you at the usual time." He was gone before Daphne could turn back.

She had just started her nightly setup when she heard feet pounding down the sidewalk. A young man hurled himself into the clinic. He was pointing back to the street, unable to get his winded lungs to push the words out. In another minute, several young men, all wearing bandannas tied tightly around their heads pushed through the door. One of their kind was stumbling along between two of them.

They laid him on the chipped tile floor just inside the clinic door. He was gasping and moaning. Daphne saw the blood soaking across the front of the tee-shirt and washing down the baggy pants. She pulled on a pair of latex gloves and grabbed a fistful of gauze squares. She quickly cut the tee-shirt. "Shit, it's a gut shot," she muttered as she gently swabbed the area with gauze squares.

There were more feet pounding down the pavement. The gang members hit the floor. Daphne looked up the see the shaved heads of a rival gang drawing down on her window.

"No," she screamed as she jumped up and ran outside.

Dennis grabbed for the radio, "Station 10, we have a gang fight at the free clinic in the Corners. Officer is 10-40." As he shoved out of his car, he could hear the dispatcher calling all units to his officer needs assistance location. He pulled his gun out from under his jacket as he ran across the street.

Daphne pushed the gun pointed through her window in the air and shoved the young man back. "What the hell do you think you're doing, Fat Boy? This is neutral turf. You know the friggin' rules. You keep your wars away from here or you can damn well bleed to death next time somebody cuts your belly open."

Dennis ran up and grabbed Daphne's arm, pulling her behind him. She shoved him back before she realized who it was.

"Fuck, it's the man," the heavy young man said. Hostility rose like noxious vapors around Daphne and Dennis.

"He isn't a cop unless I say he's cop," Daphne said. "Now get you asses out of here before I make him a cop."

The young men melted away in the dark. Dennis even heard a couple mutter "Sorry" under their breath to Daphne as they vanished.

She turned on him as soon as they were gone. "Are you trying to get yourself killed? Cops are prize game around here."

He pushed her into the clinic ahead of him, keeping his gun ready. "I might ask you the same thing. Just what the hell do you think you're doing stepping into a gun like that?" His eyes were blazing.

Sirens could be heard now coming from all directions, converging on the Corners. The streets were rapidly emptying. The young men in the bandannas were dancing foot to foot nervously. Daphne motioned to them. "Listen, Shun is going to have to go to the hospital. It's a gut shot. If they don't operate and clean up the mess in there he's going to get peritonitis and die. So you all just take off. There's nothing you can do here. I'll handle everything. Go. Now."

In the space of a heartbeat, there was no one left except Dennis and Daphne and the young man on the floor. Daphne knelt down beside him. She motioned Dennis towards the back of the room. "Get me the blood pressure cuff and an ambulance." Dennis holstered his gun as he went to get the blood pressure cuff. He handed it to Daphne and as the first officer appeared in the door, ordered him to radio for an ambulance.

After sending all but one car back on patrol, Dennis went in and watched Daphne. She was taking readings every couple of minutes and noting them down. She talked with the young man, getting information on where his body position and where the bullet had come from. The ambulance rolled up with its whoop-whoop sirens going. Two men and a woman jumped out, hauling a gurney with them.

"What we got, Daphne?" one of the men asked. She succinctly told them. She ordered IV lines started and fluids to support the young man's fight for life. As they loaded the young man on the gurney, she pulled off a glove and reached out for the woman's radio. She signaled the hospital and told them what to expect and requested they have a surgeon on stand-by when the ambulance arrived.

Then they were gone. As the ambulance's siren faded away, the silence left behind was almost as loud. Daphne pulled off the other glove and went to the back of the clinic. She tossed them in the wastebasket and washed her hands. She suddenly sagged against the sink, feeling limp as the adrenaline rush subsided.

Dennis quickly crossed to her and kneaded her shoulders, "Hey, you alright?"

She stiffened under his hands, pulling herself up straight. "Probably just low on caffeine. I'm fine." She couldn't quite mask the residual shakiness in her voice.

Dennis slowly forced her to turn around and then pulled her into his arms. It was a comforting hug, much as one gives to a distraught child, but Daphne didn't care. She could feel the breadth of his chest, hear his heart beating under her cheek, the comforting strength of encircling arms. For the moment she gave herself up and leaned against him.

Dennis was surprised at her size. Somehow her strong character made her seem bigger. But the top of her head rested below his chin and her body was small and light, like a child's.

Daphne's overriding desire was to just stay inside those arms forever, but she pulled away with a deep breath to steady herself.

"So how come you're out slumming instead of home cooking dinner," she asked him though it took all her will to look him in the face and not give away the emotion boiling within her.

Dennis had a deprecating smile on his face. "I couldn't go home and face the kids until I'd come to apologize to you."

"Apologize to me? For what?" The surprise was genuine.

Dennis jammed his hands in his pants pockets and looked at the floor while he considered his words. "I ruined a great evening by asking you questions I had no right to ask." He looked at her now, his eyes searching her face. "Daphne, you don't have to hide who you are, what you are. I saw your 'talent' the night we went out on the baby case. Grissum alluded to it some time ago. In a way I understand it. Cops get hunches for no reason. See things that look like normal everyday events and something in your gut tells you it's hinky. You interview someone and you know who's lying and who's honestly mistaken. I can't tell you why any more than you can tell me why you hear things beyond hearing. It's there. I want you to stay a friend ...to the children, and," he paused a second. "to me. Will you?" The imploring look in his eyes validated his words.

Before she could respond, the sound of sobbing reached them. A young mother came through the door with a screaming toddler clutched in her arms, a bloody towel pressed to the baby's face.

"He fell, he fell, oh, god, he's hurt bad."

Daphne ran to take the struggling baby from the mother's arms. She quickly deposited him on the examination table and reached back to pull gloves out of the box behind her. She mopped at the blood and located the gash on the hairline.

The mother stood sobbing and shaking. Daphne spoke soothingly. "Ah, that's not so bad. What'd you hit, little guy? "

It was hard for the mother to get the words out. "He fell onto the drawer in the bathroom. I was getting ready to give him a bath and I left it open. Oh, it's all my fault," she wailed.

Daphne looked up and Dennis caught her eye. He looked at the child and then raised an eyebrow. Daphne looked at the child and knew it was an accident. She looked back up at Dennis.

"He's going to be fine. Little ones this age have accidents," she slightly emphasized the word, "all the time. Mama, hold him while I get some things."

She gathered some items off the listing supply shelves and turned back to the table. She glanced up at Dennis as she shook betadine on a gauze square. "The all-nighter next door does a pretty good chicken and the potato salad is not bad. Tell the kids hi for me and I'll see them soon."

Dennis' answering smile scattered the shadows of the prior night.

The young woman watched him go. "Is that your husband?" she asked.

"Not yet," Daphne said as she applied steri-strips to close the cut. Then stopped as she wondered why she said that.

Chapter Twenty Seven

It probably would have been Daphne who made the grisly discovery in the towels if she hadn't had a tonsillectomy to admit to the unit. Kathy's scream had adult heads poking out of doors all up and down the unit. Susanne was the first in the linen closet.

Kathy pointed with a shaky finger. "I touched that."

Susanne looked. Even accustomed to the sights found in the hospital she shuddered. "That is gross. Sick."

She stepped back out of the closet, pulling Kathy with her. Picking up the phone, she pressed the paging button. "Dr. Grissum to peds stat. Dr. Grissum to peds stat."

Grissum looked up from the chart he was making notations in at the main desk in ER. "What the hell?" he looked blankly at Eydie. Her expression was innocently quizzical. "Don't ask me," she said. Grissum reached past her and picked up the phone.

Susanne answered. "Dr. Grissum, we found something in the linen closet. I think you should see it...stat."

Grissum hung up the phone with a puzzled expression. Then he shrugged. "I think they just found the drug ring is really operating out of the linen closet in pediatrics." He strode towards the elevator.

Eydie's eyes never left his back. "You'll wish it was a drug ring," she thought as she watched.

Grissum stared down at the thing nestled in the towels. It made the hair on the back of his neck stand up. He carefully covered it over before picking it up and gingerly slipping it into a wash basin. He then did a quick check of the rest of the closet, assuring himself and the two nurses no other surprises were hidden among the linen.

He looked at Kathy and Susanne. "I don't want one word about this out until I get to the bottom of it. You keep it to yourselves, do you understand?" His tone bespoke the dire consequences that would be assured if they violated his law. He picked up the basin and left the linen room. Pushing the button on the elevator, he issued another order. "Tell DelaVeque I want to see her in my office...stat."

Susanne and Kathy squeezed into the linen closet and closed the door. They kept their voices low. 'Do you think he thinks she put it there?"

"Why else would he want to see her?"

"I don't believe it. Daphne's not the kind."

"Yeah, well, but she's been acting kinda strange lately. Real moody. And she didn't work Halloween night. Said she had something else to do. And they say that women who go too long without a man begin to get all weirded out and do bizarre things."

Kathy hugged herself and shivered. "The whole thing gives me the creeps."

There was a pounding on the door. "Hey, you two. You holding the sheets for ransom or what."

* * *

Grissum sat the basin on his credenza and lifted off the towel. A fashion doll dressed in pink scrubs was nestled in the white terrycloth. The curly blonde hair was pulled to the top of the head with tiny combs. Three 'jewels' dotted the ears. And the throat had been sliced almost through with cascades of real blood soaking the top of the doll's body and the underlying towel.

Daphne burst through the door. "I have three admits this morning and I am already behind so make your ass-chewing short and sweet."

Grissum picked up the basin and thrust it onto the desk under Daphne's nose. "Somebody left this in peds linen closet." She looked down uncomprehendingly for a moment and then the image and its message impacted her. She went white to the lips and her chest began to heave as she began to hyperventilate. Grissum grabbed her arm and shoved her into a chair. He pushed her head down between her knees and held it there until she fought him to straighten up.

"That's not funny," she managed to whisper.

He sat on the arm of the chair and pulled her over to lean against him. She was trembling. He began to rub his hand over her shoulders and back. Even through her scrubs he could feel her heart pounding at breakneck speed. "It sure as hell isn't."

She was still only a few minutes accepting his ministrations. He felt the monumental effort she made to pull herself together. She stood up and turned away from the basin with a shudder. Her smile was forced. "Well, is there anything else you would like to share with me? Duty calls."

He put his arm out. "Kid, why don't you take today off. Let somebody cover for you for a change."

She shook her head resolutely. "No. Somebody is running a stupid, ugly game on me. Probably the same one that left a note stuck under the door at the clinic."

"What note? Where is it?"

"I don't know. The landfill. Edmund was with me and I had him put it in the garbage. I thought it was some kind of Halloween prank."

"What did it say?"

"Something about the end of 'Ms. Free Clinic' being near. About how the joker, whoever they are, was deciding whether to shoot, knife or bash. I'm supposed to wonder how and why." Her voice trailed off and her eyes wandered towards the basin. She looked back him. Her round little chin was jutted and her mouth set. "Nobody is going to intimidate me with some stupid juvenile pranks." She marched resolutely from his office.

He looked back at the doll. "Baby, let's pray that's all they are trying to do."

Chapter Twenty Eight

Dennis came through the front door of the police station. Vern buzzed him into the dispatch area and then waved him over. He motioned Dennis in close. "Dr. Grissum is waiting to see you."

Dennis looked through the pass through window. "I don't see him."

"He's in letting the chief fawn over him but he wouldn't let the chief handle whatever problem he's got. Told me he needed someone who knew what they were doing, not a pencil necked, paper pusher who needed a K-9 to find his ass." Dennis and the dispatcher exchanged knowing looks.

Vern buzzed Dennis into the squad room. The chief bounced up and motioned through his window for Dennis before the door clicked behind him.

"Sir?" Dennis said.

"You have met Dr. Grissum, chief of staff at the hospital, haven't you, Cobb?"

Dennis kept his face carefully under control as he answered. "Yes, sir."

"Good, good. Dr. Grissum wishes to discuss something with you. Please use my office." The chief shook Grissum's hand and then pulled the door shut.

"There goes a walking waste of the taxpayer's money," Grissum said as he watched the chief start badgering working officers.

Dennis swung a chair around and straddled it. "So, Doc, what's up?"

"That better be unintentional," Grissum growled. He reached over and picked up the basin he had set on the floor. "A couple of the nurses found this in the linen closet up in pediatrics today." He stood and set it on the chief's desk. Dennis got up and joined him. Grissum pulled the towel off.

Dennis whistled softly under his breath. "Somebody's a sick puppy."

Grissum watched him carefully study it. When Dennis' eyes widened and he drew in his breath with a sharp intake, Grissum spoke. "You see it, too. The deliberate resemblance."

"Daphne." It was a flat statement, not a question.

"Yes. I saw it and she saw it."

"You showed this to Daphne?"

Grissum tossed the covering towel down beside the basin and returned to sit in the chair. "Cobb, I guess you know I love that girl more than life but I've been around too many years to presume innocence in anyone for anything. I wanted to see her reaction. I guess I wanted to be sure she hadn't done it herself."

Dennis turned his attention to Grissum. "And?"

"She had a major shock reaction. Sudden onset of pallor, hyperventilation, palpations, clammy skin, acute tremors. Textbook classic. You can fake some of the symptoms but not basic neurological responses." He frowned. "I probably wouldn't have done it that way if I had known about the note."

Dennis sat back down although his eyes strayed to the basin. "What note?"

"She says there was a note shoved under the door at the clinic. She and Edmund read it."

"Where is it?"

"Garbage. She thought it was a stupid Halloween prank. Had Edmund deep six it."

Dennis lifted an eyebrow. "She didn't say anything about it last night."

Grissum raised his eyebrow in turn. "Seeing a lot of my girl, aren't you."

Dennis grinned. "We have been well-chaperoned. My kids have always been with us. Except for last night. We had about twenty gang bangers instead. They brought a shooting victim in." Dennis was thoughtful for a moment. "Probably slipped her mind in all the excitement. Did she tell you what was in it?"

"Said it was a death threat. That the sender was trying to decide whether to shoot, knife, or bash. Daphne was supposed to wonder how and why."

"And today this is in the pediatric unit." Both men looked at the bloody doll.

"Don't forget the two crank calls," Grissum reminded him.

Dennis rubbed a forefinger under his lip. "Yeah, they could have been a warming up exercise. The real questions are who and why? If we knew that then we could answer the last question."

"What's that?"

"How far do they intend to go?"

Grissum leaned forward and looked at Dennis with steel in his grey eyes. "You get the answers to questions one and two real quick. If Daphne's life is on the line, nobody better bobble. Anything happens to my girl and hell will be a welcome place for whoever is responsible. Do I make myself clear?"

Dennis' eyes hardened in answer. "You are not the only one who gives a damn what happens to her so I expect your full cooperation because the only thing we do know for sure is the person behind this has a link to the hospital. I will want access to personnel files, grievances, complaints, anything at all that might point us in the right direction. Do I make myself clear?"

The two men remained locked in their challenge. Then Grissum nodded. "I'll even supply the hot lights and rubber hoses if that's what you need."

Dennis smiled. "I keep those in the back of my car. I just need files and access to information on the computer."

Grissum stood up. "I'll assign one of those nitwits they hire for their boobs not brains up front to help. They are so clueless they haven't figured out where they work yet. They shouldn't guess what you are up to. I want this to be low profile. If someone gets the idea we are breathing down their neck, it might push them into action before we find them and stop them." He started for the door.

Dennis spoke over his shoulder. "Doc, we got one other problem."

Grissum swung back and looked at him, eyebrows pulled together in a questioning frown. Then his expression cleared as the two men looked at each other.

"Daphne," they said in unison.

* * *

Eydie hovered in the background after summoning Dr. Grissum to the telephone. When he returned to the floor, he had issued an order all phone calls from the Kelton Police Department were to be put through to him 'stat'.

"Doc, I got the note."

"How the hell did you manage that?"

"Daphne's cousin. He didn't like the fit of the situation. Squirreled it out of the clinic when she wasn't looking.

"And?"

"It's exactly what Daphne described. An articulate threat against her person."

"What's your take on it?"

"Frankly, it scares the hell out of me. The writer says 'it pleasures the mind to consider the possibilities'. That tells me we are dealing with someone who is fantasizing, playing out the scene over and over mentally. Eventually just thinking about it won't be enough. They will feel the compulsion to act."

"But we got some time, right. They are still thinking about it according to what you just told me."

"That's what the note says. There's just one thing, Doc."

"What's that?"

"We don't know how long they have been thinking."

"You're saying we are sitting on a hand grenade, the pin's been pulled, and we don't know the count."

"Exactly."

A chill climbed up Grissum's back. He clamped his teeth down so hard on the cigar he had absently stuck in his mouth, he bit the end off. He spat it out. He felt helpless against the encroaching threat. He would have torn open the gates of hell itself for the skinny little waif who had wormed her way to the very center of his being. But there was no face, no form, nothing he could grab and rend apart.

"So what do we do? Wait until it's too late?"

Dennis felt the man's fear and anger coming down the phone line. "Yes, Doc. We wait. Wait and watch. And while we're doing that, we do our best to keep her under wraps."

"That'll be a hell of a trick. Like stuffing a she-cobra with advanced PMS in a basket with your bare teeth."

"We'll do it one day at time and tonight is taken care of."

"Yeah?"

"She's going to babysit the kids while I'm out on a date."

"You know, Cobb, I was almost beginning to like you."

"My date is work and you are my dance partner, Doc. We gonna stage a raid on those files at the hospital. The perp knows her routine. That tells me, if they are affiliated with the hospital, they are present during the same shift she is. That's day shift. We come in during the day and we may tip our hand. We come in at night, it's quiet, a different shift, front office shut down, draws less attention."

"Not bad," Grissum said. "Only one thing, Ginger Rogers. I lead."

Eydie came to lean on the counter after Grissum hung up the phone. "Is there a problem, Hal? Would it help to talk?"

He turned his eyes towards her but she sensed she was unseen. "Yeah, I got a date and I don't have a damn thing to wear."

Chapter Twenty Nine

The night had not been restful for Lygia. She had been pursued through her sleeping moments by dark fears and her waking moments by a growing self-loathing. Instead of marching through her morning routine with her usual precision, she had stumbled about, arriving at the office minus both her earrings and lipstick.

Throughout the morning, her thoughts kept conjuring up Edmund. Everything was getting mixed in her head. The dreams were overlapping reality and the whole causing a rising sense of dread within her. By the time Rebecca returned from lunch, Lygia was gripped by a mysterious compulsion to find Edmund. She came into the reception room, her coat and purse slung over her arm. "Cancel the rest of my appointments. I'm going out. I'll have my phone but I don't want anything unless it's from Edmund Broadhurst or my mother."

"What should I tell your patients?"

"Tell them I have an emergency." And though she didn't know why, Lygia knew somehow it was the truth.

Lygia parked her Audi in the Hanson Building's parking lot. The grey drizzle sent a shiver she felt to her soul as she got out of the car. It was the season of death. The trees stood bare. Their wet branches were blackened bones rattling in the rain. The brilliant foliage fallen to a dank, decaying shroud on the parking lot. There was keening in the wind.

The panic was swelling in her. She felt pressed to action without understanding. Her heels clicked impatiently as she hurried to the door bearing the gypsy symbol. She tried the handle. It was locked. She knocked anyway.

Edmund sat in his high-backed leather chair staring out the window at the sky. It was the same slate color as his soul. He heard the knocking but found he had no interest in whoever was outside his door. The handholds in this life were running out. He was readying himself to swing out over the chasm and let go.

Lygia leaned her ear to the door and listened. It was a futile gesture she knew as the English oak door would obliterate all but loud sounds. Finally, she turned and walked slowly back towards the elevator.

Back in her car, she sat and watched the rain drops run together and form little rivulets down her windshield. She talked logically to herself. There was no reason for this sense of impending doom engulfing her. She was behaving irrationally, operating on emotion with no basis in fact. She should go back to her clinic and conclude her business for the day. Then she could go to the gym and work out whatever remained of this madness on the Nautilus equipment. Yes, that was the rational approach.

She turned on her engine and in fifteen minutes was nosing her car into the curb in front of Edmund's house in the Heights.

She was on the porch, knocking when she heard a woman's voice from behind her. She turned to see a tall woman hurrying up the second tier of stairs. "I'll be right there."

She stepped back as the woman climbed up the porch stairs, stopping to pull off a rain bonnet. Her dark red hair was coiled in a braided chignon at the base of her neck. The woman had a red-head's delicate white skin and deep aquamarine colored eyes.

Lygia recognized the heavy satchel the woman carried in one hand as being English in origin. Setting it down, she pulled keys out of her rain coat pocket to unlock the front door. Lygia was taken aback. She had not anticipated a woman in Edmund's life.

Once the door was unlocked, the woman turned back with a charming smile. "How may I help you?"

"I'm Lygia Ashe. I am trying to locate Mr. Broadhurst. He wasn't at his office. I thought perhaps he was here."

The woman bent and picked up the satchel. "Ah, yes. Dr. Ashe. Edmund has spoken of you. Won't you please come in out of this beastly weather. I am in dire need of a cup of hot tea. Would you join me? Perhaps, between the two of us we can track down the elusive Edmund."

She deposited the satchel on the floor by a coat tree before slipping off her raincoat and hanging it up. She held out her hands to take Lygia's coat. Once secured on a branch already filled with assorted attire, she led the way down the dark hall to the swinging door at the end. It led to a large, old-fashioned kitchen. Other than a microwave sitting discreetly on a cart, there was no evidence of modern appliances.

The woman filled a teapot and placed it on the gas range. Turning up the fire, she turned back with a smile. "I must go and check on Aunt Anne. Her sitter has a miserable cold and wasn't able to come today. It's mid-terms this week and I had to be with my classes. Unfortunately Edmund had already gone or he would have stayed with his mother."

Lygia quickly connected the information. "Then you are Edmund's cousin?"

The woman turned her hand up in apology. "Oh, my. I haven't even introduced myself yet." She held out a slender, strong hand. "I am Katlyn Talmek, Edmund's cousin, as you have correctly surmised. But please call me Kat."

Kat was pushing through the kitchen door again when Lygia spoke. "Would it be inappropriate to meet Edmund's mother?" She found she was intensely curious about Edmund's life.

Kat eyed her enigmatically. "No. Anne certainly won't mind."

Lygia followed Kat down the dark hall to the stairs near the front door. Kat climbed the graceful old stairs to the upper hall. She paused in front of a door to the left of the head of the stairs, and looked at Lygia as though she was about to say something. Instead she turned the handle and went into the room.

Lygia stepped in quietly behind her. She wasn't sure what she had expected to be behind the door following Kat's remark about Anne's sitter. Perhaps Grace Poole keeping watch over the mad Mrs. Broadhurst. Instead she was stunned by the pure beauty and elegance of the room. The cool white carpeting looked as though it had been woven out of moonbeams. A bed with delicately turned spindles supported a genuine Alsace lace canopy. A lilac silk duvet covered the comforter. The pillows were edged in exquisite hand embroidery. The several chairs were feminine and covered in soft rose velvet. Accents of lupine blue, moss green and a pale sunglow yellow gave the impression of walking into secret garden.

Kat went to kneel before a woman who sat looking out the window. She was dressed in a gown reminiscent of the type worn during the age of chivalry. The yoke, sleeves and hem traced over with dainty crewel stitchery. When she turned her face towards Kat, Lygia could see a pale, fragile loveliness little marked by the passage of time. Kat gently took the woman's hands and led her to the door. "We'll be right back," she murmured as she led the woman out. The woman may or may not have noticed her. The sweet smile never changing as she passed Lygia.

Lygia looked around the room and spotted a photo in a sterling frame on the woman's night table. She went to look. It was a younger vision of the same woman. The beauty was startling but it was not the beauty which captured the eye. It was the life flowing from her. She was laughing in the picture, a small towheaded boy encircled by her arms. The same laughter and life mirrored in his little face. Lygia mentally compared it with the face of the man he had become. The adult face had fulfilled the promise of masculine beauty. But the expression had become one of cold cynicism; the eyes now wary and predatory and the mobile mouth given to small mocking smiles. She wondered when the last time was he had laughed with the same joy and abandonment as was captured in the picture.

Kat came back with the woman and carefully reseated her in the chair. The woman turned her eyes again to the window. She never made a sound. Kat carefully arranged the two small feet in embroidered velvet slippers on the footstool. She reached over and pulled a pale yellow mohair lap robe off a small carved chest and tucked it around Anne. The woman paid no more attention to the ministrations than a doll.

Kat stood up and bent over to kiss her aunt on her forehead before leading the way from the room.

Back in the kitchen the kettle was whistling cheerily.

Lygia sat down at the table and thoughtfully watched Kat pour hot water in the teapot to heat it, then empty it out before measuring in the tea, and adding the hot water. It was the same way her own mother made her tea...the old world way.

When Kat finally sat across from her, the tea steeping between them, Lygia spoke. "It's not Alzheimer's, is it."

Kat reached up to pull the pins from her hair, letting the heavy braid fall around one shoulder. "No, it's not."

"How long has she been like this?"

Kat scrunched her forehead in thought. "Nearly thirty years."

"But the picture," Lygia exclaimed, then blushed. "I'm sorry. I saw it while you were out of the room. It's Edmund and his mother, isn't it."

"Yes. It was the last picture taken of them before his world imploded." Kat expertly poured the tea. She motioned towards the lazy susan on the table. "Brown sugar is all we have, I'm afraid. I can get cream if you want it."

Lygia reached out to spoon some sugar in her tea. "Tell me about it, please."

Kat sipped at her tea, then leaned back. "I'm afraid there isn't much I can tell. We don't know anything but the most general outline."

"Edmund's father was a British medical student studying here when he met Anne. They fell in love. Soon after he graduated, they married and went to England where Edward, that was Edmund's father, entered the Anglican seminary. Edmund was born a year before his ordination. It was the dream of Edward and Anne to serve as medical missionaries in Africa. They arrived in Africa when Edmund was nearly two and settled in a small village in what was then the Congo region. From letters my grandmother kept, they were supremely happy."

"Not long after that picture was taken, Anne developed a fever of some type. She needed medicine which they could only get from a nearby town. Edward and Edmund walked out late one afternoon to get the medicine, leaving Anne in the care of the villagers. They never reached the town. The next morning British game wardens found Edmund clinging to a tree in a state of deep shock. The only thing ever found of his father was his blood splattered prayer book and ordination stole he carried with him at all times."

"They are in a case in his office," Lygia said.

"Yes. The natives brought Anne to the hospital where the British had taken Edmund. His great uncle, Albert, came to Africa and took the two of them home to Manchester, England. He finished raising Edmund and cared for Anne. And that's all we know. Except a little boy lost both his parents in a sense and he has been searching for them ever since."

"No one knows what happened?"

"Edmund has no memory of that night. He has quite literally searched the world over to try and find a way to recover his memory. He has convinced himself if he could remember he would be able to reach Anne. Help her find her way back."

"Oddly enough that was how we met up with Edmund. He was in the outback of Australia with the aboriginals at the same time Elmore and I were there. We got to talking and gradually uncovered that my mother and his mother were sisters. As Albert was dead by then, we suggested he bring Anne and come live with us in this great barn of a house. We thought perhaps if Anne were exposed to the house she grew up in, it might help activate some memories. As you saw, it didn't work."

"Has he tried hypnosis, regression therapy?'

"The process required does not lie in the realm of modern medicine, Dr. Ashe. They are too limited in their understanding of man's true composition. All they see is a body or a mind."

"But what else is there to treat?"

Kat looked at Lygia thoughtfully. "When you know the answer to that question you will have the key. Your time must be very valuable. Let me ring Edmund's office and see if he's in."

She disappeared out the door and reappeared punching a number into a cordless phone. She held it to her ear for a long time. Finally she clicked off with a small frown. "How odd. Edmund always leaves his answering machine on in case Anne should need him." She punched in another number. "I'll call his cell phone. He always carries it and usually calls back in a minute."

She sat down and poured them both more tea. They made desultory talk for another fifteen minutes. Kat kept glancing at the phone, her frown deepening. "This really is most peculiar, Dr. Ashe. Edmund always keeps in closest contact with us. I can't think what he's about. I tell you what. Leave your number and I have him call you as soon as I hear from him."

Lygia produced a card from her purse and handed it over as she stood up. "My home number is on the card. I'll be there. Please don't get up. I can show myself out. And thank you for your hospitality."

Chapter Thirty

Dennis' eyes burned from the long hours of poring through records and staring at the computer screen. His head ached from being in the closed office with Grissum's interminable cigar smoke. And his gut was tight because they had walked away as empty handed as when he had arrived. He had no more idea who was targeting Daphne at 11:15 p.m. than he had at 8:15 a.m. when Grissum had thrust the bloody doll under his nose.

Pulling into the drive beside Daphne's battered little Metro, he shut off the police radio, and engine. The curtains were closed but he could see the shadow of something in his window.

When he got within a few feet of his door, the shadows took form and he found he had turkey in a pilgrim hat and another in an Indian war bonnet holding a happy thanksgiving sign in his window. He smiled as he inserted his key into the door.

Halloween's spiders and ghosts had disappeared from his front room. Now Indian corn and silk fall leaves hung in their place. A turkey sat on the shiny coffee table surrounded by a couple of miniature pumpkins, one of which bore the teeth marks of his daughter. The room smelled of furniture polish and cinnamon. Daphne's scrub jacket lay over the back of the couch, a purple stethoscope sticking out of the pocket.

He went to the kitchen door. Daphne had her back to the door as she finished putting some dishes away. A cornucopia sat amidst silk leaves and real nuts, spilling over with plastic fruit. It occupied a place of honor on a fall festive vinyl tablecloth. A plate of applesauce cookies sat on the counter beside a bowl of deep red apples, nuts, and cinnamon sticks. The kitchen cabinets were decorated with a number of drawings of turkeys. Dennis recognized the outline of tiny hands from his own grade school days, fingers for tail feathers, thumb for head. A pan was simmering on the stove and the rising steam carried the smell of wine and fruit.

Daphne turned and looked at him, a cup in hand. A little frown appeared as she studied him. "You look like you have been pulled through a knothole backwards, Cobb."

Dennis rolled his shoulders and smiled tiredly. "I feel like it." He unconsciously put his hand to his neck and rubbed as he went down the hall to see the children. They were, as he expected, peacefully sleeping, a trace of cookie crumbs still on their lips. Cortlyn had a plush turkey firmly locked under her thumb sucking arm. A toy bow and arrow set hung over the bedpost of Eric's bed. The headband, complete with feather, was lying on the pillow where it had come off in his sleep. Dennis carefully hung it on the bedpost.

He felt a small cool hand touch his. Daphne nodded towards the kitchen. "They are fine," she said. "Let's do something about you."

In the kitchen, she stepped behind him and tugged his jacket off. She shoved him towards a chair where a cup of hot mulled wine and a plate of cookies waited. Dennis automatically rolled up his sleeves as he sat down. Daphne stood behind him and proceeded to give a very professional massage of his neck, shoulders and upper back.

She said nothing as she worked. She was too busy soaking up the sensations of a female in close proximity of a desirable male. The feel of the broad muscles, the pleasure at seeing the coarse hair on the man's arm, the spray of it up the back of his hands, the breadth of the back. All of it so different from her own body and at the same time, making her appreciate her femininity as she recognized the fitting together of the two parts.

Daphne moved her hands up in rhythmic stokes to Dennis' temples. She pulled his head back until it rested against her breasts as she stroked away the lines of tension and fatigue. Dennis closed his eyes and savored her touch.

She forced herself to stop when the compulsion to kiss him became almost overpowering. She let her hands slip across and then off his shoulders as she stepped away.

She busied herself bringing the pan of mulled wine to the table and ladling more into his empty cup. Dennis took another appreciative sip. "You're spoiling us," he said.

Daphne gave a small deprecatory smile in return. "No, it's *you* who is spoiling me."

Dennis looked at her in surprise as she sat the pan back on the stove. "By letting you clean, cook, and take care of a couple of little hooligans?"

Daphne's smile became misty and her voice whispery. "Exactly. A real kitchen holds magic for someone who never had one until they were nearly sixteen. Polishing furniture that is the same last month, last week, next week means you've really unpacked. Sharing a little of the holidays celebrations with the children let's me live what I only got to watch all my growing up years. So, yes, Det. Dennis Cobb, I am being truly spoiled. And I am very grateful for these moments."

As she spoke, Dennis had the peculiar sensation of seeing a child of four or five sitting on a wet tombstone, mist leaving glistening drops in an aureole of blonde curls. The child was alone and frightened. She was hungry, thirsty, and had to go to bathroom. But she remained still and silent. The only movement were tears slipping quietly down pale cheeks.

Tears were standing in the corners of the same eyes as Daphne looked around the room. Dennis got up quietly and stood in front of her. She dropped her head to clear the tears from her eyes and voice. He cupped her face in his hands and lifted it until she was looking up at him. This time the kiss was firm and deep. As it went on, he gave into his desire to pull the combs from her hair. They clattered to the floor while the soft curls washed over his hands.

Daphne's arms moved around him as she parted her lips. His hands slid down her back, feeling the curve of her slender waist. He wrapped one arm tightly around her while the other hand slipped down over her small bottom. He pushed her into him until she could feel his hardness against her belly. Her body answered with the tingle signaling it was preparing the deepest parts of her to take him in and hold him captive.

Dennis' breath grew ragged as he moved his hand up under her scrub shirt feeling the silkiness of her back. Daphne's lips were nipping over his neck and into the hollow of his throat. He found the back of her bra and undid it. His hands slipped around to her breasts, circling them, exploring their unknown curve, weight, thrust of the nipples.

She put her head back and closed her eyes as she heard only the cries of desire her body made to be totally possessed, filled by, and ultimately satiated by this man. "Please," she begged in a low moan. Dennis slipped his arms under her and lifted her.

He carried her to the closed bedroom. He pushed the door open and deposited her on the side of the bed. Flicking on the table lamp, he pulled the scrub top off and her bra fell to the floor. He studied her, letting his hands and eyes trace the soft fullness of her engorged breasts. Her breath came in quick little pants as she arched her back towards him.

Then he stood and pulled his tie off. He reached behind him and unclipped his gun from his belt, automatically opening the closet and placing it on the shelf. He was unbuttoning his shirt when he heard a startled gasp from Daphne. He turned back to see her grabbing her scrub shirt and holding it against her nakedness, her eyes were slowly looking around the room.

"Daphne?"

She looked at him and he could see she was starting to shiver. "Dennis, we are not alone," she said quietly.

Had he frightened her with his desire for her? Had he inadvertently triggered something from her traumatic childhood? As he sat down on the bed beside her, he was encompassed by iciness as though someone had opened a window on a glacier. And as the cold engulfed him so did a sense of melancholy. It swept over him like a wave, pulling him down toward a murky empty place. Daphne was shaking so hard, she was unable to manage getting the scrub shirt back over her head. He helped her and then wrapped his shivering arms around her. Only by clinging to Daphne could he keep his head above the drowning gloom.

Daphne buried her head under his chin and sighed from the very depths of her center. "Can you hear her? She's weeping."

"I don't hear anything. Who's weeping?"

Daphne laid her hand over his heart. "Listen from here."

Dennis held her, his lips buried in her curls. He didn't understand her gifts but he realized it didn't matter. He had fallen for her. "I love you, my strange little Daphne," he thought. The moment his thoughts spoke it, he heard the weeping. It came from nowhere and everywhere. And he had heard too much of it through the years not to recognize it was, indeed, Melanie.

He jumped to his feet and swiftly scanned the room with the eye of a professional investigator.

Daphne wrapped her arms around herself and looked up at him. "You hear it."

"Yes," he said as he grabbed her arm and hauled her to her feet. He pulled her protectively under his arm as he hurried her from the room. The minute the bedroom door was shut behind them, it was quiet again.

Daphne left Dennis' side and went to slip on her scrub jacket and windbreaker.

She picked up her backpack and fished her keys out of its depths. Dennis stood watching her, willing her to stay.

Daphne came up to Dennis and stood close. She put her hand on his chest, lightly flicking the hair with her thumb. She looked up him and sadness lay in her eyes. "I am not the only one who has ghosts to exorcise. I cannot help you. You must do this alone. But know this, if you find your strength is waning, look to your heart. I will be standing there with all my love." She reached up and pulled his head down. In the tender kiss, she filled his heart.

Even before her car left the driveway, he felt the echoing emptiness of his arms and his chest swelled with rage. He stormed toward the bedroom. "Melanie!"

* * *

Daphne pulled up in front of the old manse. She grabbed at her backpack as she flung herself out of the car and raced up the tiers of steps. She flew through the front door, dropping her backpack in the doorway of the living room as she ran to the fireplace.

Her hands gripped the mantel on either side of the little crystal bell. "Mom, Mom, I need you. Please, Mom." She stared at the silent bell. "Mother!" There was desperation in her cry. The tiny teardrop of crystal on the end of the delicate chain inside the bell began to move and soon struck the sides sending out a tinkling response.

"Mom, please, you have to help him. You have to go and help him."

"Help who, darling? Help how?"

Daphne closed her eyes and concentrated her thoughts bringing his face clearly into her mind. "Dennis."

"Ah, yes. Your gentlemen friend. Why would he need my help?"

"She won't let him go, Mom. She made his life hell when she was alive and now she won't let him go. She's still trying to hold him."

"Who?"

"Melanie, his dead wife. I've heard her in the bedroom every time I'm there. She's weeping and she won't leave him. Tonight, we were making love and we went into the bedroom. She was battling us, Mom. And now, he's going to fight her. Please help him, Mom. Please do what you can to help him. Please." Sobs of fear choked off her words.

She felt the tender ice of her mother's lips on her cheek. "Concentrate on him, darling. I must use your thoughts to find him." The bell on the mantel went still but Daphne heard the faint ringing of the wind chimes outside the front door. She continued to cling to the fireplace and brought all the power of her mind to focus on Dennis.

* * *

Dennis slammed the door to the bedroom behind him as he had done a thousand times during their marriage. "Melanie. You nearly destroyed me when you were alive. You will not interfere now that you are dead. Do you hear that, Melanie, you are dead. You chose it. You made it happen."

The weeping grew louder. Once more icy waves of soul swamping despondency washed over him. He staved them off by keeping his rage hot.

"You chose Fred, remember. Fred was all you wanted. When you were alive, I never existed for you. You never wanted me. It was all Fred. You ruined every minute of our marriage with your obsession for Fred. Look around, Melanie. You see this?" He swooped up the comforter from the bed. "You bought this because it was the one you and Fred had picked out." Dennis grabbed it in two hands and tore it apart. He went to the window and tore the matching curtains down. He went to her dresser and opened the bottom drawer. "Look, Melanie, look at all the love letters you wrote to Fred. How many did you ever write me?" Dennis pulled them out by the handful, shredding them. He pulled open the top drawer and grabbed a stack of pictures. "You made me hate him. My oldest and dearest friend and you made me hate the memory of him." Dennis tore the pictures in bits scattering them over the mounting wreckage.

A little band of clowns stared up from the depths of the drawer watching his savagery. They had been given to Melanie by Fred. When he noticed them, he picked them up and one by one smashed them against the wall. The weeping was so loud, now, it roared in his ears. His rage against her was dissipating. The waves of despondency washed over him again and again, sucking the fire out of him. He dropped back against the wall, burying his face in his hands. He tried to focus on Daphne, remember the taste of her flesh, the warmth of her lips, the feel of her, but it was blurry as though the lines of her were gradually being erased.

He lifted his head and leaned it back against the wall. "What do you want from, Melanie? I have nothing left to give you."

A female voice, unfamiliar and yet, comforting, slipped across his collapsing thoughts. "Forgiveness. Melanie needs your forgiveness."

Dennis turned his head back and forth. "I can't give her that."

"For Daphne, Dennis, do it for Daphne." And she was there, clear and strong in his mind. He could feel her weight against his chest, the pressure of her arms around his neck, the heat of her lips on his. And just beyond the sense of Daphne, he saw Melanie. Weak, self-centered, confused Melanie. Melanie who had grown up so cosseted and sheltered, she knew nothing of survival.

He saw Melanie was incapable of being the wife and mother he had wanted her to be. She had clung to Fred's memory as a child clings to a blanket for comfort and to shield her from the vast, hostile adult world she was unable to cope with. She had taken to the alcohol and pills to try to find the courage she did not possess. She had been a scared child all those years and he had missed that. Her attack on Cortlyn had been a final scream for help and he had walked away from her. He had never looked beyond her failures. And that became his great failure.

He looked at Melanie and whispered. "I'm sorry, Melanie. I failed you far more than you failed me. Forgive me. Please forgive me." Then Dennis collapsed on the bed and wept for Melanie the tears he had denied her at death.

Daphne let her hands drop from the mantel. She was unspeakably tired. She staggered to the old couch and dropped. She tried to keep awake and her thoughts on Dennis. A coolness touched her forehead. "Sleep, baby, sleep.

Chapter Thirty One

After pacing the floor for hours waiting for Edmund's call Lygia had fallen into a restless sleep. She lay across her bed now, still fully clothed as she chased down the tunnels of her subconscious looking for someone.

She found him sitting in his chair at his office. A great knife plunged into his chest. She wrestled with it. If she could get it out, he would live. But she couldn't keep a grip on the handle, slippery with his blood. She looked for something to aid her and grabbed his father's stole. The knife melted as she wrapped the stole around it.

She awoke with a start. She swung around to sit on the edge of the bed. The formless dread she felt was growing to pathologic proportions, causing her heart to race in her tight chest. She ran her hands through her hair, clutching at it. Was this what madness was? Trying to find your way through an alien country where all the landmarks have been changed?

But it wasn't an alien land. It was more like a land she hadn't visited for a long time, changed only by the length of absence. She knew this country. It was part of her.

Lygia lifted her head and drew her breath in sharply. She did know this land. Suddenly, it all clicked together. Kat's talk of a part of that was neither mind nor body. It was soul country. It was the key. She had it. She reached for the telephone.

A sleepy voice mumbled on the receiving end.

"Mama, get dressed, I'm coming for you. Now." Lygia hung up and literally ran to get her purse and keys. She pulled up into the driveway of her mother's tiny shabby house in the old section of town. She left her car running and the door ajar as she ran up the steps. It opened immediately. Her mother was still tying the bright flowered scarf over her loosely bound dark hair.

"Twenty years you come only Sunday afternoon. 2 a.m. you decide you want your mama."

Lygia reached around her, and grabbing a black coat, flung it around her mother's shoulders. "Mama, hurry. It is soul sickness. The time, it runs," she said unaware she had lapsed back into the speech rhythms of her youth.

Her mother turned her face up to her daughter. The years made her look like a quizzical little monkey. Bei Ashlokev turned from the door and hurried towards her bedroom.

"Mama?" Lygia cried.

"There are things I must have," she answered and she disappeared behind the faded paisley curtain.

In a moment, the curtain pushed back and she trotted to her daughter, a fanny pack around her waist. "We should go now."

Lygia backed the car out of the narrow drive and turned towards the other side of town.

"Where is this, your patient?" Bei asked as she held on to the edge of the window with one hand and the console with the other when Lygia floored the gas pedal.

"He's not my patient, Mama. He is a man I…a man I know."

"So how do you think he needs of help like mine?"

"There is darkness in this man, I have felt it. This man has been asking something of me but I cannot hear; I will not hear what it is he needs. I shut him out. Now I feel I have condemned him to something terrible. His cousin spoke of the place that is neither mind nor body. It is there I feel he is being lost. In the soul. You know that place, Mama. You will help him."

"This we wait to be seen."

Lygia pulled the car up in front of the Hansen Building. She jumped out running to the glass doors. They were locked. Lygia dug in her purse and pulled out the identification the police department had given her when they contracted for her services. She knocked on the glass and placed it flat against the window for the security guard to view. He moved slowly as he studied it before carefully unlocking the door.

"Come on, come on, you dumb bastard," Lygia muttered between clenched teeth.

When he finally held the door open, Lygia pulled her mother in. "You have keys to all the doors in this office building, don't you."

"Yes, ma'am. But I need a warrant or something to unlock anyone's door."

"You have the right to unlock any door if you believe there is the possibility of someone being harmed or doing harm to themselves."

"Well, yes." His eyes widened. "You're that psychologist. . .ah . . .ah, the baby killer case. You think someone is going to get hurt."

"Yes. One of my patients didn't report in today. I have been treating him for severe depression. He has not returned to his home and his family called me, fearful for his life."

"Wow. I'll help if I can."

"I need the key to 313 at once."

"Mr. Broadhurst's office. I would never have thought. Come to think of it though, he's pretty strange acting at times."

"If we don't get moving, we may be too late."

The guard hurried away and returned in a moment with a gold key hanging from a small medallion. He held it out as they pushed the button for the elevator. "It's a roman coin, he says. Very valuable."

Lygia nodded as she willed the elevator to move more quickly. At Edmund's door, the guard hesitated. "I don't know, Mr. Broadhurst has a lot of expensive stuff in there. Maybe I should call my supervisor."

Lygia was just opening her mouth to call down the guard when they all heard the crash of glass being smashed. The guard swallowed hard, his hands shaking as he opened the door. They pushed into the waiting room where they could see Edmund leaning on the edges of the case enclosing his father's icons. The glass was shattered and blood ran from his hands.

"Geez, lady. You want me to call the police?"

Bei pushed him toward the door. "I want you should get your ass out of here, is what I should want."

Lygia guided the guard to the door. "I believe we can handle it. We'll call if we need help."

The guard looked back at Edmund and nodded. "Just push the 6 on the telephone. That's rings directly to me."

Lygia gave him a reassuring smile as she shoved him into the hall, closing and locking the door.

Her mother was already at Edmund's side. She was speaking in the old language. He turned his face slowly towards her as though he were listening from a far place. Bei reached out and lifted his hands. "Lygia, find me something to wrap. It is not good here."

Lygia hurried around the desk and opened the door she presumed led to the bathroom. There were no first aid supplies but the hand towels were linen. She grabbed one and carried it to the desk. Opening the center drawer, she found scissors to cut strips which she handed to her mother.

Bei carefully wrapped the hands though the still flowing blood immediately stained the white linen. Edmund watched disinterestedly as if it were happening to someone else.

Bei spoke to her daughter as she worked. "You, too, should go, Lygia. You know not of this."

"I will stay, Mama."

Bei fixed a stern eye on her daughter. "Then you will do as I say. To do anything without me to tell you could cause that which you do not want. You are understanding me?"

Lygia nodded.

"Then you go and sit there on the floor. You should hold his head in your lap."

Lygia went into the waiting room and sat down, her back against the leather couch. Bei turned her attention to Edmund and spoke to him in words Lygia could not make out. Bei placed her hands on either side of Edmund's face and drew his face down till she could look him in the eyes. Then she led him in the reception room. He came docile as a child. She stopped to slip him out of his blood spattered suede jacket. Reaching up, she undid his tie, pulling it off. She unbuttoned the neck button on his shirt and the bloody cuffs, rolling them back. Taking him lightly by his wounded hands, she pulled him towards the floor. He dropped to his knees. She pushed at his shoulders until he lay down and rolled onto his back. Lygia maneuvered quickly to catch his head in her lap.

His eyes were hollow and empty, his skin pale and cold. It was as though he was already in death's ante-chamber.

Bei unzipped the fanny pack and set out a small bottle of holy water, a crucifix, a pouch of herbs, a silver dish, matches, and her rosary.

As she sprinkled the herbs into the bowl, she spoke to Lygia. "We know not what we will see as we enter into the place of this man's soul. But, daughter, you should be remembering it will only be the memories we see. They cannot hurt us. They have no power. Do not judge them. Do not have feelings towards them. Let them blow away like the dust."

She put a match to the herbs, infusing the air with pungent smoke. She sat the dish close to Edmund's head. She slipped the crucifix inside Edmund's shirt, just over his heart. "You will say not a thing. You will keep within your heart and mind the picture of this man with no shadows. You will pray for this that is about to happen. You are understanding?"

Lygia nodded and gently smoothed a lock of hair back from Edmund's forehead.

"We should to begin."

Bei knelt quietly, her rosary slipping through her fingers as she prayed. Then taking the small bottle of water, she turned it, wetting her finger and lightly touching it to Edmund's forehead, eyes, mouth and chest.

She murmured soft prayers as she moved her hands in ritualistic strokes over his face, chest, and hands. Edmund stiffened and arched away from her. They repeated this pattern a number of times. Finally Lygia could see his resistance gradually diminishing.

"He is strong, this one," her mother said softly as she continued, "How hard he fights." Finally, Edmund gave a small moan and went limp. Bei looked at Lygia and whispered, "His name?"

"Edmund."

Bei took Edmund's wounded hands tenderly in her own. She held them, her thumbs circling over the backs as she spoke to him. "Edmund, you are now safe within my arms. You cannot be harmed. It is the blackness to which I want to talk. Give to me your blackness."

Edmund's head began to turn back and forth on Lygia's lap. "You will make the circles on his temples even as I do here," she said to her daughter. Lygia placed her fingers on his temples and began to make gentle circles.

"The blackness, Edmund. We will look at it together. Tell me."

When his voice came, it was not a man's deep voice but the light voice of a young child. "Mummy is sick. She doesn't know me. Daddy says we need medicine from Bomongo. He is going to walk to get it. I want to go with him. It scares me because Mummy doesn't know me."

"He is letting you go?"

"We are walking out now. It is only a four miles. I have made the walk many times. It will be dark when we get there. Daddy says they will bring us back in their lorry with the medicine."

Edmund's breath began to come more quickly as though he were running.

"What scares you, child?"

"It's getting dark, I can't see very well. But I feel something is following us. I can hear movement in the bush. Daddy feels it, too. He is holding my hand too tight and hurrying. I have to run. I'm getting scared."

Lygia looked at her mother. She knew where he was. It was his dream she had been drawn into. She opened her mouth to speak, but bit back the words when Len Bei shot her a warning look.

Edmund was breathing hard and making little whimpers of fear. "Where are you running to?"

"The banyan tree. Daddy is pushing me up it now. Telling me to climb high and stay put. To make no sound. He will stay at the bottom and protect us."

Edmund's body began to tremble violently. Lygia jumped when a scream came out of the very depths of him. "Daddy! No!"

Bei released his hands and slipped her arms around his neck, pulling him to her ample bosom, and rocking him like a child. "You are safe. In your safety, tell me what you see."

"Cats, big cats with the faces of men. They are hurting my Daddy. They have terrible claws. They are tearing him. I can smell the blood. He is crying out in pain. It's dark. I can't see my Daddy. I can't hear him. Mummy, where's Mummy." He began to sob against Bei.

"Hush, *tikno*. Little boy, be at peace. The blackness is melting away. It is fading into the light. It cannot not come for you anymore. It is old, this blackness. It is weak, this blackness. It must leave because you know this blackness now. You can name it and when it is named it cannot be blackness. You have made it through this night. This long, black night. But now the day must claim you. The day with its light. To prepare for this day, you must rest, *chavo*. Sleep, boy, sleep. And wake a man in the light."

Edmund's breathing gradually became quiet and his death grip on Bei's dress relaxed. She helped to lay him back down in Lygia's lap. "Now, you must hold him. Stroke him. Comfort him in his sleep. He is weary and he must still the journey make back from the dark place."

Bei knelt another minute, her eyes closed and her lips moving silently. Then she reached out and began to gather up her things, slipping them back into her fanny pack.

She stood up and snapped it around her waist. "I am to take a cab home." She pulled up her full skirt, revealing an electric yellow silk petticoat. Safety pinned to the waist was a ribbon sewn to an old fashioned cloth change purse. She opened the change purse and took out several bills. Snapping it shut, she let it drop and shook her dress down over it. Lygia wondered how many hundreds of times through her growing up years she had seen her mother perform this exact same act. It used to embarrass her, but this morning, it was a profoundly comforting ritual to watch again.

Bei pointed to the slumbering Edmund. "He wakes up, you feed him. And none of this phoney baloney stuff neither. You feed him real food. You understanding me?"

Lygia smiled at her mother. Second only to her mother's prayers for people was her need to feed them. "I will, Mamma. "

"Okay, I go now. That young man, he can phone me a cab." Bei started for the door. Lygia spoke. "Mamma, I am needing a kiss."

Bei looked back around the door at her daughter. "He wakes up. You come kiss me."

When the door closed, Lygia looked down. Edmund was in a deep, natural sleep. She touched his soft hair. She could smell the expensive cologne he used. It had a rich smoky smell. She slid her hand down his chest. His shoulders were wide and his waist narrow. There were no bulked up muscles, but she could feel hardness and strength under the fine cotton shirt. He made a small sound and rolled onto his side burying his head against her, his arm circling her waist. She cradled his head in one arm. She lightly stroked his shoulder and back with her free hand.

She looked up at the dark window. In a little while, this would be over and she would return to her life. Her narrow, sterile, empty life. The thought weighed down her heart. She no longer wanted to move through her days an obedient robot to her day planner. She suddenly desired color, flavors, risks, passion. She craved life in all its brilliant, messy, unpredictable hues.

She thought of her mother's house. There was always a procession of people. They came for advice; for her to *dukker*, speak the future for them, to comfort them, and when the occasion merited, to scold them. They brought their spouses, their children, their friends. The house always smelled of herbs, spices, rich coffees, Turkish tobacco, hot breads. There was noise in the little house. People laughed deeply, sobbed loudly, yelled passionately. It was a messy house, the colors clashed, cats hung on every window sill, plants spouted everywhere. There were too many cushions, too many shawls and scarves, too many pictures on the walls and too many knick-knacks on every surface. But god, it throbbed with life.

When she was growing up, her friends always wanted to go to her house. How funny she should have forgotten. Her mother let them dress up in her clothes, put on her make-up. She made them treats, fresh and hot from the stove. Lygia remembered the little girl with the bright red hair and million freckles. She didn't even know cookies came from anywhere but a cellophane package. She let them make noise, laugh and play their cassette tapes till all hours of the morning. She gave them unconditional affection and attention. All of which her daughter had come to disdain.

Lygia developed a passion for gorgio homes after her humiliation in junior high when she was accused of being a thief only because she was part gypsy. She had been cut by prejudice and she had let it bleed away her heritage. She had determined someday no one would know she was gypsy. She would be all gorgio, all non-gypsy. And she had succeeded. She had buried the gypsy in herself, leaving only the white portion. She hadn't remembered, to her mother's people, white symbolized death.

Edmund stirred. He moaned as he put weight on his injured hand. He rolled onto his back and opened his eyes.

She brushed his hair back. "How do you feel?"

He looked up at her. "What happened?" he asked hoarsely.

Lygia smiled. "You met my mother."

"What is she, a lorry moonlighting as a sumo wrestler?"

"No. She is *rawnie*."

"A great lady?"

"Yes, very great lady."

"*Tacher rat?*

"Yes. True blood."

Edmund put his hand down to push off the floor and groaned again. He leaned on his forearm and maneuvered to a sitting position. He looked at his hands. The torn linen strips were dark with blood.

Lygia got to her knees beside him. "You smashed your father's case last night. I'm afraid I tore up one of your towels to make bandages."

"Smashed the case? I don't remember."

Lygia got to her feet and helped Edmund to his. He swayed dangerously for a moment. She moved against him, putting her arm around his waist, to support him.

"Maybe you better sit down."

"No, no. Just give me a moment." He put his arm across her shoulders and leaned for a moment, his forehead resting against the top of her head.

Still using her for support, he turned to his office, pulling her with him. He dropped his arm off her at the case. There was blood on the glass he had broken with his bare hands, blood had dripped down the side and made spots on the carpet.

He leaned on the case much as when she had first seen him last night. "It's all so dark. Like looking into a deep shadow," he said.

She came around to the side of the case and took hold of his arms. "Look now, Edmund. Look for the dark. The dark chamber within you. It is empty."

Edmund stared into the case; then turned his face to Lygia. "You know? You can tell me?"

"Come, sit. I will tell you of a small, terrified boy."

Guiding him to his chair, she knelt at his feet and carefully held his hands as her mother had done. She told him what they had witnessed the night before. Edmund listened intently and when she was through, laid his head back, rolling it to look out the window. "I still don't remember."

"You may never remember. You were a very young child and it was a horribly traumatic event you lived through. It is not necessary to remember. You know the name of your darkness now so it has no power over you."

He continued to look out the window silently. Lygia reached up and placed her hands on either side of his face, bringing it back to her. "I speak the truth my mother spoke to you last night. You have come out on the other side of the long night into the day."

As Edmund looked at her, he heard the echo of her words within him. He knew his darkness, but what he sought within it was not there. He looked over her head, murmuring, "But nothing for her. There was nothing for her."

Lygia knew he spoke of his mother. She reached up to wrap her arms around his neck, pulling his head down to rest in the crook of her neck. His hands clutched at her sweater even as they had at her mother's dress last night. "No. There was nothing," she whispered.

He only gave himself up to her womanly comfort for a few minutes. Last night Bei had held the boy. Today, Lygia held the man. He straightened up, his gaze turned inward. Lygia saw the tiny flicker of hope extinguish. Only infinite sadness remained. Finally, he came back to the room and looked at her. Her face was pale with fatigue. There were bluish circles under the black pools of her eyes. Her mouth, innocent of artifice, was soft and vulnerable like a child's.

"You are exhausted, Dr. Ashe."

His use of her formal title sent a spasm through her. It had the effect of negating the intimacy she had felt through the long night. She reached out and grasped the corner of his desk, pulling herself to her feet. What had she expected? They were the same people they had been before. An ocean of differences still surged between their two worlds.

So why did she feel rejected by him and why did it hurt? Thoughts and feelings staggered and stumbled into each other. She didn't even possess a sense of who she was anymore.

It was probably because Edmund was right. She was tired…tired to the bone. Too much had happened in too short of time. She just needed time and space to get her world back in order.

She gave a wan smile and went to the reception room to get her purse. It was under Edmund's jacket. She lifted his jacket to pull it out. Before she could lay it back down, he was taking it out of her hand. He hung it over his arm as he tugged down his cuffs and buttoned them, wincing a little.

"I shall take you home."

Lygia fumbled in her purse for her keys. "That won't be necessary. I can manage. In fact, I should take you home."

He reached out and took the keys from her hand. "Nonsense. You are much too fatigued to be trusted behind the wheel."

He opened the door and stood back as she went through.

He gingerly handed her into her car. She didn't sleep on the way to her condo but she drifted close to it.

She was struggling to stay on her feet by the time Edmund unlocked the door and drew her in. He guided her to the bedroom and sat her on the edge of the bed. He knelt, slipping off her shoes. He tugged her sweater out from under her bottom and over her head before pulling her back to her feet to strip off her leggings. He reached behind her and turned down the bedding. He pushed her down on her pillow and drew the sheet up. Reaching under the sheet, he unfastened her bra, slipping it off while maintaining her modesty. Lygia rolled on her side, already drifting into sleep as he tucked the blanket around her bare shoulders.

Chapter Thirty Two

Kat came down the stairs, her long hair streaming over her royal blue quilted robe. She was tapping her finger on her upper lip, a sure sign she was worrying something in her mind. She had climbed to Edmund's attic room and found no sign he had been in during the night. He had not phoned either. Edmund was eccentric in his habits, but he was always courteously careful to make sure the family would not worry and could reach him in an emergency. It was just so odd.

She was mid-way down when the door opened, the pale grey of the dawn a mere sliver on the horizon. "Edmund?"

"M'dear." He reached out to turn on the little hall lamp in its dusty pink ruffled shade. Kat could see the makeshift bandages clearly for a moment as he withdrew his hand.

She hurried down the stairs. "My lord, what happened? Come here let me get a better look." She motioned him to the living room where the wall sconces still burned. She untied the strips and carefully pulled them away. They stuck to the deeper cuts.

"I'm going to get Daphne. These need proper tending," she said letting the bandages hang.

A sleepy voice came from the couch. "Get Daphne for what? Ow."

"Daphne?"

A tousled blonde head rose above the back of the couch and an arm holding a stethoscope flopped over the zebra skin. "Do not, I repeat, do not sleep on one of these. My right kidney is now permanently dented."

"What are you doing on the couch?"

"I was helping Mom."

"Helping your mother do what, for pete's sake? Grow moss?"

The bell on the mantle tinkled indignantly.

"What's with you, cuz?" Daphne worked at getting the sleep out of her eyes. Finally, she was able to focus on the visible cuts and the still hanging bandages. She slipped off the couch at once and came to check his hands. "Arm wrestling piranha? Juggling razor blades? Donating blood the hard way?"

Daphne looked up at him, although the familiar small smile played on his lips, he looked drained. "You need to soak off those bandages in warm water and I need to get ready for work. Come on, I'll race you to the shower. First one there gets the hot water."

They stared at each other for at moment, then Daphne felt Edmund tense and she moved. Edmund was only part way up the stairs when Kat heard Daphne's bay of triumph. "Mind tricks don't work on me, Edmund Broadhurst. I *know* there is not a huge, hairy tarantula in the bathtub."

Kat shook her head as she headed towards the kitchen. "This place is getting positively dotty."

Daphne was running late by the time she had gotten ready for work and bandaged Edmund's hands. She scampered down the outside stairs and stuck her key in the car door to unlock it. When she grabbed the handle and jerked, she found she had locked it instead. "Shows how valuable you are," she said to the car as she unlocked it and slid in behind the wheel.

She started it up and pulled out down the hill. Thoughts and feelings clattered around noisily in her. She had relived every moment of last night. It was a fire in her. She could taste Dennis' mouth, feel his aroused masculinity, his hands and mouth moving over her skin. But morning also brought with it doubts, insecurities, fears. Was his desire for her real? He had been tired. She had given him several cups of the mulled wine. And she had been eager, maybe too eager. Lord, she would have made love to him right there in front of the stove.

Daphne was experienced enough in the ways of the world to know that hot, passionate nights could turn into ice-cold regrets in the light of day. Maybe it was fortunate Melanie was still trying to hold him. Maybe any regrets would be small and they could continue on their more platonic footing. He had come and asked her to stay his friend, not lover or beloved. Friend. She was willing to live with that if it was all he had to give her. Indeed, she would be grateful. She knew in the deep place where hopes began and crushed hopes went to die, she was an ill-fitting half to any man. She had no reason to look for more.

But she also knew she had stepped on very dangerous ground last night. It would be hard to look at Dennis now without wanting to feel his lips, to be held in his arms, to be tempted to light the fire within him again. No, the best thing would be to stay away until she had trapped all the scurrying emotions and locked them back in the closet of reality.

She felt the tears rising. She would have to get her mind off him or she would be an emotional basket case by the time she reached the hospital. She reached down and pushed the cassette sticking out of the player in and hoped it wasn't love songs.

She hit the brakes and swerved wildly causing the car behind her to honk angrily when a scream on the tape suddenly filled her car. She pulled over and sat shaking as a hoarse whispery voice spoke to her by name.

"Daphne. How much I look forward to the day when the screams I hear are yours. When I see you sniveling and begging me to spare you life. What will you give in exchange? Your pretty little face to carve into the monster you are? Your hands for the thief you are? How about your body? Not to kill, but to damage so you spend the rest of your life looking out from a living tomb? Think about it, Daphne. Make your decision with care. And while you are thinking, look into each face you see. Wonder if they are friend or foe? Who is it? What face do they wear? Be scared, Daphne. Be very scared. Time is running like water through your fingers. It will soon be gone." The words trailed off into more theatrical moans and cries.

Daphne wrapped her arms around herself to quell her shaking. Her first thought was to run to Dennis, to throw herself into his protective arms, to shield herself against his strong body.

She closed her eyes and forced herself to draw in deep breaths. No. She couldn't do that. She had always cared for herself. She had been frightened before. She had faced ugly things before. She had been alone before. This was no different. Let them come. She would fight them if she could and if she couldn't, then she would just have to go down.

She ejected the tape and dropped it on the passenger seat as though it burned her fingers. She put the car into gear and drove the rest of the way to the hospital, screwing her courage to the sticking place.

Chapter Thirty Three

The pale grey of day filtered through the uncurtained windows. Dennis rolled onto his back. He had fallen asleep on the bed. He sat up and rubbed his eyes. They felt swollen and crusty from the tears he had shed last night.

He stumbled over the debris as he made his way to the bathroom to splash water on his face. As he dried it off, he became conscious of a change in the room. It had the cool, serenity of a new day. When he stepped back in the bedroom, he knew Melanie had gone. "May you find peace, Melanie," he said softly. A shard of one of the shattered clowns crunched under his shoe. He had better clean up this mess before the children or Mrs. Mac saw it. It would be hard to explain.

He got a garbage bag and began to shovel in the debris from the night's savage emotional storm. He had filled the bag and was going for the carpet sweeper when he spotted one more fragment lying on the floor. He picked it up and saw it was Daphne's purple bra, discarded when their passion had been frozen. He held it to his lips and breathed in the perfume that always put him in mind of sunlit meadows. He closed his eyes and he could feel her slender arms around his neck, the heat of her lips on his skin, the fragility of her body in his arms. Slicing abruptly across the sensations welling up was a picture of a doll with its throat cut. He was overwhelmed with the desire to find her and shield her inside his arms, keeping her safe against his body. He went to call her. But as he picked up the phone, he saw it was 6:40 a.m. She would be on her way to the hospital.

He put the phone down, realizing how little he knew about her daily life. He didn't know her days off, her home phone number, if she had a cell phone, what she did during her time off other than run the free clinic, who she saw or where she went. In fact, he had only seen her once in anything other than scrubs. He hadn't even seen her legs uncovered. "Some detective you are, Cobb," he thought. "You're in love with a woman whom you couldn't find if your life depended on it." Ice touched his backbone. "Or if her life depended on it."

Chapter Thirty Four

The day had passed routinely in pediatrics. Several of the nurse's were charting as they prepared to finish their shift. Karen was sorting through the notes in her pocket when she gasped. "Oh, lord, Daphne. There was a phone call for you hours ago. It came in while you were doing the appendectomy discharge. I meant to give you this as soon as you got back. I am so sorry." She handed the note over. It was from Dennis.

Daphne's heart skipped a beat but she kept her face a cool mask. She reached over and picked up the phone and dialed the police department. When the dispatcher answered, she asked for Dennis.

"I'm sorry ma'am, he is not in right now. Can I take a message?"

"This is Daphne DelaVeque over at Kelton Community. Did he leave a message for me?"

She could hear the rustle of papers being shuffled about. "No, ma'am, he didn't. I guess it couldn't have been too important. I'll make a note that you returned his call though."

Inside, her heart choked on his words 'it couldn't have been too important.'

"No, that won't be necessary," she said keeping her voice level.

Susanne looked at her curiously as she hung up the phone. "Seeing the detective, Daphne?"

Daphne kept her head down and continued to make notes. "I have seen the detective. He's the one who answered the call on the Floyd baby murder."

"Yeah but that was a long time ago. Why would he still be calling you?" Susanne was ducking her head trying to get a better view of Daphne's face. Daphne satisfied her by looking directly at her. "It probably has to do with the gang shooting that came to the clinic a couple of days ago. He showed up with the ambulance." She shrugged with a nonchalance she didn't feel.

Karen shuddered. "I don't know how you can keep going down to that place. One of these days you're going to get yourself killed."

Daphne looked at her sharply, then realized that Karen was just dithering as usual. "Maybe yes. Maybe no. It wouldn't really matter either way, would it?"

She tossed her notes in the garbage, flipped her pink stethoscope around her neck and walked to the elevator.

Something clicked in Susanne's head and she was twitching by the time the elevator doors closed behind Daphne. "Karen, it just hit me. Remember that doll you found."

Karen made a face, "Ugh. How could I forget? I'm still having nightmares."

"Think about it. Didn't it look just like Daphne?"

Karen stared at the closed elevator doors and then turned to look at Susanne. "Wow," she said.

Daphne had clocked out and run to her car in the November damp when she remembered she had not picked up the rose from the hospital's flower shop. It was November 3rd. The day her mother died. She was just turning around when she spotted the tape laying in her car seat. She unlocked her car door and picked it up gingerly. She'd take it in with her and dump it somewhere.

Once back in the hospital, she realized she probably should give it to Grissum. He had made her promise she would bring anything else that showed up to him. She had never broken faith with the man. She wouldn't start now. She carried it down to his office and peeked in. He was out on the floor as usual. She ripped a sheet from a prescription pad and penned a quick note.

"Doc. Another love letter to yours truly. Don't play this while driving and don't turn the volume up when you listen. You'll empty the hospital. Otherwise enjoy. D."

She slipped a rubber band around the tape to hold the note in place and headed to the flower shop.

Daphne climbed the asphalt paths glittering with rain to her mother's crypt. She carefully laid the single pink rose on it and then leaned against the pink marble. "Happy anniversary, Mom."

"I like him, Daphne. He's a good man."

"Yes, he is, for what it's worth to me."

"Darling, if you want him, you have got to go after him. You need to get yourself out of those scrubs and into something glitzier. Fix yourself up for him. Let him know you are interested."

"Oh, I let him know last night, Mom. I practically raped him."

"And I thought my generation was liberated."

"Yeah. I probably blew it right out of the water."

"I don't think so, baby. It was thinking of you that helped him resolve everything with his dead wife."

"It's over?"

"Yes, it's over. Melanie has moved on to a healing plane. She won't be back."

"I'm glad for him."

"Honey, I could help with Melanie but I can't help you fight off the living. He is a very attractive, red-blooded man. He can't live like a monk forever. And you're not getting any younger."

"You know, Mom, you can really boost a girl's ego. Make her feel good through and through."

"Go to the mall. Buy a sexy dress. You'll feel better."

The rain was beginning again. Daphne flipped up the hood on her coat and jammed her hands into the patch pockets. "A sexy dress is only closet filler for me. Later, Mom," she said as she dashed for her car.

Once inside her little car, Daphne flipped her hood back and knocked a piece of paper from above her visor. She jumped when it fell down by her feet. She sat a long moment looking at it. Surely no one followed her here. She finally forced herself to reach down and pick it up.

"God, DelaVeque, you have nerves of steel," she scolded herself as she looked at it. It was the confirmation of her registration to a seminar scheduled for the morrow. In all that had happened, she had completely forgotten about it. The last thing she wanted to do was get up at the crack of dawn and drive 80 miles to listen to some expert expound upon interpretations of pediatric blood values. But she had plunked down $225 for it and she needed the hours for her license renewal. She crammed it back above her visor.

Back at the main intersection, she found she was turning towards the mall. She wasn't interested in shopping and she generally avoided the malls, but they were full of people, light and noise. She suddenly had aversion to being alone.

Chapter Thirty Five

Grissum stared at the tape player in horror. He had listened to the tape twice. Daphne's stalker now had a voice. A poisonous whisper relishing the atrocities it described. What had Daphne done to attract such a monster?

Grissum reached for his phone and punched in Daphne's home number. It rang about five times before Kat's voice answered. His hand tightened on the phone as he heard her rich contralto. "Kat, this is Hal."

"Hal, what a pleasure. How have you been?"

"Fine, Kat. Fine. You?"

"Doing well for an old professor."

"I was a fool to let Elmore get you away from me."

Kat's warm laugh came down the line. "I would have made a terrible doctor's wife, Hal. I am far too independent, politically incorrect, and loathe all the socializing that is required. You would never have made chief of staff with a woman who thinks, perhaps, there is better medicine in roots, herbs, and the shaking of bones."

"You may not be wrong in your beliefs, Kat. The longer I am in this game the more of a sham it seems. But, that aside, is Daphne there?"

"No. She hasn't come home yet."

"Do you expect her soon?"

"Hal, you know this place. People wander in and out at all hours. We look for them when we see them."

"Do you have any idea where she is? The clinic maybe?"

"She may be. But in truth I have no idea where she could be. You know Daphne. She could be anywhere. Do you want me to have her call you when she gets in?"

"Yes. I don't care what time it is. Have her call me here or at home."

"I'll leave her a note."

Grissum didn't hang up but dialed the police department immediately upon disconnecting his call.

"Give me Cobb."

Dennis' voice sounded distracted when he answered.

"Cobb, I want you to tell me Daphne is waiting for you in your bed."

Dennis felt a flush creep up his neck but his voice was even. "I'd love to, Doc. But I haven't even talked to her today. I called this morning but she never returned my call. We got a break in a string of car thefts. I've been busy with that most of the day."

"Shit!"

"Why? Something else come up?"

"You could say that. I want you to listen to this." Grissum held the phone close to the little tape player's speaker and played the tape for Dennis.

Dennis' hand tightened on the phone until his knuckles were white. He was silent when Grissum came back on the phone. "You there, Cobb?"

"When did she get it? Where was it left for her? How did she take it?"

"I don't know. I don't know. I don't know." Grissum's voice had a sharp edge. He was a man fast being pushed to the brink. "I found it with a note from her just a few minutes ago on my desk. It wasn't here earlier this afternoon. I'm guessing she left it after she got off shift."

"Where is she now?"

"God, man, I don't know. That's why the hell I'm calling you. I was hoping you knew. She's not at home. I checked. There's no phone at that friggin' clinic."

"Cell phone?"

"She doesn't have one."

"Look, I was just heading out of here. I'll go by the clinic and check on her."

"Call me. Tell me what you find. Here's my numbers." Grissum proceeded to rattle off his office phone, home phone and cell phone. "I'm going to call some of the gals she works with and see if she mentioned what she was going to do to any of them."

Dennis was on his feet even before hanging up the phone. The moment he sat it in its cradle, he was moving out the door. He had to restrain himself not to resort to the lights and sirens so he could speed to the clinic. The building was dark when he pulled up in front of it. He wavered between relief and consternation.

Just to be sure, he rattled the door and shone his flashlight through the windows. It was empty. He drove home, his mind racing in a wheel of fear.

Where *was* Daphne? Why hadn't she returned his call? Why hadn't she come to him when she got the tape? Why did the damn little fool always have to try to gut things out alone? Didn't she understand what he was feeling for her? That he was there to shelter her, protect her?

A cooler side of his brain answered. Why would she know? You haven't really shown her much except you wanted to get her into your bed. Women are used to men wanting to bed them without any strings. Get your rocks off and then arrivederci, baby. Only the very young equate bed with any more then sex.

He remembered once again the image he had caught of the little child on the tombstone. He thought about the 15 year old who had hitchhiked to find her mother's grave. The woman who had casually mentioned she had thought herself old enough to be left alone all night in strange motel rooms at age eight.

He realized she had never even mentioned the doll or the note to him. Everything he knew was through Grissum and Broadhurst. He doubted Grissum would have known of their existence if the doll hadn't been fortuitously found by someone other than Daphne.

Yeah, Daphne would try to handle this alone. She had never had a reason to believe she could turn to another human being and receive any kind of care and protection. She had survived in a land of neglect and estrangement much of her life. She didn't know there were other worlds. He would have to show her. And, please God, don't let him fail her.

He quelled the children long enough to take the phone to the bedroom and call Grissum. He was still at the office. "The clinic is closed tonight. I checked it. It's empty. You find out anything?"

"Not a damn thing except I think she got the tape early today, before she got to work. Susanne said she was kinda pale and a little shaky when she got to work. Said she was real quiet all day. Susanne thought maybe she was sick. Daphne hasn't said a word to anyone about any of this. Not even her own family. I could tell when I talked to Kat. There was no worry or alarm. They don't know. By the way, Susanne made the connection between the doll and Daphne. Susanne did say Daphne got a little jumpy when Karen made a comment about Daphne getting herself killed if she kept working the clinic."

"How did she respond to that?"

"She told Susanne and Karen it didn't really matter one way or the other." He was silent a moment. "That's what scares the hell out of me, Cobb. She won't come to either of us. She'll go head to head with whoever is behind this. Alone."

"I know, Doc," Dennis said quietly. "Call me if you hear from her. I don't care what time it is. I'll do the same for you."

Chapter Thirty Six

Lygia sat curled up on the corner of her mother's chintz covered overstuffed couch. She had tossed several pillows on the floor to make room. Bei came in from the kitchen and set a demitasse of heavily sweetened Arabic coffee on the corner of the crowded coffee table. She carried her own cup to the overstuffed chair opposite. She shooed two cats out of the chair before sitting down with a welcome sigh.

"So you should want to talk? You look like your last friend, they have ridden the bus out of town."

"I don't know, Mama. I'm just restless and edgy. Probably just a reaction to last night. I'll be alright when I get a good night's sleep."

"So you had a good day's sleep and you're still all glum in the mouth. But I think you are in the right. That man last night. He disturbs you. You should want to tell me?"

Lygia shrugged. "There's nothing to tell. We've met a couple of times professionally. That's all."

"So there's nothing to tell. How come you know he is in need of help? How come you know where he is? So now he is better, how come you don't just get fat fee and go happy to the bank instead of sitting there all sad. Maybe because this man speaks to you in a place you do not listen for."

"Mama, I know you didn't see him as he normally is last night so you wouldn't know. Mr. Broadhurst is of, how shall I say it, a different persuasion."

Bei snorted indelicately. "Shows what you should know with all your fancy book ideas. This man is not of the gay people."

Lygia picked up her coffee and looked with mild amusement at her unworldly mother. "And how did you decide that?"

"Remember I tell you there is a vibration to the soul. It is higher and faster in the girl people than in the boy people?"

Lygia nodded. Her mother had accurately predicted which sex was to be born for years before ultrasound took over the responsibility.

"It is the confusion of the vibration which tells me when someone is of the gay people. For the men, it is higher and faster than it should be. Not as high and fast as woman's. But more than it should be. I hear this man's vibration last night. It is right. He puts on a face that is not his own. So who should know why?" She shrugged eloquently.

When she had awakened in her bed wearing nothing except her panties, she suspected Edmund had undressed her and put her to bed. When she had gone to the kitchen, she confirmed her suspicions. Propped against the coffeemaker was a note written on one of his cards in his elegant copperplate. "L. Called your office and instructed you would not be in today. E." It hadn't bothered her because of his sexual orientation. Now she felt embarrassed.

She had just gone to the kitchen to refill her cup when the doorbell rang. Her mother sighed and heaved herself out of the chair.

Edmund stood in the doorway. Bei looked closely into his face and was gratified with what she saw.

"Ah, my Lygia's friend, Edmund. You no longer stand in the grave."

Lygia's head snapped up when she heard her mother. She went to stand in the shadow of the kitchen door and watch.

Edmund took her mother's hands in his own and lifted them to his forehead. "No. It has closed without me, thanks to Rawnie Bei." He kissed the back of each hand, turned them over and kissed the palms. Then still holding them face up with one hand, he reached in his jacket pocket and removed a small fabric bundle which he laid in her hands. "A blessing given must be returned, lest it become a curse on one's soul."

He leaned forward and kissed her forehead.

Lygia was amused to see her mother flush with pleasure. "It has been long since I have met with one who knows of the old ways. The young they have no time for such as this. Please to come in and share in some coffee."

"I would be honored." He sat on the end of the couch where Bei indicated and when one of the cats jumped into his lap, he simply stroked it, disregarding the cat hair settling on his dark brown slacks.

Bei called to the kitchen. "Lygia, you should bring a cup for Mr. Edmund."

Lygia could not hold back the blush creeping over her face as she sat the cup in front of Edmund. Only a few hours before, he had stripped her almost naked. He looked at her with no interest, though. Well, it looked like her mother had been wrong after all.

Lygia curled back up on the corner of the couch and watched him. He reminded her of someone who was recovering from a near fatal illness. He was alive but there was no animation or life in him. He was still pale and his movements slow as though it was an effort to make them.

Bei studied him as well. There was a small moue of worry on her mouth. "You have found some answers, yes?"

Edmund sat the cup down as though it were too heavy to hold.

"Yes. I spoke with a friend at the university in Zimbabwe. He grew up in the same region where my parents had their mission. He told me of a cult of natives who practiced what would be the equivalent of the black arts in European countries. They believed they were shape changers and could become the animals of the jungle. They donned animal skins, strapped claws to their hands and became the animal."

"They wished to drive the white missionaries from their region. Education and enlightenment, of course, being the enemy of superstition. I believe it was they who attacked my father that night." He glanced at Lygia and then back to Bei. "You said I spoke of cats with men's faces. That fits." He fell silent.

Bei nodded slowly as she studied him. "You are alive, *chavo*. You know your darkness and still you carry much pain. Something else tears at your heart," she said softly.

Edmund closed his eyes briefly. "I had always believed the answer to my Mum's situation would be in the understanding of the darkness. The darkness is now open to the light and I find nothing I can carry to her."

"I should come to see your mama, yes? We should look together, yes?"

"That would honor me greatly, Rawnie Bei."

"Then we should come in day or two. You are not strong yet. We wait till your strength, it comes again."

Edmund pulled himself up from the couch and kissed her cheek. "You give me hope. I should leave you now." He started for the door.

Bei's voice was sharp. "Lygia, you should go as well."

Edmund turned back. "Forgive my rudeness. I should be delighted to see your daughter safely home." The words were a mechanical recitation of proper upbringing. There was no warmth or animation in the voice.

Still obedient to that tone of her mother's voice, Lygia jumped up. As she gave her mother a hug and kiss, Bei whispered in her ear. "Look with your heart. I have done my work, you should now do yours."

Bei stood in the door waving as the car backed out of the drive. Only when they were out of sight did she reach into the pocket of her dress and pull out the little bundle Edmund had given her. She untied the square of material and when she held up is contents, she burst into tears. She knew the hands that crafted the cross on its chain. They belonged to her people across the ocean.

Edmund parked the car outside Lygia's apartment. "Shouldn't I drop you somewhere first?" Lygia asked.

"I believe I promised your mother I would see you safely home, m'dear." He got out of the car and came around to open her door. His hand was like ice when he assisted her out. Throughout the silent drive home, her mother's words rang over and over in her head. Do her part. Do her part. But what was her part? Escorting her to the door, Edmund unlocked and opened it, reaching inside to flick on the lights. Then stepping aside, he indicated she should go in. She hesitated on the doorstep. "Look with your heart," Bei's voice echoed in her head.

She looked at Edmund, not with her eyes or mind, but with her heart. She saw clearly the emptiness in the man. Her mother had wrestled him back from the jaws of death but she had not infused him with life. He was still in danger. He could still be lost.

And then she knew what she needed to do. Immediately, her mind jumped in. "What if he rejects..." "Oh, shut up," she told her logical self, and went instead to Edmund. She cupped her hands behind his head and stared into his eyes. Nothing flickered there. She drew his head down till their mouths met. His lips were cold and bloodless. She pressed the warmth of hers into them. He did not move to respond. Lygia pushed back the sneering voice of her mind as she kissed his eyes, face, and traveled back to his mouth.

His hands came up to rest on her waist. "Drink deeply the gift of life being offered." His arms slipped around her and he pulled her tight against him. Like a starving man, he devoured the life flowing from her mouth.

Chapter Thirty Seven

Dennis had finally fallen into a fitful sleep when the phone rang. He automatically looked at his watch as he reached for it. It wasn't quite 6 a.m. Maybe it was Daphne. He snatched the phone off the charger. "Cobb."

"You didn't hear from her, did you?" It was Grissum's voice.

"No."

"Me neither. I'm telling you when she gets to work today, I'm going to kick her little ass all around the hospital just before I staple her into my pocket. I didn't sleep worth a damn."

"It wasn't too good around here either." Dennis hesitated before he asked the question that plagued his night. "Ah, Doc, there isn't anyone else she is involved with, is there? Where she might, er, have stayed the night, ah, might be?"

Grissum read Dennis' misgivings. "Not a chance. The only men she has hung out with is that motley crew she patches up at the clinic. I haven't seen anyone get her engine running in years, that is, until a certain cop showed up. Don't know what the hell she sees in him."

"I don't either, but thanks, Doc. Call me as soon as you talk to her."

Although concern still gnawed at him, Dennis' spirits were buoyed as he went to shower. As soon as Grissum called, he was going to make a beeline to the hospital and set his little blonde straight on a few things.

Grissum was chewing his cigar from one side of his mouth to the other as the elevator crawled to the second floor of the hospital. It was 7:15 a.m. and he was about to have a heart to heart with females who failed to call when ordered to. Susanne was just coming out of the linen closet with an armload of bunny and ducky decorated sheets. The sight of them reminded him of years ago when he had his gall bladder out. He had awakened on a set of those courtesy of his irreverent girl. Half the damn hospital had been lurking around his door to hear him bellow which incidentally had hurt like hell.

"Where's the blonde bomb, Susanne?"

Susanne looked at him blankly. "It's her day off, Dr. Grissum."

Susanne continued to stare after him as a string of epithets poured out all the way to the elevator.

Back in his office, he dialed Daphne's number again. He caught Kat sounding breathless. "Hal, of course I left a note for Daphne. I told you I would. No, she wasn't home when I went to bed about 10. Let me look. No, her car isn't here. I'll have to leave a note. I have an early class today."

Grissum's brows were drawn together in an Olympian rage as he dialed the police department. "It's her friggin' damn day off. No, she's not at home. I just tried. Her goddamn car isn't at home now. Kat said she wasn't home by 10 last night. Kat is going to leave another note. I tell you, Cobb, I'm going to strangle the little broad myself. Yeah, yeah. I'll keep you posted."

The emergency room staff knew it wasn't going to be a good day when Grissum hurled a pack of sterilized instruments against the wall, spraying the contents onto the floor. Even Eydie kept her distance.

Chapter Thirty Eight

Lygia opened her eyes slowly, fearful it was another of the strange dreams and the wonder of it would vanish in the day's light. But he still lay beside her, his face peaceful as he slept. She touched it and felt the warmth. Ever so lightly, she brushed back the waves of hair. He stirred and his arm slipped over the curve of her hip, pulling her until his head rested against her heavy breasts. She eased an arm under his neck and sheltered him against her heart.

Last night he had worshiped at the altar of her body. Even now she floated on the waves of remembered ecstasy. Edmund had carried her to heights that were surely the borders of heaven.

Slowly undressing her, he had loved each part of her he bared. He had gently urged her to reciprocate. His hands had left trails of fire, his mouth fanning the flames as he brought her to the brink again and again. And when he had finally joined with her, she experienced an explosion climbing from the depths of her up her spine, shattering the walls she had lived within. In that great rocking moment, she had touched the stars, swum the ocean's depths, and felt the magnificent web of life joining her to worlds known and unknown.

The stagnant pool had broken free to rush forth in a glorious, tumbling river. No matter where it carried her, she wanted to experience the fullness of the journey.

He stretched and rolled away. Then rising up on his elbow, he looked down on her. His eyes were glowing amber and his hand was light as he traced the outlines of her face. Looking up at him, she saw the strength and courage returned. She touched the jagged scar running along a rib. A wash of images welled up in her mind. She felt the dark places he had gone in his search, the price demanded and his unflinching willingness to pay it, the depth of the love driving him, the height of his reverence for life.

Tears filled her eyes, one slipping down her cheek.

Edmund brushed it with his thumb. "What is it, m'dear?"

"I saw. I saw who you are and it makes me ashamed. I have been so little while you have been so much," she whispered, dropping her head to hide the embarrassment burning in her face.

He put his hand under her chin, lifting her eyes to him again. "No, my luv, you were merely dormant, keeping safe within you the gift I would need to survive. And when the time was come, you poured it forth by denying the self you were. You found the courage to give the heart with no promise of return. That is a rare and wondrous act." His voice grew husky as he pulled her against him. "You saved my life, Lygia, and I thank the heavens for you."

Lying wrapped in his arms, their legs entwined, Lygia felt the sharp tang of life's possibilities in her mouth and coursing through her veins. She gave a shiver of pleasure. Edmund's body responded and he lowered his head to capture her mouth.

Chapter Thirty Nine

By late afternoon, Grissum had moved from rage to ice. Although he and Dennis had communicated several times during the day, neither had yet heard from Daphne. At quarter after five, Dennis called Grissum again.

"Nothing. Nothing. Nothing. I have heard nothing from anyone. Any luck?"

Dennis had issued a 'be on the lookout' for Daphne's car. "Nothing on the BOLO. Look, I'm going to have an office full of cops in a couple of hours. We're going to raid the place the auto theft stuff is being fenced through. Here's my cell phone number. I want to hear regardless. I'll call you when I get through unless I hear from you before that. I'm going to run down and check the clinic. If you hear from her before I do, I want you to do me a favor."

"What's that?"

"Lash her to your chest until I shake free."

Grissum hung up the phone and swung around to stare out the window at the darkening sky. He didn't remember ever feeling so old and tired.

There was a knock at the door, it opened and he could see a head reflected in the window. "What is it, Eydie?"

She came in and closed the door. "I'm worried about you, Hal. You've been like a bear with a sore head all day. Is there something wrong? Is it anything I can help with?"

Grissum swung around towards her although he remained slumped in his chair, his hands hanging limply over the arms. "Not unless you can tell me where DelaVeque is?"

Eydie shook her head and sat down. "Sorry, I'm not the assigned babysitter this week."

Grissum closed his eyes and rubbed them wearily.

"She's really crawled inside your skin, hasn't she?"

"Eydie, I couldn't feel more strongly about that girl than if I had actually fathered her. Anything happens to her and I. . ." His voice trailed off.

"And what, Hal? What would you do?"

He looked past her. "I thought about it a lot last night for some reason. I would walk out of this place; liquidate everything I have, set up a pediatric trust fund in Daphne's name and move far away. I couldn't go on working or living here. I would never stop looking for her if I did."

Eydie's voice was soft. "And what about all the other people who care for you, Hal? What about all the other people who depend on you? What about them?"

"They got along before I showed up and they'll get along when I'm gone. Without my baby, there isn't one damn thing here that matters."

Grissum reached into an empty pocket looking for a cigar. He patted his other pockets. Eydie got up and came around his desk. She opened the top right drawer where he kept his cigars. She rummaged around until she found one. Her hand brushed cold steel. She shoved some papers side. "Is that a gun, Hal?"

He glanced in the drawer. "Yeah. Got it ages ago from the police department. Guess they thought I might need protection from the mangled dead. Go out once a year and qualify. Other than that it just collects dust."

"You don't keep it loaded, do you?"

"Of course, I do, Eydie. An empty gun is pretty damn useless."

She unwrapped the cigar and handed it to him. He pulled a clipper out of his pocket and snipped the end. Eydie struck a match and held it just below the end of the cigar. He took a deep puff and sent the smoke spiraling. Eydie went to crack the window so he wouldn't set off the smoke detectors again. She paused at the desk. He was staring out the window again.

"Anything else I can do for you, Hal?'

"Nope. Unless you see DelaVeque. Tell her she ain't going to have an ass when I get through with her."

Eydie opened the door. "I'll do that, Hal. I'll be sure to do that."

Chapter Forty

Twilight was settling on the horizon as Dennis walked through the cemetery. He had a small bouquet in his hand. He climbed the paths to the place where Melanie lay buried. He stood looking down at the flat headstone with the bronze plaque. "Melanie Denise Garber Cobb, 1974-2007" was all it said. He had been unable to think of any loving words to place on it at the time of her death.

He had stood in nearly the same place that day, alone, apart at the grave side services. The Garbers and O'Conners had all banded together weeping and directing dark looks in his direction. His own parents, Susan and her husband, Chris and his wife had stood around him in a protective half circle staring back and defying anyone to approach him with anything other than the usual bland condolences.

And when he had walked away that day, he had never come back until tonight. Tonight he wanted to close the circle by saying farewell to Melanie. He laid the bouquet on the grave. "Good bye, Melanie. I wish you well on your journey. I hope you can find peace and happiness." The guilt devouring at him all these months was easing. Calm was settling as though she were bidding him the same. The circle closed.

The damp seeped in under his coat, chilling him. He turned away from the grave and stared towards Kelton's lights and the lights lining the highway as it left the city. The modern jungle where predator and prey still moved in obedience to laws as ancient as life. Somewhere out there was a faceless predator stalking Daphne. Which would be the savvier animal?

As he swung back around for one last look at Melanie's grave, he caught sight of a light on the top of the hill. It looked like someone was standing with a flashlight albeit one with weak batteries. His curiosity was aroused. He started up the hill.

When he reached his destination, he swallowed hard as he realized the light was a kind of rosy-gold globe hovering above a crypt. In a moment, the globe began to shape itself into a woman, a beautiful woman. The woman flashed a smile at him and spoke but not so his ear heard. It was as though the words went straight to his brain where he recognized them. "She is truly at peace now, Dennis. She's moving to the healing plane. She wishes you well in your life."

There was something familiar about the woman as though he had seen her before. He made the connection. "Are you Daphne's mother. . . ah?" He was drawing a blank at her name.

"Althea Wyckham, Dennis. My daughter has done well to choose you. I believe you will heal the damage I did."

She was beginning to dim visually. "I can't do this long, too fatiguing."

"Althea, do you know where Daphne is?" Dennis asked the dark. He only heard the sound of raindrops bouncing off her tomb.

* * *

Daphne felt as though a whole chain gang was in her head breaking her brain into little pieces by the time she pulled up in front of the old manse. After being stuck for eight hours in an overheated room listening to the endless droning of a lecturer, she had the ninety minute drive home nearly tripled because some stupid truck decided to roll over and play dead on her side of the freeway.

All she could think about was downing about half a bottle of ibuprofen, crawling into bed and sleeping for a week. She climbed the stairs to her room and found five notes stuck around the sign on her door that announced "Daphne's Dump". Everyone of them was from Grissum demanding she call immediately. She tossed them all on her night table, "Yeah, sure, Doc, I'll call. In about three years."

She went to the bathroom and downed the medication, then came back to drop her clothes on the floor and her body into bed. Just as she was sliding into sleep, she tried to remember if she had locked her car. Oh, well. Maybe she would get lucky and someone would steal it.

The raid went like clockwork. Dennis left the officers logging in evidence and taking statements. He headed back to the police station. There were no messages for him. He hunted up Daphne's statement from the baby case and recorded her address in his little notebook. He got back behind the wheel and turned towards the Heights.

He didn't realize he had been holding his breath until it escaped in enormous sigh of relief when he spotted her car parked in front of the old house. He pulled in behind it and got out. He looked up at the house but it was dark. He satisfied himself by checking the car. The doors were unlocked. He looked inside. There was a McDonald's bag on the floor and a pile of papers on the passenger seat. He could smell her perfume in the car. He closed his eyes and breathed it in slowly. Then opening his eyes, he locked both car doors.

He peered at the sticky slip he had fastened to the top of the police radio and dialed Grissum's home phone number. He started the engine, pulling away from the curb, phone to his ear.

"Doc," Dennis said to the answering growl. "I just went by her house. Her car is there. I checked it and it looks okay. I think I know how she got the tape. She didn't have the car doors locked. No, I didn't talk to her. The house is dark. At this hour they are probably all in bed. Yeah, I'll talk to you tomorrow."

Chapter Forty One

Eydie's eyes were red-hot and swollen. She hadn't cried with this ferocity for many, many years. She had cried so many tears in the beginning when she had been unable to cope with the endless tide of young, nubile nurses flowing through the hospital doors. For Hal, it had been like living in a garden with endless blossoms to pluck. But it was almost over. All the pain, all the waiting, all the empty, lonely years. Tomorrow she was going to exact her vengeance on Daphne and then cut out of this life. She had found the perfect method. It would haunt Hal, wherever he ended up, knowing it was his gun that ended the life of his precious Daphne. And it would be her final act of love to use one of Hal's bullets to end her own miserable state.

Chapter Forty Two

After Dennis' call, Grissum had drifted into sleep while still sitting in his recliner. His beer went flat while the ball game ended, the news was delivered and the talk show droned on. When the phone rang at his elbow, he was able to pull himself into consciousness at once. It was a trick he had learned during his internship when sleep was grabbed whenever he had three minutes together.

"Yeah," he answered. His brain went to full alert as he listened to the same whisper he had heard earlier on the tape recorder.

"Your pretty little dolly is tucked up all asleep in her little bed, safe tonight. But her time is running out and dolly won't be so pretty when she takes her final nap. Your dolly is going to be all smashed by the end. No big blue eyes. No pert little nose. No sweet smile. When it's over, death will be the best gift she can have. Have a nice night, Dr. Grissum."

Grissum's haggard face had whole staff whispering nervously in corners as he paced up and down in front of the time clock eying every swipe of the name tags as they clocked in. Finally at three minutes to seven, the elevator opened and Daphne went to the clock to swipe in.

Those hurrying from the area froze in their tracks as Grissum's roar reached a record level. "DelaVeque."

Daphne calmly clipped her tag on her pocket before turning to face him while the hall emptied as fast as people could cram into the elevator or take the stairs. He stormed to her and grabbed for her arm. "You and I are going to have words, young lady."

"At that volume the third floor will be privy to our conversation, and I'll go peacefully, you don't have to drag me off."

"You'll be friggin' lucky I don't throw you over my knee and beat your ass."

"Kinky."

She followed Grissum to the Physician's Lounge which also emptied as soon as he slammed the door against the wall. He grabbed her arm and shoved her in ahead of him.

"Do you want to tell me just where the hell you have been since three o'clock Friday? And while you're at it, why you couldn't be bothered to pick up the goddamn phone and call me like I requested."

"If it's any of your damn business, Friday was November 3rd. I took a rose to Mom like I have done every year for seventeen years. Then I went to the mall until it closed at 10:00 p.m."

"You at a mall for four or five hours? Hah."

She turned away from him but he still caught the undertone in her voice. "I just didn't feel like being alone."

He came up behind her and put his hands on her shoulders pulling her until her back rested against him. She was wound tight. "Baby, it's alright to be scared. You should be scared."

He turned her around and lifted her chin until their eyes met. "But don't fight this out by yourself. You're not alone. I'm here for you and Cobb's here for you. We practically tore this town apart trying to find you. I want you to be with one or the other of us when you aren't working. I'll just have to hope his intentions are honorable."

Daphne put her arms around Grissum's waist and rested her head against his chest. He felt some of the tension go out of her body. "I hope they aren't."

He kissed the top of her head. She didn't see the fear in his eyes.

When he had sent her to the ped unit, Grissum strode to his office and called Dennis. "She's here. She's fine physically. Scared as hell. She spent all of Tuesday evening at the mall and that's more time than she has probably spent in the last decade. Safety and anonymity in the crowds. Yesterday she had a seminar, continuing ed hours. Got home late due to a wreck on the freeway." Grissum paused.

"Cobb, I got a call last night. Same voice as on the tape. No, I couldn't tell if it was a man or woman. The voice was an ugly whisper just like on the tape. They called her my little dolly. They said," Grissum's voice broke. He cleared his throat. "They said they were going to smash up the little dolly before she was killed. No, I haven't said anything about to Daphne. She's holding on by sheer guts now. I told her I wanted her either with you or me whenever she isn't working until we can get to the bottom of this. Your intentions better be honorable, Cobb. She hopes they aren't. You coming by later? Yeah, yeah, I'll write it down as best I can remember. Okay, look for you."

Dennis hung up and checked his watch. Daphne was safe. He would wrap up the last of the paperwork on the car thefts and then he was going to ask for a couple of days off. Get Grissum to order Daphne off. He was going to load her and the kids up and head to the beach. By the time they got back, the state crime lab should have some info on the note and tape. Grissum could keep working on the hospital angle. He'd work on Daphne while they were away. If she felt safe enough, she might remember something that could help them.

Chapter Forty Three

Lygia picked up her mother and drove to Edmund's house to meet with him as arranged.

He was waiting on the porch for them. Bei was thoroughly winded after making the climb up the three tiers of stairs. She patted his arm. "When you two should be getting married, I want you should buy nice ranch on flat street, one floor."

Lygia blushed and looked away. "Sleeping together does not equate to future marriage, Mama," she scolded in her mind.

Edmund guided Bei to the living room to sit and catch her breath before they tackled the last of the stairs leading to his mother. Kat, on hearing their arrival, came out of the kitchen bearing a large tray with a samovar and glass cups in silver holders.

 Edmund took it from her and carried it to the living room. There were fresh baked baklava and lemon pound cake on the tray as well. Bei clapped her hands in delight.

"Oh, it is too wonderful. It is like being at home again." She reached out and caught Edmund's hand pulling him down till she could kiss him on the cheek. Then she stood and kissed Kat as well. They embraced like old friends.

Lygia was feeling a trace of embarrassment for her mother's grandiose gestures. She looked around the room to avoid any more notice of her mother only to be startled to see it was as eccentric and, in its own way, cluttered as her mother's house. A somewhat moth-eaten zebra skin hung over the back of the couch. The dusty wood floor was covered with worn Persian and Kalim rugs. The tall cabinets held collections of weapons. Lamps came from every possible era. African tribal art hung with blue willow ware. Yes, her mother was quite right. She was at home here. Lygia looked curiously at Edmund. She had been in his office and his mother's room. They were exquisitely decorated and yet, he was perfectly comfortable in this room. Another side of a very complex man. Lygia wondered if one lifetime would be enough to know him.

Bei drank a cup of the sweetened tea and ate a piece of both the baklava and the pound cake. Then wiping her fingers on a napkin, she held her hand out. "Come, Edmund, it is now the time to see your mamma."

He led them up the stairs. Daphne was just coming out of her bedroom. Edmund introduced the two women to her. Daphne looked Lygia up and down carefully before flashing a happy smile at her cousin. "Very good, cuz. I knew you had it in you somewhere. My best to you both."

Bei in turn had been studying Daphne. She reached out and took Daphne's hand. "Please to be very careful. There is one who hates for reasons you know not. They want much harm to come to you."

Edmund and Lygia both looked in alarm at Bei and then Daphne. Daphne's face had gone white but she was nodding her head. "True, too true. Well, I best be off. I've had the clinic closed for two days and there will be a line around the block I'm afraid."

Edmund caught the tail of her windbreaker as she started for the stairs. "Whoa there, kitten. Is there something you need to be telling me? P'haps you should wait until I can go with you."

Daphne smiled and shrugged. "Just keep your ears on." It was their private code to stay tuned into each other's thoughts.

Bei watched her disappear down the stairs and out the door. When she was gone, Edmund looked at Bei questioningly. She looked up at him and smiled. "There is also much love around the little one. It should maybe be enough. Your mamma?"

Edmund opened the door to Anne's room. Bei went to her and knelt before her taking her hands. Anne brought her eyes back and they held on Bei's face a moment longer than Edmund had seen for some time. Bei carefully placed her hands first on Anne's face, then on the sides of her head. Gently Bei touched her hands, neck, and heart.

She sat back and closed her eyes, meditating. When she opened them, she shook her head sadly at Edmund. "There is no soul sickness. It is the body that has failed. The fever of so long ago, it damaged the head. Like the wires getting burned."

Edmund came to stand quietly behind his mother, hands on her shoulders. She never moved or acknowledged his presence. "Then there is nothing?" he said very quietly.

Bei shook her head. "But do not be cast down, my son. There is one who stands guardian to her. It is one who loves her even as you do. No. One who loves her as a man. He is with her always until it is time he should take her hand and bring her to the new home."

"My father," Edmund whispered.

Bei started to get off the floor a bit stiffly, Edmund came around to give her assistance. "Ah, the knees. They are too soon old."

Bei reached up and pulled Edmund's head down until she could wrap her arms around him. "*Tikno*, she is not unhappy. She is at peace. It would grieve her to know the pain you carry for her. This you must let go so her peace is complete."

Chapter Forty Four

Oddly enough, Daphne felt safe as she walked into the Corners. This was her tribal ground. She knew the danger did not come from here. It came from outside and few would hazard the Corners just to get her skinny ass. Here she would not have to look over her shoulder.

She opened the clinic and prepared for business. It sure beat the mall any day.

Chapter Forty Five

Grissum sat down in his chair and reached into his pocket for his cigar. Cobb didn't know it but tonight he was getting Daphne duty. Cobb was young and could afford to lose sleep trying to keep up with the blonde tornado. At the rate she was aging him, he would be dead next week. A patting of all his pockets produced no cigar. He turned back to his desk drawer and opened it. A letter lay on top. The writing looked familiar. He pulled it out and ripped it open.

My dearest Hal. By the time you read this I shall be dead by your gun. But I shall not be alone. I intend to take your darling little Daphne with me. For thirty five years, I loved you, waited on you, served you every way I could. And not once in that thirty five years did you toss me so much as a crumb of affection. Instead you poured everything out on your little dolly. I heard you that night Sawyer was killed. I heard you tell her how much you loved her, needed her. I watched my god turn into just another man with feet of clay begging for the affection of a sweet young thing. I can't hurt you physically. I have loved you too long and too deeply for that. But I will cut your heart out and bury it with her so that you can live the remainder of your life as I have had to live. Alone, empty, wanting.

Eydie

Grissum's hands were shaking so badly it took him three tries to dial Daphne's home number. Kat answered. "Kat, I need to talk to Daphne now."

"She's at the clinic, Hal. Is something wrong?"

The phone hit the desk as he raced for the parking lot. He lit up the tires on his Bronco slamming it from reverse to drive. He flipped the switch setting his headlights to flash and the added blue lights to strobe. He pulled out his phone and punched in the police number as he dodged in and out of traffic.

"For god's sake man, get me Cobb."

"Dennis. It's Eydie Nettles. My emergency room nurse. Son of a bitch." He swerved to miss a motorcycle. "She's got my gun. Eydie means to kill her." He disconnected the call never realizing he hadn't told Dennis where he was headed.

Dennis tore out of the office and flung himself into his car. He revved the engine and backed out of the city lot, hitting his lights and siren. At the street, he suddenly realized her didn't know where to go. He pounded the wheel. "Goddam it, Doc. Where?" He grabbed for the phone when the cool voice spoke. "The clinic, Dennis. Daphne's at the clinic."

He stepped on the gas. "Thanks, Althea."

Chapter Forty Six

Daphne had just come out of the little bathroom, smoothing sanitizer over her hands when Eydie pushed through the door. She looked at her in surprise.

"Eydie, what on earth are you doing in this part of town?"

"Came to have a little chat about man stealing, sugarcakes."

"What are you talking about? I haven't stolen anyone's man. I don't even have a man."

"Oh, yes, you have. You took the only man I ever loved. The only man I ever wanted. You took my Hal."

"Grissum? Eydie, Doc thinks of me as a kid it amuses him to look out for."

Eydie's voice was hemmed with hysteria. "No. No. I heard him that night. I heard him tell you that he couldn't, wouldn't want to go on if anything happened to you. I saw. I saw the way he looked at you. He worships the fuckin' ground you walk on, you filthy little bitch."

Daphne calculated her strategy as she moved toward Eydie, carefully inching her way around the examining table.

"And because of that you are going to die, DelaVeque." Eydie pulled the gun from her bag and waved it in Daphne's direction. "Do you recognize this? It's Hal's. I want him to know every minute of every day the rest of his life that it was *his* gun that killed you."

"Guns don't kill people, Eydie. People kill people. He'll hate you, Eydie. He'll make your life a living hell."

Eydie shook the gun at Daphne. "My life is already a living hell. It's been a living hell for years."

"Then I'm not to blame for all of it. Why me. Why now?"

"Because the others didn't mean anything to him. He took them to bed the way he took me to bed. He used us and tossed us aside like so many surgical sponges. But you, that's where you're different. He thinks he loves you. You can hurt him for me."

Daphne had cleared the examining table. She tensed to leap, her hand closed over the switchblade. Eydie, in the hypersensitive state of obsession, caught it. She leveled the gun at Daphne and fired.

Daphne flung herself to the floor but not fast enough. The bullet tore a deep channel across her upper arm. She gasped. When the numbness washed away in her blood, she sent the pain on.

Edmund and the women were back in the living room. As he leaned his arm on the fireplace mantle he, too, gasped and grabbed his upper arm, looking down as if he expected to see blood. Then the bell on the mantle began to ring wildly. "My god, Daphne."

He was out the door and taking the steps two and three at a time. At the foot, he sprinted towards the Corners.

Daphne pulled herself off the floor. Blood was soaking down the sleeve of her scrub jacket.

"Does that hurt, Daphne? Think what two or three more bullets will do. I don't want you to die instantly. I want you to hurt. To bleed. To beg me to kill you. I want to hear you beg." Eydie was moving closer to her.

Grissum's vehicle slammed to a stop in front of the clinic, one tire up on the curb. He hurled himself out and into the clinic.

"Eydie," he screamed.

"Oh, this is even better, Hal. You will get to see your little girl die. I like that."

Grissum looked towards Daphne and caught his breath sharply when he saw the blood soaking her torn jacket. He took a step. "Oh, my god, baby."

"Baby, baby. She's always your baby. But me who loved you, stood by you, gave up everything for you, I'm dirt under your feet. If I died right now you wouldn't remember my name tomorrow."

Grissum spread his hands. "That's not true, Eydie. If mistakes have been made, they are mine. I'm the one who should pay. Daphne never asked a thing of me. I chose her. She didn't choose me. It's my fault. If you must kill someone. It should be me."

"Oh, that would make it so easy, wouldn't it, Hal. One big bang and it would be all over. No more pain for you. *No!* I want you to suffer. I want you to live another hundred years suffering."

Daphne worked her way back around the table while Eydie had her attention fully on Grissum. She took a flying leap at the woman.

Dennis slammed on his brakes, spinning the steering wheel as he barely avoided the end of Grissum's Bronco. He threw open the door of his car and stepped out just as a gunshot shattered the old front window sending shards of glass splintering over the sidewalk.

He ducked behind the car door before approaching in a low broken field run. At the door, he could see Daphne and Eydie wrestling on the floor. Daphne was trying to get control of the gun but she wasn't big enough to match the woman's weight or fury. There were large splotches of blood where Daphne's wounded arm was hitting the floor as they struggled. Dennis drew down on the two women trying to get a clear shot while Grissum stood bellowing for him to "Shoot, damn it, shoot."

Daphne was tiring rapidly. She couldn't keep the gun from coming back at her. Dennis couldn't get a good shot with Daphne's body blocking Eydie's.

Running feet could be heard coming down the sidewalk. Edmund grabbed the door frame and spun into the clinic. He took it all in a split second and then spoke with a voice sounding as though Satan himself had arrived. Every action froze. Edmund reached into the fray, grabbed Daphne by the back of her jacket and flung her back towards Dennis and Grissum. Dennis shoved her behind him into Grissum's arms. Coming up on one knee, Dennis leveled the gun at Eydie. Edmund was standing between them as Eydie started to get up. Dennis was sighting in when Daphne reached out and grabbed his arm, "No, wait," she panted.

Edmund was speaking in a voice too low to be understood by the people behind him but Eydie's eyes were growing bigger and bigger. Just as she reached her feet, he grabbed the gun out of her hand with a speed that defied the eye to catch it. He calmly handed it back behind him. Dennis stood and took it. Eydie fell back, sinking slowly down the wall to the floor where she began to sob bitterly.

It was over. As the realization hit her, the world took a bad pitch for Daphne throwing her into a land of woozy shadows. She collapsed against Grissum, her curls falling away from the pallor of her skin. Her eyes were open but unfocused. Slowly, her lids drifted down. Her hand clutching Grissum's lab jacket fell away.

Dennis dropped to one knee. Daphne seemed to be bathed in blood. "Doc?" Dennis asked in a frightened whisper.

Grissum fingers went to her carotid artery. Thin and thready, the pulse barely pushed against them. His face was ashen, his voice tight. "Get an ambulance, Cobb. Tell 'em it's a code."

From her place against the wall, Eydie's sobs slowed as she watched the tall, detective get to his feet. Daphne's body lay limply in Grissum's arms, her blood on his hands. It was smeared in bright streaks across his white lab jacket and shirt. Eydie began to laugh.

Dennis stopped and took a step in her direction. Edmund pulled his eyes away from his cousin's pale, still face. "For god's sake, man, go. I can handle this."

"Is your dolly all broken, Hal?" Eydie's voice was a hideous cackle.

Grissum's head snapped up and he stared at Eydie, pure hatred in his face. But slowly his expression began to change to one of contempt. Then she watched him erase her very existence as it settled into a neutral expression. She was no more.

He looked back down into Daphne's face. Tenderly he brushed a curl back from her cheek and Eydie knew. She knew it wouldn't matter if Daphne lived or died. Grissum would always love her with everything in him and he would carry her and her, alone, in his heart. He had obliterated Eydie from him. He had wiped out whatever meager acknowledgment he may have had. She had succeeded only in killing herself.

Dennis came back and squatted in front of Grissum, his eyes fastened on Daphne. "They're rolling, Doc."

Grissum touched the carotid again. It was steadier, a little stronger. He looked at Dennis and could see the anguish in the detective's eyes as he stared helplessly.

"You got it bad, don't you, Cobb."

Dennis hung his head and nodded. "Yeah, I got it bad. I've never known anyone like her. I think I fell for her the moment I saw her backing that drunk across the sidewalk. A kitten taking on a pit bull, all spit and hiss, scrappy as hell."

Grissum nodded. "I know. When she very first came to work as a ward clerk, she walked in on me one day as I was reducing one of the young nurses to hysteria, a hobby of mine back then. She slammed those charts down with a whack I can still hear and came at me. Here I am six foot three, newly named chief of staff with an ego to match, and I was being backed literally into the wall by this little hellcat. That was the first time I fired her. Know what she did? She stripped out of that grey jacket the clerks wore then, looked at me and said, "A hospital is only as good as its staff and staff is only as good as they are treated. This place won't be worth a shit." Then she threw the jacket in my face. Took me three months to get her to come back."

They lifted their heads as they heard sirens. In another moment, red lights began to flash across the walls. As soon as the ambulance crew appeared with the gurney, Grissum took command, ordering IV's, oxygen, and cardiostrips. Dennis stood up as they carefully lifted Daphne into the gurney and covered her. As they started toward the ambulance, Dennis caught Grissum by the arm.

"I have to mop up here, Doc. Take real good care of her until I can get there, please."

Grissum reached out and squeezed his arm. Dennis watched until the ambulance was whooping its way toward the hospital. Then he turned back, his face set in icy somberness.

He reached down and hauled Eydie to her feet. He automatically recited her Miranda rights as he hooked her up with his cuffs. He pushed her ahead of him from the building. Outside, there were curious knots of people standing, watching. The street was full of blue lights. He handed Eydie over to one of the uniformed officers. "Book her. Attempted Murder in the First Degree, Especially Aggravated Assault, Theft of Property, and Stalking for starters."

As the officer began to stash Eydie in the back of the car, Edmund came up beside Dennis. He was adjusting his tie back into position and straightening his jacket. "She's going to be fine, old man."

Dennis looked at him startled. "How. . .?"

Edmund smiled. "In this family, never ask how. Just accept." He looked around. "Five foot two, eyes of blue, but, oh, what damage our little kitten can do."

Dennis did a slow sweep of the area. Shattered glass glinted like blue diamonds in the lights of the police cruisers. Grissum's Bronco was half on the sidewalk. His own car was parked nearly sideways. He realized a couple of the knots of people were rival gang members eying each other. He spotted several drug dealers edging around in the shadows. The girls who worked out of the motel were shivering in their skimpy clothes, their cigarettes glowing in the falling night like fireflies.

One of them called to him. "Hey, copper. Daphne alright?"

He waved his hand and realized he was still carrying his gun.

One of the gangs was edging up. "Hey, man, like would you tell Daphne not to worry. We'll keep everything safe for her." The other gang also was moving up. "Yo, man. Like there's some glass in the old Kress building. We can get it to fix the window. "

The girls glanced at each other. "Come on let's get this place cleaned up. Business is kinda slow anyway."

Edmund brushed his finger over his lip. "I do believe it's all under control here. I'll take Grissum's lorry back to the hospital. We'll see you there."

One of the drug dealers called out from the shadows. "Neutral turf?"

"Neutral turf," Dennis answered. "Anyone screws up and they will answer to Daphne."

"Yeah, then there will be some major league ass kicking," someone said.

Chapter Forty Seven

It was nearly two hours later when Dennis finally came through the emergency room doors. Eydie was locked down and the preliminary reports were in.

He met Edmund, Lygia, Kat and Bei walking toward the doors discussing where to get something to eat.

"How is . . .?"

Edmund cocked his head. "Listen for yourself."

Dennis paused. He could hear Grissum bellowing and a softer reply.

"I suggest you go and rescue the good doctor, Det. Cobb," Kat said with a smile.

Dennis held out his hand to shake Edmund's. "I didn't get a chance to thank you. Any chance you could teach me some of your tricks of the trade?"

Edmund glanced at the source of the noise. "Sorry, old man. Can only be passed onto family, you know."

Dennis followed Edmund's glance. "Yeah."

Following the voices, he stepped into a cubicle. Daphne was propped into a sitting position on the gurney. Her upper arm was heavily swathed in gauze under an elastic bandage. It rested in a sling over the top of a hospital gown. Still looking very fragile and pale, her expression was nonetheless mutinous.

He went to stand beside Daphne as Grissum loomed over the other side, his arms crossed, his cigar working from side to side. "Cobb, do you think it is too much to want this piss poor patient to spend the night in the hospital?"

"I have spent fifteen years in this place and, if I have learned one thing, a hospital is the last place to be when you are in a debilitated capacity. They let anyone who found a license in a Crackerjack® box practice medicine on you."

"If I let you go home, I won't get a moment's peace wondering what asinine stunt you'll be pulling next."

Dennis took up. "Lady, I have just left a neighborhood that looks like a bomb was dropped in the middle of it. I have spent half my courtship with a gun in my hand," he said. "Are you going to be this much trouble all of our lives?"

"You ain't even seen the half of it yet, Cobb," Grissum growled. "But you might as well find out for yourself. Here." Grissum picked up a blanket from the chair and threw it at Cobb. "Take her. Tie her to the damn bedpost. I'm going home, get a stiff drink and sleep like the dead. I'm too old for this."

Dennis moved around the table and carefully wrapped Daphne in the blanket. He slipped his hands under her legs and back and lifted her off the table. As he started towards the door, Grissum called after him.

"I want her down for twenty four hours. Bring her in stat if she starts bleeding through the bandages, running a temperature, or behaving like a normal person."

Grissum followed them out of the cubicle. Daphne had her good arm around Dennis' back and her head resting against his neck. "Lots of luck, Cobb. You're going to need it."

Epilogue

The wintery church glowed with the freshness of spring inside. It was a lively gathering in the reception hall. The gypsy band played music setting the blood afire and the feet moving. Bei was bouncing Dennis through the folk dance. Edmund had Cortlyn in her white lacy dress in his arms, the tiny halo of flowers slipping as they danced. Lygia had her bridal train flung over her arm as she taught Eric the steps to the old dance. Anne sat nodding her head to the music. The shimmery ribbons plaited in her hair keeping the rhythm. Elmore, his Barbadian dark skin glowing above the starched bib of his tuxedo, moved with Daphne expertly through the dance.

Grissum stood in his tuxedo, spilling cigar ashes in everyone's champagne. "I tell you, no man has given away two more beautiful girls in his life let alone at the same wedding. See the little ones. Eric and Cortlyn, aren't they something." The hospital staff in attendance rolled their eyes behind his back. They could already count the pictures they would have to view and the stories they would have to endure.

Kat was beside the table where the double wedding cake stood, clapping her hands and laughing. A movement caught her eye. She flagged Daphne and pointed.

Around and around the wedding cake, a little crystal bell twirled blissfully.

Coming in 2008

Monster Child

by Lois Lee Shaw

Born to wealth, 13-year-old Alyson Maguire is plunged into a dark world when death claims the people who love her. Her mother, Rhonda Maguire, wields the money and its inherent power without mercy. Forced into a devil's bargain with her daughter, she extracts payment through abuse and privation. It is only Alysons's gift of clairvoyance that Rhonda cannot wrest from her.

Riding the back of a storm, the girl's plea for release permeates the dreams of those living at Spirit Wind Ranch. A facility for psychically enabled young people, it is home to twelve students attended by an eclectic staff.

When its director, Boomer, is requested to appear at juvenile court on another case, he finds his path intersecting with the girl haunting his thoughts.

But in taking Alyson into their care, the Ranch finds itself being swallowed by the darkness surrounding her. In order to exorcise the monster in Alyson's soul, they will need the help of one man…a man no one knows exists.

www.bohobooks.com

About the Author

L. Lee Shaw pursues her passion for words from a farm perched on the side of a mountain. She has had her work appear in such diverse publications as *The Oregonian* and *Quilting Magazine*. She has taught fiction writing, formed a long running writers' group and had several of her plays and playlets produced. She produces *Mo' Allie*, a journal of writings, and co-coordinates a regional writer's faire.

www.bohobooks.com